THE
BILLION DOLLAR
SURE THING

THE
BILLION DOLLAR
SURE THING

Paul E. Erdman

Charles Scribner's Sons   New York

Prologue

It was just after seven in the evening of Monday, October 27. The fall weather had been fantastic all over Europe that year, and was still holding. The trees in the small park adjacent to the cathedral had not yet lost all of their leaves. But the brown leaves that remained rustled in the light breeze coming over the Rhine from the hills of the Black Forest, darkly brooding on the horizon.

The cathedral of Basel did not rank among the most famous of Europe. Its interior had been completely gutted—including even the stained-glass windows—in the hurricane of the Reformation which had swept through in 1529. But the church's twin towers and ancient red stone façade remained a symbol for the city which, since medieval times, had served as a metropolis of trade and culture for the Germanic peoples in the surrounding area of the upper Rhine basin. Today these people live in three different countries—Switzerland, Germany, and France. And Basel, the centre of the Christian world during the Council of 1431, later the cosmopolitan home away from home of Erasmus of Rotterdam, of Hans Holbein, of Nietzsche, had sunk into provincialism. In fact, the last of the city's greats, Karl Barth, had claimed that his fellow citizens were about to become the village idiots of Europe. (Sic transit gloria Basiliensis.)

Such thoughts could not have been further from the mind of the man sitting under the trees. Sammy Bechot was a professional safecracker. This should not necessarily reflect negatively upon all professional thieves. They also have their moments for reflection, even Sammy. But not during working hours.

Sammy Bechot was twenty-seven years old; he could claim 137 successful jobs to his credit—and two rather unsuccessful ones. The latter had led, unfortunately, to prolonged involuntary pauses in his career development. They had also required Sammy to change his technique. His approach to safes had become known throughout Europe. The intricate pattern of borings he left were as sure an identification as ten clear fingerprints. Less devoted types might have despaired. Sammy, however, had persevered and had developed a new methodology which, due to its simple beauty, would have brought recognition, even acclaim, had he been active in a more acceptable field.

Sammy rose just as the tower clock struck the quarter hour, and what emerged from the shadows was not the crew-cut technician one might have expected. Rather, a chubby, long-haired man, burdened down with the standard equipment of modern troubadors. Sammy, with electrical guitar, amplifier, and loudspeaker, crossed the cathedral square and disappeared into the narrow Rittergasse. At the fifth house on the left, lying dark behind a small garden enclosed with iron grillwork, Sammy rested. The street was deserted. Dinner time.

Suddenly Sammy darted down the Rittergasse. It ended at the steep steps which descended to the banks of the Rhine below. A favourite walk for evening lovers. But it was a bit early for that. Within seconds, Sammy, baggage and all, had clambered over the grillwork into the garden, and, after the quick elimination of a pane of glass and the turn of a lock, he moved into the deserted house. It took him seven minutes to locate the wall safe.

He laid the guitar case aside but unpacked the amplifier and plugged it in. He then unravelled two electrical cords. He used the first to connect the loudspeaker to the amplifier. The second wire normally led from the amplifier to the guitar. Sammy, however, employing a rather peculiar attachment on its end, fastened it to the combination dial. He put the amplifier to full power. The resulting hum indicated that all systems were go.

Sammy patiently began to turn the safe dial. Slowly, slowly. "Ping." The first tumbler was identified, loud, crisp, and clear, through the loudspeaker. And now in the other direction.

"Ping." The second.

The combination was revealing its secrets in an almost perfect high C. Every time he applied his innovation Sammy could not help but glow with an inner pride. Absolutely foolproof.

The safe door was soon open. It took Bechot no more than thirty seconds to locate what he was looking for. A dossier with a red cover.

Five minutes later Sammy had disappeared into the city. Unknown to him, he had just triggered a process which would lead the world toward one of the most sensational financial happenings of the century: either a total crash of the U.S. dollar or a setup which would allow for the biggest private financial coup in history.

Or both.

Imagine what a Papa Kennedy, a Bernard Baruch, or even a Karl Marx would have done with a situation like this! And all Sammy was going to get for his night's work was 10,000 Swiss francs.

Oh, to be either Irish or Jewish!

1

The president of the United States did not suffer from such disadvantages of birth. He claimed both Irish and Jewish blood, a contention which, though never proven, was of itself sufficient to carry New York State regularly for his party. Sceptics pointed out that the man was neither rich nor drunk very often. The behaviour of his crony and secretary of the treasury, Henry Crosby, they said, was much more in keeping with such ancestry; he never refused a drink, and he had been the roughest and thus most successful banker in the history of Ohio before assuming public office. What was proven was that these two men represented as potent a political pair as Washington had seen in many a year. Henry Crosby's brash imagination, tempered by the president's cool judgment, was known to be the source of most of the administration's successful policy innovations.

Their connection with Sammy Bechot? None, of course. Except for the fact that it was a meeting between Crosby and the president which had led to the creation of that ominous dossier with the red cover. It had happened on September 29. That morning Crosby had burst into the presidential office for their usual ten o'clock appointment and, unilaterally waiving all greeting formalities, exclaimed:

"Those bastards in Rome are out to screw us. And by God, this time I think they're going to get away with it!"

"Henry," replied the president, "take a seat and take it easy. What problem could we possibly have with the Italians that could get you into such a state?"

"Italians, hell," replied Crosby, "It's the Germans, the Japs, and of course those fuckin' Frenchmen."

The president's eyebrows rose but he did not appear unduly alarmed. For he realized that Crosby had a thing about most foreigners and that his lack of appreciation of offshore cultures was absolute where the French were concerned. The origin of this, as the insiders knew, had been a dinner party in San Francisco back in the fall of 1957, given in honour of visiting General Charles de Gaulle. The Midwestern banker Crosby, liked for his money if not for his manners, had been included among the guests summoned by the Western Establishment. Not one to pass up an opportunity, he had broken into a circle of people conversing with the great man during the preliminary cocktails to inquire about the future of what he had termed "the eternally sick French franc."

The general had first blessed him with the iciest of stares, then had spoken to the aide at his side: *"Qui a fait entrer ce cochon?"*

Then he had turned and strode across the room. The rather pronounced lull in the conversation which he left behind had been first broken by the startled Crosby: "What'd he say?"

A refined lady from Atherton, who obviously felt a closer spiritual affinity to Colombey-les-deux-Eglises than Columbus, Ohio, offered a translation: *"Monsieur le general* inquired," she said, " 'who let that pig in?' "

After that Crosby's views on France were something less than strictly objective and everybody in Washington knew it. With this obviously in mind the president said, "Henry, surely you're overreacting. But to what is still a total mystery to me."

Crosby, by now seated, seemed to have regained control of his emotions and answered, "Mr. President, you know that the annual meeting of the International Monetary Fund is taking place in Rome this week. Well, some of our so-called friends there have decided to gang up against the dollar. They plan to present us with a fait accompli."

Now the president's face did cloud over. The monetary issue, and the international weakness of the dollar, had been plaguing him ever since he had taken office. The problem had become critical with the breakdown of the gold-dollar link which had occurred in 1971. Until that time the world's monetary system had functioned reasonably well. Under the rules established at the close of World War II when the IMF was founded, each nation had related its currency—marks, yens, francs, pesetas—to the U.S. dollar. Thus one Swiss franc had been "worth" about 23 cents, one German mark approximately 28 cents, and so forth. Everyone agreed that the dollar was the natural benchmark for all other currencies. For one, it was the currency of the largest and most powerful economic unit in the world. For another, the dollar was the *only* currency which was officially and directly tied to that most ancient medium of exchange and store of value—gold. Since 1934, by law, one U.S. dollar was worth 1/35 of an ounce of gold. The United States had declared to one and all throughout the world that any foreign government which wanted to cash in dollars for gold, or vice versa, could do so at the rate of $45 per ounce.

All this was very agreeable, since it meant that everybody in the world could look toward one standard of value, the American dollar. And for those really sticky types who did not especially hanker for newfangled money, there was always the ultimate comfort that if not they, at least their governments, could always get the real thing—gold.

In August 1971 this thought occurred to some of the more tricky Europeans who suspected that the dollar was getting a bit dicey. So they decided to opt for gold. The Belgians, the Swiss, the French of course, and even the Vatican. As you can imagine, this moment was more than just slightly awkward for the United States. How could it pay off over $65 billion in debts, when there was only $10 billion of gold left in Fort Knox?

The president's advisors came up with what appeared to be a clever solution. The United States simply announced that the dollar was no longer convertible into gold. As simple as that. Payment was just stopped on all those IOUs which the United States had been issuing to the world in the form of dollar bills for many years past. Having done that, the American government proceeded to tell other nations that it was up to them collectively to find a solution to the world monetary crisis. A few months later the finance ministers of the eleven most powerful nations in the world met in Washington for just that purpose. But as so often before, the wise men of the world played midwife to a mouse. European governments and Japan agreed to revalue their currencies by a few percentage points if the United States devalued the dollar a few percentage points by raising the price of gold from $45 to $48 an ounce. With great pomp and ceremony at the Smithsonian Institution an agreement to this effect was signed, and with a huge sigh of relief the world went back to work as usual.

But there was an extremely serious flaw in the entire Washington settlement, which the U.S. president termed the greatest monetary agreement in the history of the world. It solved nothing. The dollar remained greatly overvalued. Convertibility of the dollar into gold was not restored. It could not be restored at $48 an ounce. If it had been, within hours the entire $10 billion worth of bullion in Fort Knox would have disappeared into the hands of foreign governments. The fact remained that there were still 65 billion unwanted dollars floating around the world, with more going out all the time, which anybody in his right mind would have exchanged for U.S. gold with the speed of light at the price of $48 an ounce. For the free market price of gold was moving inexorably toward $80 an ounce!

Inevitably, new crises occurred. In February of 1973, as a result of yet another run on the dollar, Uncle Sam had no choice but to devalue again, by raising the official price of gold to $42.22 an ounce. But, as before, it was just a temporary patchwork job. The dollar was still not convertible; it was still overvalued.

So the malaise lingered on—until the IMF meeting in Rome.

"Henry, what precisely happened?" asked the president.

"Well, I sent my undersecretary to the meeting with the usual instruction. Just keep the lid on. Do nothing, promise nothing. Stall. Tell 'em we're working on it."

"Which he did, I suppose."

"Of course. And in the public sessions everyone could not have been more sympathetic toward our position. They all agreed that time would heal."

"So?"

"So behind this public smokescreen, the French in their usual underhanded fashion, worked out a deal."

"Go on."

"The French first got to the Germans and convinced them that the time had come for the Common Market to take charge of the world monetary system. Together they bullied the rest of the member countries into going along with the plan. The Japs, our great friends in the East, got wind of it and joined the club immediately."

"And their plan?"

"They will jointly tie their currencies directly to gold. At a higher price, of course. And all their currencies will be freely convertible into gold. Now you know what that means for us."

"That the dollar becomes a satellite currency."

"Right. In about the same class as the Polish zloty."

"Those dirty bastards."

"I've been telling you that for years."

"All right," responded the president, now irritated, "but first tell me how you know all this."

"Our man in the German Ministry of Finance. He was asked to help work out the draft agreement. I've got it here. And as you'll see, it's already been initialled."

Crosby reached into his briefcase and produced a bundle of Xeroxed documents.

"There can be absolutely no doubt of their authenticity."

"O.K., Henry," said the president, after taking just a cursory glance at the papers. "I believe you. What's their timing?"

"On January 2 they'll be making a joint announcement from

Paris. They plan to make the whole thing operational immediately the next day."

"But how in the world do they expect to get away with it? Surely they must realize that we will hear of this?"

"They probably do. But they figure, and correctly so, that they've got us over a barrel."

"But are we? I'm not so sure," said the president.

"What do you mean? You know as well as I do—"

"I know this: I'm not going to let the dollar become the laughingstock of the world. I'm not going to let Europe and Japan take over the international monetary system at our expense. God knows what they'll try to take over next."

"But how?"

"Quite simply. We'll make a pre-emptive strike. We'll put the official gold price right up to $125 an ounce and simultaneously return to full dollar-gold convertibility. And well before January 2."

"But," reasoned Crosby, "what will we do if there's a run on gold? There are by now $75 billion out there that would become potentially convertible. I hardly need remind you that our gold supplies—"

"Look, Henry," said the president, "Franklin Roosevelt was in the same position in 1934 when he raised the gold price from $20.67 to $35 an ounce. But he figured that the new price would attract a lot more sellers than buyers. And that's exactly what happened. On dollars you can earn interest, good interest. On gold you cannot."

"Yes," said Crosby, "but the problem will be the speculators."

"I disagree," replied the president. "Look, it's now more than forty years since Roosevelt made that last big hike in the price of gold. You can be damn sure that when I announce this I'll let the world know that I do not expect another change will be necessary before the year 2000."

"Mr. President," said Henry Crosby, "you've got it! Goddammit, you've really got it! And everybody thinks you're some kind of a nitwit where economics is concerned. Brother, I would just love to see the faces of those Frenchmen when they hear about this!"

"Well, you can be sure they're not going to hear about it until I go on TV to announce it. Henry, this thing has got to be kept totally and absolutely secret right up to the last minute."

"I know. That could be a problem since it's still going to take time to work out all the details. In fact, Mr. President, I think that while you're at it, you should go one step further. Put gold up to $125 an ounce, yes. But also devalue the dollar by another 15 percent against other currencies. Those guys keep yapping about the dollar being overvalued, about our balance of payments always being in deficit, about having to swallow more and more dollars. Look, if we devalue by that much we'll be able to outcompete almost every nation on earth again. Even the Japs. As long as we're doing it, we might as well go all the way. Hell, all this should go over great with the voters. You'll be restoring America's leadership of the free world, protecting American jobs, putting the country back on the road to prosperity, restoring the position of the dollar to its rightful place as the currency not only of the United States but of the entire world!"

"Henry," said the president drily, "let's not get carried away. But you're right. As long as we're taking the plunge, let's do it right. Now how much time do you think we'll need?"

The two men discussed the matter for another two hours and finally decided that D day would be Saturday, November 8. The announcement would come on the evening of November 7, after the banks had closed.

During the next few weeks the plan was duly put to paper and five copies only were made, each bound in top-secret red. The White House pair, now complemented by the secretary of state and the chairman of the Federal Reserve Board, decided to bring a fifth man into the plan. He was the secretary-general of the Bank for International Settlements. You probably have heard relatively little about this bank. Yet, next to the IMF, it is no doubt the most important institution in the whole complex network of the international monetary system. It acts as the central bank for the world's central bankers.

It is, for example, the Bank for International Settlements—known as the BIS in professional circles—which, when the pound sterling or the Italian lira periodically comes under pressure, massively intervenes to prevent a blowup. When everybody else is selling, the BIS is buying, and vice versa. It has almost unlimited funds available for this purpose from its owners. For its owners are the major central banks of the world, ranging from the Bank of England to the Swiss National Bank to the National Bank of Hungary. Most important from Washington's standpoint, during every currency crisis since 1971 the BIS has provided major and consistent support to the dollar. It was a friend in enemy territory.

The cooperation of the BIS, and especially its secretary-general, would be absolutely necessary to restore international order after the first major gold price increase in over forty years. Such an event could trigger a tidal wave which would rock every financial market on earth.

It was decided that U.S. Secretary of the Treasury Henry Crosby should brief BIS Secretary-General Bollinger in a private meeting. Discreetly. If Crosby turned up in Basel, the home of the BIS, it might start speculation. It was agreed that London would be better.

A very brief transatlantic phone call and the date was fixed. Four in the afternoon of October 16, at the Savoy.

2

On that same October 16 Dr. Walter Hofer landed in London on Swissair flight 168 from Zurich. It was shortly after seven in the evening. He hurried through the long corridors after leaving the plane, trying to beat the mob to the immigration desks. This was not all that easy for Dr. Hofer since he had unusually short legs. He would never forgive his Creator for this, perhaps deliberate, slight.

Everything else regarding Dr. Hofer was perfect. Impeccable clothes, silver grey hair, perfectly manicured hands; a face which reflected intelligence, culture, wisdom. And a bearing which obviously set him worlds apart from the thousands of others who were also striving toward English soil at this moment.

Hofer was most aware of the "otherness" of himself. His position as chairman of the board of the second largest bank in Switzerland demanded it. He regarded his post as not just a job, but rather a calling. There was little doubt in his mind that his role had been long foreordained by that Power which had seen fit to extend an especially benevolent hand over the people, and especially the currency, of his country.

The rather grubby immigration official gave him a practiced look of disdain which, however, changed into what might even have passed for a slight expression of respect when he noted the profession listed in Hofer's passport.

"On business, sir?" This was only the second "sir" that month, a privilege reserved for quite special occasions.

"Of course," replied Dr. Hofer. He seemed quite unaware of the honour being bestowed.

After ten impatient minutes at the baggage carousel and a

wave of the hand from the customs official, Dr. Hofer was once again back in the hands of private enterprise.

"Your car is right outside, Herr Doktor." The manager of the local branch of Hofer's bank was blessed with a central European handshake—firm but correct—and delegated the responsibility of carrying Hofer's overnight bag.

The two exchanged few words on the way to town. This was not unusual. Local bank managers were very seldom granted any insight into affairs which demanded the attention of the top fellows in Zurich. One of the absolute prerequisites for a managerial position in the bank was lack of curiosity, not to speak of imagination.

At the Savoy they had the usual suite ready—on the Embankment side, of course. Two messages were handed to Hofer at the reception desk. He opened them upstairs after the porter had left. Sir Robert Winthrop had sent his verification of the arrangements for the next morning. The car would be waiting for him at nine, and the meeting was scheduled to begin at nine-thirty. Fine.

The other message was obviously not so fine from the expression it created on Dr. Hofer's aristocratic features. There was heavy fog at Orly, and she could not make it that evening.

"Damn it," thought Hofer, and he actually thought it in English with quite the correct accent. He had an amazing facility for completely adapting to the language of the country he was in. During the past century the Swiss had come a long way from their cuckoo clocks.

Claudine was one of his few little pleasures in life. Four years ago he had met her at a reception given by the minister of finance in Paris. She was the niece of the minister's deputy. Her history was not too unusual or interesting. After an early marriage and an early divorce she had established a boutique and a generous number of friendly relationships. After leaving the reception with Walter Hofer, she established the basis for a rather intimate link with the Swiss banking community. It was not just his fame and fortune which attracted her. She had a thing about short men, even though she herself was almost six feet tall. Especially short men with moustaches. For Hofer had one of the most distinguished little moustaches ever to grace the reception halls of the French Ministry of Finance. And, as he proved much later that first evening, he knew how to use it in a way which exceeded Claudine's most optimistic expectations.

Hofer, for his part, just loved tall women, especially big-breasted ones. Since Claudine had come into his life, Paris no longer meant complicated foreign exchange controls, an eternally wobbly franc, and hordes of uncouth Americans. No, the City of Light had become a haven, a place of respite, where he could snuggle his rather Roman nose, and moustache, between those mounds of ever-refreshing pleasure.

Claudine had appeared at the end of a most unfortunate incident in Dr. Hofer's personal life. His secretary, Heidi, had been endowed with both the height and bust measurement so prized by the five-foot-five Alpine magnate. Also she had been willing to provide comfort to her boss even during banking hours. This should not appear as perverse as you might imagine, since banking hours in Switzerland are unusually long. It was also not as imprudent as you might suppose. For in the General Bank of Switzerland, all top executive offices were equipped with a signal system very common in that country. Right next to the door leading into such offices is mounted a quite unobtrusive light. When switched on, it serves to every law-abiding Swiss as a sacred barrier never to be violated, regardless of the emergency, no matter how urgent.

But bulbs will burn out.

Dr. Hofer now had a male secretary and a greatly increased sympathy for astronauts, Grand Prix pilots, and the like whose lives were constantly exposed to the vagaries of modern technology. After a certain period of introspection, long office hours had to some degree given way to an increased regularity of overnight trips within Europe.

And now because of that damned fog in Paris he was going to face a complete waste of the better part of the twenty-four hours in London which, as so often in the past, he had planned with meticulous care.

He picked up the phone. "Give me Paris, Trocadero 7534, please. This is suite 717–20."

"I'll call back, sir."

At least they could sympathize with each other by phone. He unzipped his bag and sorted out his toilet articles, eleven in all. It was just a short trip. He decided to take a shower and then eat downstairs. After five minutes the phone rang.

"I'm afraid that Trocadero 7534 does not answer, sir."

"Well, try it again."

"I've dialed three times already to be sure. No one answers."

"Then cancel the call. One moment, though. Could you now connect me with Zurich, 51–35–94." He hung up. This time he had the connection immediately. "Martha, this is Walter. I'm at the Savoy and everything is fine," said Hofer.

"Oh, I'm so glad," replied his wife. "You know how I always worry about you when you fly. Especially in the fall, when there is so much fog."

Oh God, thought Hofer. Fog again.

His wife continued: "Walter, are you sure you will come home tomorrow night as planned? You know, you promised. But it seems that everytime, something comes up, and then . . ."

Hofer didn't really listen any longer. After five minutes or so he finally interjected, "Martha, I'm expecting a call from New York about this time, so I think we had better hang up. I hate to leave you alone so much as a result of these trips, but you know they are simply unavoidable. I'll try, I promise, to make it home tomorrow."

"I know, Walter," replied his wife. "Just don't work too hard."

Twenty minutes later he entered the Grill Room. It was very crowded, but the headwaiter, recognizing Hofer though not quite placing him, found a quiet table by the windows in the far corner.

16

This was probably the third time in ten years that Hofer had dined alone in a public restaurant. But he made the best of it and enjoyed his steak Diane, which, he found, was almost as well prepared as at the Carlton in Brussels. Over coffee, which was certainly not up to Swiss standards, he pored through the *Economist*. Glancing up, he suddenly noticed two men in an intensive discussion well across the rather large room—men whom he knew quite well.

Damn peculiar! Crosby and Bollinger, alone together in London? He had just seen Bollinger the other day in Basel, and no mention had been made of any special meeting this week. To be sure, as secretary-general of the Bank for International Settlements, Bollinger had to be rather close-lipped. But still. It was also rather funny that he had heard nothing about the American secretary of the treasury being in London right now. Crosby was a type who relished publicity. Evidently this was not a chance meeting. Both were, at times, referring to a document which Crosby had obviously brought with him. Bound in glaring red. Only the Americans would do that.

By now all lingering thoughts about the phone call that had remained unanswered in Paris completely disappeared. Dr. Walter Hofer was trying intensely to calculate the possible significance of the scene he was witnessing across the room. He deliberately tarried over his coffee, even ordering a second cup, something which was by no means in keeping with his usual dining habits.

Finally the pair got up to leave. It was Bollinger, not the American, who now was carrying the red-covered papers. Both appeared extremely solemn.

Fifteen minutes later Hofer was in bed. But the peculiar happening in the Grill Room kept him awake for at least an hour. Something was up.

3

The next morning at nine on the dot Dr. Walter Hofer stepped into the waiting Rolls. Fifteen minutes later he was in the City. Sir Robert Winthrop was there to greet him at the door of the bank. Bad sign. First a meeting scheduled for nine-thirty, the crack of dawn by City standards, and now the personal touch.

"Walter! So good to see you again. It was extremely kind of you to come over at such short notice."

"You know it is always a pleasure for me to come to London, Sir Robert," replied Hofer. "Is David here?"

"Yes. I think we might as well go right up to my office and join him."

They took the oak-panelled elevator to the fourth floor. Hofer was always infected with more than a touch of envy when he visited this old merchant bank. Everything at Winthrop's was in such good taste—unplanned taste. In a way it was a pity that such tradition was being wasted on these increasingly incompetent bankers. But at least the people here at Winthrop's were the best of the lot in London.

A tall gentleman rose to greet Hofer as he entered Sir Robert's office. It was David Mason, president of the third largest bank in New York. Mason was more than a banker. He was Establishment. A staunch Republican, he had served his government in various posts, most recently on the Cabinet level. Mason had the easy manners of eminently successful men. But when the three men took their chairs at the coffee table, these easy manners immediately gave way to extreme alertness and wariness. The American knew that there was more than a shade of cunning in the apparent superciliousness of Sir Robert. He also knew that the practiced straight-forward-ness of Dr. Hofer was often a perfect cover for the most deliberate deceit.

Both Europeans shared quite the same opinion regarding their American friend. As experience had so often shown, the glad handshake could be followed by almost naked brutality within minutes. The ever-present American humour was rarely amusing, all the more so since it so often contained deliberate barbs, designed to serve as ill-disguised warnings, or even insults.

In other words, the attitudes in his room were quite typical of those present at so many meetings which bring businessmen from both sides of the Atlantic together. The difference, perhaps, was that these three men had been arm's-length cronies for almost twenty years. This was not by any means the first time they had met in the rather peculiar office of Sir Robert Winthrop.

Sir Robert did not particularly like formality and liked to think of his office in the bank as a, well, place of refuge. The furnishings reflected this. The pièce de résistance was the huge model of his family yacht, built in 1936. The more one's gaze wandered around the room, the more apparent the marine touch became. Here a painting of somebody or other in an admiral's uniform; there an extremely old telescope, on a massive circular mount. A look inside the bar would have revealed an unusually high ratio of rum to whisky.

The explanation was quite simple. The Winthrop family had always had really two responsibilities: the navy and the coin of the realm. Sir Robert, as a result of the wisdom of his father who had recognized quite early the rather limited intellectual capacity of his second son, had been delegated as the family guardian of the seas. The elder brother, James, had been selected for the bank. Robert had been happy in the hearty company of his peers, until tragedy had struck in the form of the very early demise of his brother. Overnight Robert became a banker. But, though he bumbled his way through, he had never really got into the spirit of the whole thing. He had never felt the need to spend sleepless nights over falling profits or to gloat over the humiliation of a competitor. He was steadfast in his faith that Winthrop's, come what may, would always find its way through, He was willing to serve his time at the helm out of duty, not pleasure.

This particular morning was proving a bit awkward to get underway. It was too early to offer something to drink, and in view of the solemnity of the occasion, it would definitely be out of place to get too involved in small talk. Sir Robert decided the situation called for a no-nonsense, to-the-point sort of approach. So he plunged right in.

"Gentlemen, since I have the privilege of being the host at this meeting, I would like to confirm that we have just two matters on the agenda, namely, Transcontinental Airlines and Canadian and Western Oil. I propose that we get right to them."

Both Walter Hofer and David Mason nodded their agreement, so Sir Robert went on.

"The Transcontinental situation, which our American colleague brought to us some time ago, has created a very serious problem for my bank. I'll summarize the background for your benefit, Walter. The company, like so many airlines, developed a very serious cash flow problem as a result of its massive equipment purchases and almost stagnant passenger growth. Bills to pay, and insufficient current income to meet them. Transcontinental has always had the Republican Book in New York as its prime bank, and thus David, here, is on their board. He arranged for the company to get the maximum line from his bank, namely $80 million, and also helped them establish quite substantial lines with other banks in the West over the years. Under the unusual circumstances, the company still ran short of cash, so our American colleague assisted the company in raising an additional $50 million in Europe. We at Winthrop's agreed to serve as the managing underwriter in

London to place the two-year promissory notes selected as the vehicle for obtaining these funds."

Sir Robert now focused his attention on David Mason.

"We have put our name very firmly on this issue, but it still proved difficult for us to put together a syndicate. In the end, after much arm-twisting, we were able to place most of it; 75 percent to be exact. The rest, of course, we are still stuck with."

Winthrop shifted his gaze back to Hofer.

"At the end of last week David informed me that the company is not coming back in the way hoped for. There is a real possibility that Transcontinental might be forced into receivership within the next six months. At least that's what David tells me. And I think we have no reason to doubt his opinion. After all he is vice chairman of the company's board.

David Mason winced slightly at these last words. Sir Robert knew quite well that, as a director of that company, Mason had perhaps bent some rules in expressing this opinion—although it was a strictly private opinion, of course.

Sir Robert went blithely on. "In all fairness, David has indicated to me his most strong feelings of moral responsibility and regret, but unfortunately it seems that he cannot help us out at the moment. Maybe you could expand a bit on that aspect of this mess, David."

Sir Robert was highly relieved to have got all this off in such splendid order. Normally, he was not burdened with such difficult details. His most able management had repeatedly stressed to him—for many years now—that his genius lay in the big picture, in defining principles, in soothing the outraged client. The more mundane aspects of the bank were, indeed, better left to others. But today Sir Robert had no choice. All this cut a bit too close to the quick.

The head of the Republican Bank of New York, fifty-nine years old, with an eleven handicap, five grandchildren, and a slight hangover, would also have most gladly left this somewhat painful discussion to others. But unfortunately . . .

"Well, I don't really think the situation needs much expatiation," said Mason. "My bank is at the legal lending limit to one company with the $80 million we've got out now. So as much as I would like both to pump some more money into that company and to take some of that paper off of the hands of our friend Sir Robert, I'm afraid that I cannot do either. We are going to have one hell of a time explaining the amount we already have on the books without taking on any more. If that airline goes belly up, we are going to have to create a special reserve of at least $40 million next year against our loans. Uncle Sam will pay for half of it, but the other half will have to come right out of earnings. So that will mean that the shareholders are going to be looking for blood. My blood."

Mason sighed before continuing. "So that's about it, Robert. We got you into this thing, but I'm afraid that at the moment we can't get you out. Let me say this, though. The situation at Transcontinental is by no means hopeless. They may very well squeeze through this thing. But if the people here in London start getting panicky about those promissory notes, and the word spreads, then we're all in trouble—and for damn sure."

David Mason leaned back. Obviously both he and Sir Robert were expecting their old buddy from Zurich to pick up the ball. But Walter Hofer seemed completely oblivious to such expectations. He reached across the coffee table and helped himself to a cigar. He was soon deeply involved in the ritual of lighting it.

The morning was proving to be extraordinarily strenuous for Sir Robert, for he had no choice but to resume. "Well, I think both of you deserve to know that we at Winthrop's find ourselves in a most awkward position at present. If, as you put it, David, the market here does get panicky about the Transcontinental paper, it would mean that we would be hit with a bomb of major proportions for the third time in almost as many years. As you know, we involved our partner banks and clients in the Penn Central fiasco of 1970. Last year, just three months after we sponsored the prime underwriting of a £20-million new issue of the Zambian Nickel Mines, the whole story of that tremendous ore find turned out to be fictitious, complete tommyrot. Damn embarrassing, that. The City took the first thing rather well. After all, even Winthrop's makes a mistake once or twice a century. But they took the Zambian debacle much less well. If Transcontinental goes bad, I'm afraid that we will be out of the underwriting business for a while. The only answer for us is to take back that paper which we sponsored in the market. We will have to take it back at near par. In other words, we are going to be stuck with the whole $50 million of the original issue, notes which, if not worthless, at least will probably not be repaid for years. Gentlemen, this would exhaust our liquidity. We simply cannot afford to have that amount of money tied up indefinitely."

Sir Robert Winthrop probably should have looked somewhat crushed after having to admit that the bank he had been responsible for during the past twenty of its 267 years of existence was facing a possible catastrophe. But not a sign of the slightest discomfort marred his cheerful features. He rose and picked up the somewhat dusty telephone from his desk. "Mary, could you have some coffee sent in, please?"

A rather nice-looking girl appeared immediately, and while she fussed with the cups, Dr. Walter Hofer's mind was working at very high speed. The situation was amply clear. Mason had got Sir Robert into one hell of a jam and couldn't get him out of it. If Winthrop's hit the skids, David Mason would be finished in Europe. Sir Robert's plight could only be solved if somebody took a good part of those Transcontinental notes off of his hands—and fast. And both of them expected him to do so. Especially Mason. For the American knew quite well that if it had not been for his massive and continuing intervention in Washington, the people there would have come down on the Swiss banks with every weapon at their disposal years ago. That would have meant the loss of at least $1 billion a year in new deposits from the increasing number of Americans who were finally learning to appreciate the benefits of the Swiss bank secrecy laws. So he would have to help. The only question really open was the nature and amount of the reciprocity. That, no doubt, was the reason for the second item on the agenda—Canadian and Western Oil.

David Mason turned directly toward Hofer, after adding two lumps of sugar to his coffee. "Walter, I think you realize by now that we are going to ask your help in this situation. Robert was most hesitant to approach you due to the rather large amount involved. But I assured him that as long as we took a quite realistic approach to the problem, I was convinced that we could plan on your assistance."

Hofer finally broke his silence. "There can be no doubt that the amount is extremely large, even for us. Fortunately, I am faced with neither a liquidity problem such as you have, Sir Robert, nor the necessity of immediately setting up such immense reserves for possibly endangered assets as you must in America, David. Nevertheless, if we should agree to assist in removing the Transcontinental paper from the London market, at some point the piper will have to be paid. The cost of the piper could run very high, especially if that airline goes from receivership into liquidation—which seems most probable if the U.S. government does not step in."

"But do you feel that something can be worked out?" asked Sir Robert.

"I think it will not be impossible. But I can give you no commitment, Sir Robert, until you come with a quite precise suggestion and give me ample time to study your proposal with my colleagues back in Zurich."

"Just a minute," interjected David Mason. "I think it would be prudent to stick to a general discussion at the moment. I'd like to touch on the second item on the agenda before we get bogged down in details."

Mason knew Dr. Walter Hofer. Provided the price—he, of course, always termed it cost—was right, he could give a flat commitment before the day was over. If Hofer decided something, his so-called colleagues back in Zurich would not even be consulted. They would be duly informed at the next meeting of the bank's executive committee, and that would be that.

Hofer once again broke his silence. "I think that's a quite reasonable suggestion, David. What's the problem with Canadian and Western? I can hardly believe that they are also headed for receivership."

"Well, Walter," replied Mason, "actually both Robert and I have a certain amount of interest in this company, directly or indirectly. Let us explain."

The explanation did not take long. Winthrop's had been serving as the financial advisor to the British-Canadian company for many years. The reason for this affiliation went back to the mid-1950s when the merchant bank had first introduced the shares of the company to the London market. For more than a decade the company had remained relatively unknown, until major oil reserves were discovered on the shores of Lake Athabaska. Overnight the company's vast properties in that area had achieved a value, or at least potential value, of huge proportions. It was, however, known that this development had greatly outstripped the capabilities of the management of the company. It was likewise known that no changes were in the offing. The English founder of the corporation, and its one and only chairman, ran the company with an iron hand and with a quite placid distaste for either urgency or change. So, after substantial initial enthusiasm, investors had slowly lost interest in the shares of the corporation. At the rate Canadian and Western was moving, the petroleum under its properties would still be exactly there in the year 2000. The fact that Winthrop's were the corporation's merchant bankers only added to the conviction that things would move very slowly.

But the Source of All Energy, in His wisdom, had intervened. Just a month ago, the chairman of the company had advised Sir Robert that he was dying of cancer. He instructed Winthrop's to seek out a merger with a major international oil group. Apparently the man knew the weakness of his management. He wanted to secure the future of the corporation before bowing out.

Sir Robert Winthrop had immediately taken the opportunity to the president of the Republican Bank in New York, his friend David Mason. For Mason, in addition to his board membership at Transcontinental Airlines, had also served for many years in the same capacity with Oriental Oil, which was, in fact, his bank's most important single customer. Oriental was immediately and definitely interested. Canadian and Western was a downright steal. Its shares were trading at just under £2 on the London exchange. They were worth at least double, based on the Canadian properties alone. Oriental was prepared to make a takeover bid at £4, under the condition of pre-acceptance by the chairman of all the shares which he controlled, either by direct ownership or by proxy. The bid would be sweetened by separate agreements which would guarantee long-term employment for each and every member of the current management and would provide for additions to, but no deletions from, the existing board of directors.

The offer had not yet been made. But David Mason knew that it would be soon forthcoming. In fact, just the week before, he had attended the board meeting at Oriental during which the exact terms to be offered had been agreed upon. Sir Robert had already assured him that the offer as outlined by Mason would receive the chairman's blessing and that of all of his associates active in the company. Their acceptance would undoubtedly guarantee shareholder acceptance of the Oriental bid.

According to Mason, Oriental Oil was currently in the process of selecting its merchant bank in London to handle takeover operations. It was expected that the offer would become official within thirty to forty days. This process of inserting two merchant banks between merging companies was new to the Americans, although it was quite the normal pattern in London. It usually made good sense. For the London merchant banks served not only as continuing financial advisors to their corporate clients, but quite often also had the roles of lawyers, company doctors, and in awkward instances even confessors to British firms. They were, as a result, ideal marriage counselors. The whole system, to be sure, stands and falls with discretion, and the understanding that such merchant banks would never use inside information for the purpose of private gain. Thus, in a situation like this, it would have been unthinkable for Sir Robert or his bank to have started buying up the shares of Canadian and Western Oil at £2 in the sure knowledge that just a few weeks later they could be sold to Oriental Oil at £4 or better. It would not have been in the spirit of the game, as defined by the City Code on Takeovers and Mergers.

It was equally unthinkable that the president of the Republican Bank of New York would have let such a thought even cross his mind; especially since in the United States, the misuse of inside information was at least theoretically subject to legal penalties. To be sure, such misuse was most difficult to define. But one could not be too careful these days.

Dr. Walter Hofer had no such problems. Switzerland had neither traditions nor laws along such ridiculous lines. If an insider decided to take advantage of the information which was duly his as a result of the responsibility he had to bear in a corporation, it was only just that he should be free to employ such knowledge as he saw fit. The laws of other countries were equally of no concern whatsoever to Dr. Hofer. Switzerland, and especially its bankers, were not missionaries for foreign causes. If the governments involved could not enforce their laws, or enact laws which were enforceable, it was their fault, and theirs alone. But Hofer knew the mental contortions which his Anglo-Saxon colleagues were forced to perform when faced with sticky issues which could not be solved by legal contortions. Experience had demonstrated to him the necessity of helping them construct an "out" which would free them from any possible future remorse. So at the end of David Mason's long monologue, he asked the question which both of his partners were waiting for.

"That is all highly interesting, David. I can see the importance of your coordinating this whole transaction in a most careful manner with Sir Robert. But where can the General Bank of Switzerland be of any help?"

Mason solemnly explained. "Well, as you no doubt appreciate, one can never be quite sure of whether or not a takeover bid will be fully acceptable to the seller in its proposed form. The current idea of Oriental is to put the whole thing on a paper basis; it would be strictly a share-for-share transaction. The current owners of Canadian and Western equity would receive one new Oriental Petroleum share for each ten old Canadian and Western."

Hofer quickly calculated it out. Right. That would put the new post-takeover bid market value of Canadian and Western at almost exactly £4 per share, at yesterday's closing market prices.

David Mason continued: "But it may prove necessary to throw in a cash kicker. We don't know at this point. My question is whether or not you would be ready to provide Oriental with a very short-term, non-collateralized loan of, say, $50 million to bridge the gap, should cash be required in this operation? My guess is that the company would need the funds for no more than ninety days. They would be willing to pay, probably, 0.75 percent over the three months interbank Eurodollar rate in London."

Dr. Hofer knew bloody well that Oriental Petroleum was no more short of cash than was the Bank of England. But now the circle had been closed—and fairly elegantly at that.

Hofer replied, "David, please let me make a quick phone call to Zurich to see whether such an arrangement will be feasible. Sir Robert, would you mind asking your girl to put a call right through? By the way, David, when would Oriental probably need the funds?"

"My guess is January 1," answered Mason, with that completely straightforward manner so necessary to success in the banking industry.

Hofer moved over to a chair opposite Sir Robert's desk and waited for the connection to come through. In the background the other two men had started on golf. Sir Robert knew that it had become highly fashionable for American executives to combine their European business trips with a weekend on the links in Scotland, so the arrangements had already been made. He was not one to buck American trends, especially when $50 million of rather suspect paper was at issue.

Dr. Walter Hofer's phone call was, of course, totally superfluous, but it gave him the necessary time to once again mentally check out his calculations. His male secretary had already briefed him well on the situation, following Sir Robert's phone call a few days earlier, when the items on the agenda had been mentioned. Canadian and Western had 75 million shares outstanding. About 30 percent of these were locked in, either through ownership or control by the company's chairman, or stuck away in British trust and thus unavailable. But there were smaller blocks on the Continent which would be available. His guess was that three phone calls would get him about four million shares at maybe 5 percent—or even 10 percent—premium over the current market price. On the basis of the average turnover of C & W shares on the London exchange during the past six months, it seemed further probable that he could buy an additional three, maybe three and a half, million shares on the open market during the next month without unduly upsetting the price. That, combined with the blocks, would give him about 10 percent of the total outstanding equity of the company before the takeover bid started to come into the open. In gross terms, he stood to make a capital gain of over £15 million or about $36 million. This would allow him to take just about that amount—say, $35 million—of the Transcontinental notes off Sir Robert's hands. His quick analysis of the Transcontinental balance sheet in Zurich had indicated beyond any doubt that even if that company was liquidated, the creditors would receive at least 40 cents on the dollar. That would mean $14 to $15 million gross profit in the worst possible instance, less the cost of tying up the funds in the Transcontinental notes for maybe two or three years, say, $7 million maximum. Which would leave . . .

When the telephone came through, Hofer asked a number of questions regarding the bank's liquidity schedule during the next quarter and appeared to be receiving satisfactory answers. The charade was complete.

He returned to the coffee table and listened politely as the golf conversation drew to a close. He then decided to waste no more time. "Gentlemen, I think I can help you out regarding both items on this morning's agenda."

Neither Sir Robert Winthrop nor David Mason appeared especially surprised. "First, we are willing to provide Oriental with the $50 million under the condition you suggested, David. The commitment will remain an oral one, directly from me, good until January 15. Please let me know in time if you decide to draw down the funds. There will be no standby fee. Second, Sir Robert, due to the acute situation you find yourself in, we will be willing to take up to $35 million of the Transcontinental notes off of your hands. I will instruct our chief securities dealer to accept all offers up to this amount from you until the end of this year. Of course, you realize that following our usual practice, we will be using quite a number of different nominee names as the official purchasers. The only provision is that we will not pay over 90 for the notes."

The latter thought had just occurred to the good doctor. If he got the notes at 10 percent under par, it would provide an additional cushion of a couple of million dollars. You never knew. That old bastard Robert had undoubtedly been overdoing things regarding his problem anyway.

"If you are willing to accept my word, gentlemen, I do not think that there will be any need for additional talks or documentation regarding either of these subjects."

The response was most positive. Nothing could possibly be more acceptable than the word of Dr. Walter Hofer. Thanks were duly exchanged, but no handshakes. Sir Robert had a strong dislike for this foreign habit. The conversation returned to golf and then to interest rates.

As noon approached, Sir Robert suggested that they proceed to lunch. The dining room was exquisite. David Mason, and many of his colleagues in New York, Chicago, and San Francisco, had tried to duplicate the facilities which every respectable bank in London had. In almost every case the result had been disastrous, at least to the slightly discerning eye. The less polite called it phony. After hundreds of years, the Americans still could not quite make it when it came to natural elegance.

Sir Robert offered sherry. He apologized for not inviting any of the other executives of his bank to lunch. He had not known that they would finish their business so quickly and had anticipated that their talks would continue well beyond lunch. Neither Dr. Hofer nor David Mason appeared especially offended.

The lamb chops were excellent and the wine which accompanied it superb. It was always astounding to Walter Hofer to realize that it was often easier to get a good bottle of French wine in London than in Zurich. After coffee had been served, Dr. Hofer very carefully broached the subject over which he had been mulling during the entire meal.

"David, do you by any chance know what your secretary of the treasury is doing in London this week?"

Mason replied, "No, in fact I'm fairly sure he's not here, but in Washington."

"No, I saw him at the Savoy last night."

"Peculiar."

"Yes, I thought so also."

Hofer turned to Sir Robert Winthrop. "Another odd thing. I also saw Bollinger of the Bank for International Settlements here last night. Would you know, Robert, is there some meeting going on right now in London that would demand his presence?"

"None whatsoever that I know of," replied Winthrop.

Both Sir Robert and David Mason were extremely alert now. It was totally out of character for Dr. Walter Hofer to gossip. Hofer did not leave them in suspense. He repeated every detail of the scene he had witnessed in the grill room the previous evening, placing particular emphasis on the document with the red cover which apparently had entered the restaurant in American hands and left in the custody of the man from Basel.

"Damn peculiar," concluded Sir Robert. "If you would like, I could perhaps ask around and—"

He was interrupted by Hofer, something he rarely did. "No. I would prefer that we keep this entire matter completely, and I mean completely, to ourselves. I trust I have your word on this."

He then very succinctly outlined his opinion concerning the possible purpose of the get-together at the Savoy.

They agreed to keep in touch on the subject.

Sir Robert accompanied both of them back to their hotels, first dropping Walter Hofer at the Savoy and then proceeding on to Claridge's with David Mason. "Robert," said Mason as they arrived, "why don't you come in and join me for a quick scotch?"

"Don't mind if I do. After all, it has been quite a day."

The driver was instructed to wait, and the two men entered the hotel through the revolving doors. The concierge handed David Mason a whole stack of telephone messages with his key. Mason did not even bother to glance at them. He had his suite on the third floor, and after a tortuously slow elevator ride and a long walk during which they seemed to have turned at least five right-angled corners in the corridors, they finally made it.

"A bit of a rabbit warren, this place," commented Sir Robert.

"Yes, but the appointments of the rooms cannot find their like in Europe," replied Mason.

Sir Robert carefully hung up his coat and hat, and within minutes once again had a glass in his hand—a very stiff scotch, with too much ice, of course.

"Well, here's to our friend Walter Hofer," said Sir Robert.

Mason raised his glass all of two centimetres and stated, "Pompous bastard, isn't he?"

"Yes, but he knows his business. Hard as they come, of course. You can never really trust any of those continental chaps, you know."

"Robert," laughed Mason. "You've been telling me that for the last twenty years. Say, I have not had a chance to tell you the latest one going around New York—after your Zambian Nickel Mine stroke of genius."

Winthrop winced. Here we go again, he thought.

"It seems that this merchant banker was on a cruise in the South Seas and accidentally fell overboard. His friends watched in horror as a shark swam swiftly toward him. They expected to see him eaten alive. But at five metres the shark turned and disappeared as swiftly as he had appeared. The merchant banker clambered back aboard and his friends cried, 'Miracle!' 'Nonsense,' was the reply, 'professional etiquette.'"

Sir Robert Winthrop joined Mason in his booming laughter. With all the money that had been at stake this day, Sir Robert would have turned cartwheels if necessary.

But every dog has his day, he thought. His wife turned livid when she caught Robert in his "be buddies with Americans" act. Women were seldom able to accept small tactical defeats. They lacked talent for overall strategy. But there was no use explaining. Times had, after all, changed. They would change again.

Mason made his way toward the discreet bar across the room. "Care for a refill?" he asked. The first one had taken all of two minutes.

"Why not," replied Sir Robert and then continued: "Tell me, what do you really think of that little story Hofer told us after lunch?"

"I'm sure it's true. Hofer would hardly dare make up a tale like that."

"That's not what I mean. I was referring to his conclusions."

"Obviously he did not draw his conclusions based strictly upon that little incident at the Savoy."

"So you think he knows more than he's admitting?"

"Of course."

"But then why tell us?"

"That also puzzles me a bit."

"This could be very serious. Would it mean a whole new round of devaluation and revaluation?"

"I'm really not so sure of that. How did you make out in 1971?"

"Badly. Very badly."

"So did we. But I heard that Hofer did very well."

"I heard the same."

"But I've also heard that he's run into a pack of difficulties lately on some of his foreign loans—Yugoslavia, Argentina, Greece. All very bad news for the Swiss, and Hofer is in deepest of all. There's also some talk about rather heavy commodity commitments—silver, or some such thing."

"Frankly, I wouldn't take such talk too seriously," commented Winthrop. "Do you think Hofer is really going to keep in touch?"

"I'm sure. Otherwise he would never have brought the whole matter up in the first place in such a cozy fashion."

"But why?"

"I really can't say, Robert. I would just suggest that you keep your shirt on and hope that nobody upsets any applecarts on the Canadian and Western takeover. A bit more ice?"

It was almost six before Sir Robert left the hotel. By this time Dr. Walter Hofer was already airborne. He had gone immediately into action upon his return to the hotel. He had instructed the hall porter to book him on the four o'clock BEA flight to Paris. Three phone calls had followed from his room—one to his bank, one to his wife, and one to Paris. He had decided to extend his trip for just one more evening.

The limousine took thirty-five minutes to the airport. He

had boarded his flight on schedule from the new terminal. If he had taken the flight he had originally scheduled back to Zurich, he would have had to use the rather crummy facilities of the Number Two building at Heathrow, reserved in all its glory for non-British airlines. There he would no doubt have bumped into Reinhardt Bollinger of the BIS and Igor Melekov, deputy chairman of the Foreign Trade Bank of the Soviet Union. Both were headed toward Zurich.

4

Igor Melekov was travelling alone. This, in itself, was unusual for any Soviet citizen outside Eastern Europe.

But Melekov was an exception not only to this rule but also to many others in the Soviet Union. For he was Number Two in what was beyond any doubt the most unabashedly capitalistic enterprise in modern Russia. As such he enjoyed a type of idiot's freedom. His seven-room apartment in the Moscow Hills area was as plush an establishment as could be found in what was, at least by Moscow standards, an already very plush neighbourhood. It was furnished in the most expensive Knoll style, had bathroom and kitchen fixtures right out of California suburbia. It was stocked with everything from frozen Texas steaks to at least eight different varieties of the finest Scotch whiskies. Melekov drove a Thunderbird, much to the regret of his nearest friendly Ford dealer in Helsinki who went frantic trying to meet Melekov's regular telegraphic demands not only for spare parts, but the very latest stereo tapes. The machine was, of course, air-conditioned. There was also the dacha—small, but still a dacha—in Uspenskoje; membership in three different Moscow clubs; a pass to the Dom Kino.

Despite all this, Melekov was not that much of an exception as one might think. He was a producer, and like such in any country or any type of society, he demanded and received privileges. A country which developed H-bombs, Sputniks, and a gross national product of half a trillion dollars obviously had to have a good number of producers among the drab millions. Each of these was as jealous of his "rights" as any IBM vice president or Madison Avenue genius in the somewhat more reward-oriented environment of Manhattan. Naturally, both groups of executives also had to learn to live with the knowledge that every minute of the working day, the axe hung over their heads. In Russia, of course, by tradition this axe sometimes took on more than literary form.

To be sure, Melekov was not exactly the Horatio Alger type. He had inherited privilege and also the self-assurance that goes with it. As the son of a great Russian agronomist, he had not only been able to study at the Moscow University—not more than a mile away from where he now lived—but also had attended the London School of Economics in 1937 and 1938. His field had been money and banking.

Papa, who had made all this possible, had not survived beyond 1937. He made the mistake of zigging for corn instead of zagging for soy beans.

Igor, fortunately, was out of sight and mind in England at the time, and after completing his studies slipped quietly into a glorified clerical position in the London branch of the Moscow Narodny bank. He hung low, inching up the ladder for almost a decade. Then in 1949 he hit the jackpot. Scoffers among you may doubt this, but Igor invented the Eurodollar! Not all by himself, of course, but it was his staff paper, dated July 17, 1948, and duly initialled I.M./o.1., that provided the conceptual basis for a money and capital market which went from nothing to $65 billion within twenty years. The o.1. was the inevitable secretary, whose uncalled-for ambitions died with the birth of the Eurodollar. In fact, they died somewhat earlier, but Olga Ludidovna, today back in Smolensk, still must believe otherwise.

It happened like this. The Soviet Union, since the 1920s, had always conducted the majority of its foreign trade in U.S. dollars. Even in the darkest days of the cold war this did not change. As a result, the Soviet Union's banking system—and especially the Foreign Trade Bank as well as its affiliates in London and Paris—were forced to maintain high quantities of dollars as lubrication for the system. As our young Igor noted, those dollar balances simply lay idle, as sinful a procedure as is imaginable in banking circles. There were, however, good reasons for this. For, under what everyone had assumed to be the immutable law of nature, dollars were only lent and borrowed in the United States, just as financial transactions in sterling were restricted to the United Kingdom, rubles to Russia, and so forth. For the Russians to lend dollars in the United States at that time would have been something less than prudent. In fact, this is probably no less true today. For according to the books, Russia is in hock to the States for umpteen billion dollars, for everything ranging from defaulted czarist railroad bonds to lend-lease debts from World War II. Sequestration, expropriation, outright theft loomed over every Russian dollar which might seek to make a capitalistic buck on Wall Street.

Cunning Igor's solution was quite simple. Lend the dollars in Europe! The audacity of this thought—stated just that bluntly on page 64 of the July 17, 1948, memo—was not recognized for a full year.

After that, Igor Josef (*sic*) Melekov's career was made. His father's corn was forgotten; his years among the fleshpots of London were forgotten; and of course Olga was forgotten. In 1959 Melekov was recalled to Moscow and appointed deputy assistant manager of the Foreign Trade Bank of the Soviet Union. By 1968 the Eurodollar market had become the most dynamic money and capital market in the world. The Soviet Union had earned hundreds of millions of dollars in this market in the meantime. In that same year Igor became deputy chairman of the bank.

As deputy chairman of the Foreign Trade Bank of the Union of Soviet Socialist Republics, Melekov was a powerful man. He literally controlled all payments between Russia and the rest of the world. Either his signature or that of his boss (we'll come to him later) appeared on all hard-currency borrowings or loans exceeding one million dollars entered into by Russia. In terms of sheer numbers, he made our friends Dr. Hofer, Sir Robert Winthrop, and even David Mason, look like managers of branches of a Montana savings and loan association. But, and there always seems to be a but, he was still only Number Two, and by the early 1970s it slowly became apparent to Melekov that he had squeezed the absolutely very last ounce of impetus out of his 1948 coup. Even highly original and immensely successful ideas have their inevitable life cycle. This truth was slowly facing Igor.

Of course in London, where Melekov had just completed his periodic check of the bank's affairs in that money centre, this was not felt. There, the older the ideas, the better. What irked Melekov no end was that this was apparently becoming true at home—in so-called revolutionary Russia. Most of his colleagues were fully prepared to accept the Brezhnev rule of collective mediocrity. But by no means all of them. The latter wanted new action. Not a la Khrushchev, however. His clowning, primitiveness, inconsistency had almost nauseated Melekov at times. But still, the man had shown dash and initiative. He had been willing to experiment. He had shown guts; demonstrated willingness to take enormous risks in Cuba, in Cairo, and even at home in 1956. But he had lacked cool logic. Which brought to mind Melekov's Number One at the Foreign Trade Bank. To list everything that that Georgian hack lacked would have exhausted even the Biblical (Old Testament) capacity for articulating human flaws.

"Good evening, sir. May I see your boarding pass please?"

Melekov duly ceased dwelling on any radical political thoughts as he entered the neutral territory of Swissair and handed his card to the rather dumpy, though well-scrubbed, stewardess. She showed him to the last row in the first-class section and pointed to the window seat on the left. He removed his top coat and handed it to the girl. He pulled his copy of the *Financial Times* out of his briefcase, and settled back to wait for takeoff. The flight to Zurich would take one hour. Just about right. Melekov enjoyed flying but hated the boredom of long trips. Sixty minutes in the front end of a DC-9, mostly spent coping with a couple of cocktails and a decent meal, represented in his mind just about the optimum way of moving across Europe.

The Lombard column in the paper had Melekov's full attention when the final person to board the plane, somewhat out of breath, took his seat directly in front of Melekov. Well, it almost had his full attention. Melekov had lived all his life in an atmosphere where constant surveillance of the people in his vicinity was a necessity for survival. To be sure, due to his age and geographical location, he had missed the very worst of the Stalinist purges. But things had been touch and go twice—in the mid-50s and again in 1964. He knew that he had reached a level of power where he was by definition vulnerable—to everything and everyone.

The last man in was Bollinger.

Should I? thought Melekov. No. Not yet, you never know.

The two men knew each other well. Both had attended the London School of Economics in 1937. Melekov went back to his newspaper, once again fleetingly wondering why in hell they insisted on printing on paper of that colour. There must be a reason. There must also have been a reason for Bollinger being in London and nobody talking about it.

Bollinger appeared fidgety. He adjusted the back of his seat for the third time. He looked a bit worn, too, when he came in. Well, not exactly worn. Burdened. No, that wasn't the right word either. Melekov's thoughts kept switching back and forth from his paper to the man now more or less settled in front of him.

The door of the plane was closed, and gradually they started working their way toward the end of the runway for takeoff. In spite of a huge volume of traffic, by far the greatest in Europe, for some reason one never had those ridiculous lineups like in New York. Within five minutes they were airborne.

Melekov liked to watch London from the air—especially at this time of the evening. The spread of the city was simply enormous. The gas vapour lamps forming their endless lines below, part in yellow, part in a most pure white, gave the impression of an infinity of densely packed people. Los Angeles gave something of the same impact. But not really the same. There the horizon was broken by upthrusting mountains. Here the rows of lights seemed to travel as far as the eye could reach.

Melekov ordered a dry martini—with gin, on the rocks. He observed that Bollinger had done the same. Melekov took out the olive and ate it. He always did that.

Bollinger had needed that one. He called the girl back within no more than two minutes and asked for a second. He then began wrestling with his briefcase. By the time the girl had returned, he had apparently retrieved the object of his grappling search—a rather ridiculously bound dossier, in bright red of all things.

It's really not all that easy to watch somebody sitting right in front of you in an airplane. But Melekov had the advantage of the sudden darkness which had closed in on the plane as it abruptly moved into the cloud cover at over two thousand metres. It made a perfect mirror of the windows, provided the angle was right. Melekov remained hunched over his window, apparently awed by the fact that there was absolutely nothing to see. It was impossible to follow the text of the document in the hands of the man in front of him. But a flash impression of the capitalized words in mid-page, apparently following a lead-in paragraph, burned into Melekov's brain: ADJUSTING THE GOLD-DOLLAR PARITY.

What the hell, thought Melekov. If—but no. Probably just another new study on monetary reform by some genius at the Bank of England. But why does Bollinger appear so—harried! That's the word I was looking for. Harried. He's not the type.

Bollinger slammed the dossier closed, and with a bit more bouncing around—which normally can prove damned annoying for fellow passengers in the vicinity—once again retrieved his briefcase, put the document back in, closed it, locked it, put it on the seat beside him, and settled back to finish his drink with an almost audible sigh.

Melekov settled back in his seat and ordered a second one

himself. They were already starting to cross the Channel, according to the loudspeaker. The rumblings beyond the curtain indicated that dinner would shortly be underway.

Apparently the drinks had already gotten to Bollinger. He rose and headed toward the washroom. Melekov's eyes automatically followed his movements. Bollinger was taking his briefcase with him to the toilet!

Three minutes later Bollinger returned toward his seat. This time he seemed less preoccupied than when he had boarded. He surveyed the five people up front with no apparent special interest. Melekov put aside his newspaper and looked up. Recognition struck both faces simultaneously, and Melekov rose from his seat as Bollinger moved toward him.

"Igor!" exclaimed Bollinger. "What a surprise!"

"Extremely nice to see you again, Reinhardt," replied Melekov. "Why don't we have a drink together?"

"Well, actually I've already had one."

"Me too. But they're free up here. And I'm sure that you are just as pooped as I am after a day in London."

Bollinger accepted the invitation to join Melekov without any further hesitation. But first he deposited his briefcase at his window seat. The girl accepted the order for a third set of dry martinis as gracefully as airline stewardesses accept any request these days and returned with the glasses immediately. Probably a hint that it was time to eat, not drink.

"*Zum Wohl*," said Melekov, and Bollinger reciprocated with a tip of his glass. "Well, well," said Bollinger, "you're going to honour us with a visit to Switzerland?"

"Just a very short one. It's been six months since my last trip. You remember, we had lunch in the Baur au Lac, Reinhardt."

"I remember well—especially the three, or was it four, kirschwassers, following dessert. Tell me, are you satisfied with the progress of your new venture in Zurich?"

"Quite," answered Melekov. "We actually never did intend to make our Zurich operation too big. But still, we thought we had to get our foot into Switzerland just like everyone else these days. The money and capital markets—and, of course, the foreign exchange business—is just too big to be ignored. But London and Paris will remain our chief operational centres in Western Europe."

"How about the personnel problem?" queried Bollinger.

Melekov chuckled, "Reinhardt, you'd be surprised. We have much less of a problem getting good people than most of the domestic banks. I think that it's probably curiosity."

"Tell me," continued Bollinger, "is there by any chance anything we at the BIS can do for you fellows these days?"

"Actually there is. I think some of our people—from Moscow, not Zurich—will be contacting you again within the next couple of days. We have decided to sell twenty million ounces of gold, and as usual we would like your people to handle it. This is the first time in years that we will be selling, and we hope that you will be especially careful to handle the transaction with the usual utmost discretion."

"Right," replied Bollinger. "No worry there, as you should know by now. You must think the gold price is going to hold for a while right where it is, I assume?"

"That's always a difficult question. For years the free price in Zurich and London has been moving back and forth between $55 and $75 an ounce. It's really just luck if you pick a week where you are selling nearer one than the other. We can't always choose just that exact moment we would like, you know. It's no secret to you or anybody else that we are going to have to make some big payments soon on our wheat imports from the United States. Our supplies of grain, as you must well know, have fallen to catastrophically low levels. So we will need to gather up a few more dollars than usual this winter. Do you think we are making a mistake on timing?"

Melekov watched Bollinger's face with the greatest possible concentration. No doubt about it, there was a flicker of hesitation before he answered.

"Well, Igor, as you know we really do not have any opinions at the BIS except for those which we publish in our annual report. But I can say this: every central bank in the world has faced the same dilemma for years, namely what proportion of their international reserves they should hold in gold relative to dollars. Of course, your country is in a special position. Like South Africa you produce gold in quantity, and for you it is not just a currency reserve unit but an industrial product, if you like. I would guess that in your case, as you just indicated in fact, to sell, buy, or hold gold is not just a decision upon your judgment of the world monetary situation but is closely related to your varying needs for dollars for foreign trade settlements—gold for wheat, in this instance."

"Thanks for the advice, Reinhardt."

"Now Igor, who started this whole Eurodollar merry-go-round in the first place, anyway? I should be asking the questions, not you."

The girl arrived with two trays. Both bankers attacked their somewhat overdone steaks with gusto. No sooner had they finished than the coffee was served. Both helped themselves to cognac. Neither apparently had any desire to talk shop any longer, and the conversation had drifted back to the late 1930s: to mutual friends, Chamberlain, pubs.

During disembarkation Bollinger extended an invitation to Melekov to drop over to Basel for lunch, if he had time. Melekov declined with thanks. He only planned to be in Switzerland for one day. But he did mention that he would greatly appreciate any courtesy which Bollinger might extend to his colleagues and their 20 million ounces of gold. They agreed to keep in touch.

Bollinger had to hurry to make his connecting flight to Basel. Melekov proceeded through the labyrinth, and after unusual formalities at the immigration desk—they take Russians seriously in Zurich—was met and duly escorted to the waiting car by a reception committee of three. He was back in the fold of the Soviet collective.

At nine-twenty-five the next morning Melekov boarded Aeroflot flight 61—nonstop to Moscow.

5

Two days later, on October 20, Stanley Rosen landed in Beirut, coming from New York via Paris. He looked beat. He also looked a bit wary. This was the first time he had ever ventured into Arab territory. Sure, he was quite aware of the fact that Lebanon was not strictly Arab in that sense. Nevertheless, there was no doubt about a certain tightness in his stomach which had nothing to do with the usual effects of long-distance air travel.

For some reason the plane had been waved off on its first approach from the sea and had had to make a very wide lazy circle, high over Lebanon, before landing. Rosen had been amazed, and even shocked, when the captain had pointed out that Damascus could be seen as a small spot on the horizon in the flatlands behind the mountains against which Beirut snuggled. So close to the lion's den.

Rosen was, of course, Jewish. But a very watered-down American version. After his childhood in New Jersey he had had absolutely no connection with his ancestral religion. This was not deliberate: it was just so. When he was in New York, it was seldom that he ever gave any thought to his origins. But in Europe, on every trip his consciousness of the fact was somehow refreshed. He was never reminded in a really nasty sense. But reminded just the same.

The facilities at the airport were no great shakes, and it seemed to take ages before he had cleared customs. Outside the building he immediately found a cab, American-size, and after a thirty-minute ride through what seemed to be a surprisingly European city, he arrived at the Phoenicia. Except for the Arab getup of the doorman, he could have been in Miami

Beach. While he was waiting for the check-in formalities to be completed, he was served a cup of Turkish coffee right from the brass urn, or whatever it was called. Phony, but interesting. He hated this kind of coffee, but when in . . .

His room was strictly non-Arab. The menu featured hamburgers along with shashlik. The bellhop was all smiles. The maid was dark but cute. Stanley was slowly regaining his equilibrium.

It may seem strange that a man worth at least $20 million could ever lose his equilibrium in this world of the 1970s. But though quite aware of the safety and protection which money assured, Stanley Rosen was equally sensitive to the fact that he had earned it quickly. And although he had earned it on Wall Street, it had been on the wrong side of that narrow street. He was known as one of the cleverest financial operators in New York; he was a regular for lunch downstairs at the "21" Club; his phone calls were usually accepted without hesitation. But he had never seen the inside of the New York Athletic Club, and he had never been asked upstairs to lunch at Lehman Brothers. Yet it was known that he managed over $1 billion in assets. Some people put the figure appreciably higher.

The success of Stanley Rosen lay in the fact that he was endowed with a mental adeptness of almost unique character. Furthermore, he was willing to apply his mind to everything—literally everything—that had to do with money, its management, its use to make still more money.

But he never gambled.

During the days of the great bull market in the mid-1960s Rosen did not plunge into new hot issues with his clients' funds. He specialized in merger arbitrage and was satisfied with a more or less 20 percent return per annum. He deliberately rejected opportunities for doubling his money through access to a block of shares of sure-fire new companies. In those days of euphoria, instead of using margin facilities, he kept at least 25 percent of his funds in certificates of deposit and Treasury bills, and as the Dow Jones Industrial climbed toward

1000 steadily, he increased the cash or near cash components of the portfolios he managed. He was one of the first to detect that one could get a substantially higher return in dollars by lending them out in Europe for periods of three to twelve months (less one day—for tax reasons), against essentially no risk whatsoever, for the borrowers were the largest financial institutions in the world. And there was where he had most of the funds he managed, while the New York Stock Exchange was dropping week after week and month after month in the grim days of 1969 and early 1970. In mid-1970 Rosen had massively switched continents once more, putting almost everything back into New York: T-bills, Fannie Mae, and blue chips. By early 1971 he was back in Europe. This time he concentrated on German chemical company stocks and shares of the Big Four Swiss Banks. He stayed there quite a while and made another pile in the process. Then he moved to Tokyo and made still another. Rosen knew how to consistently make money in both bull and bear markets. Obviously a good man to know.

When people first met Stanley, they found all this most difficult to appreciate. He was short and fairly tubby. His clothes hung. His shoes were rarely polished. A blue tie and a green shirt were not unusual. He spoke rapidly, most indistinctly, and with a truly atrocious New York accent. When riding with him from Wall Street to midtown, more than one of his new clients had the thought that Stanley would have much more aptly fitted behind the wheel of the limousine than in the back seat.

There was another feature of Stanley which one could not overlook. He liked girls—lots of them. And the damndest thing was that girls really liked Stanley, with or without limousine, with or without the "21." It never failed to astound his associates when Stanley inevitably ended up with the real stunner at a party, whether in Beverly Hills, the Bahamas, or Greenwich Village.

Rosen did not fool around with small clients. The minimum portfolio he would take on was $5 million. He never solicited

47

clients, and in fact he had not taken on any new unsolicited ones during the past four years. Who needed them?

More than a few people in both New York and Washington wondered who his clientele were—in fact, more than just wondered. Stanley knew this quite well, and therefore he ran his New York shop in a fashion which was impeccable—a model of accounting practices, up-to-dateness, orderliness, supervised with ultra-scrupulous attention to all laws of the land. No, Stanley did not run The Vatican's money. The blunt fact was that Rosen handled the funds of a group of gentlemen who ranked among the most successful businessmen of the twentieth century—in Las Vegas, Miami, Chicago, Boston, New Jersey. All of them had backgrounds as humble as that of Stanley himself. All of them had accumulated immense liquid wealth since World War II. But none of them had direct access to the legitimate money and capital markets of the world or to the reputable money managers of the world—be they the trust departments of banks, the big-name investment houses in New York, or the la-di-da private counselors in Boston. So you see, there are also disadvantages in being in the Mafia. Not many of course, but still . . .

In 1959 one of their number had met Stanley. They had worked out one of the first private offshore investment company setups to be established in the Carribean area. Stanley Rosen, in true character, had discovered Curaçao not too long after the Dutch had, it seems. He had carefully developed the necessary bank connections there, had gained the services of a first-class law firm and a world-renowned, non-American accountancy and auditing company. The corporate structure that had been worked out was as near to perfection as one could get in a world crawling with tax inspectors, and plagued by ever-changing tax laws, currency restrictions, death duties, reporting requirements, et cetera ad nauseam. The Curaçao corporation was duly capitalized and received a long-term loan of a very substantial nature. All in-payments were, of course, in cash. The shares and notes were, naturally, all issued in bearer form. Under the rather lengthy bylaws, Stanley Rosen had been charged by the corporation's officers—all third-generation European residents of the colony—to manage the company's assets on a carte blanche basis. By 1963 Rosen had managed to triple the original cash input. That sufficed. The word spread —quietly.

In the course of the next five years he had established twenty-seven such entities; their structure increased each time in terms of complexity and finesse. Curaçao had been joined by the Bahamas, the Cayman Islands, and of course Liechtenstein as corporate domiciles. Often two or more of these offshore havens were strung together within one corporate complex, with separate directorships, separate balance sheets, separate auditors. The only thing they all had in common was a man-agement contract with Stanley Rosen, or one of *his* corpora-tions in Bermuda, Panama, or Luxembourg. By the early 1970s the combined assets of this system added up to a ten-digit number. Rosen managed all of it—successfully.

Exactly this thought was passing through Stanley Rosen's mind as he relaxed into an easy chair in the sitting room of his suite. Running over a billion bucks, and still not satisfied.

The decision that had led to his presence in Beirut had been taken just two weeks ago, over lunch at Delmonico's. His "partner," Harry Stahl, had been waiting for over half an hour before Stanley had finally turned up.

"Where the hell you been so long?" Harry had inquired.

"Talking to a new client."

"Talking to a what? I thought we agreed years ago that we had more than enough to handle. Stanley, I'm warning you. I've got my hands completely full now with all the back office work. Christ, you ought to know better!"

"Now wait a minute. First let me tell you what kind of a client. Boy, what's wrong with you today?"

"Nothing. It's just that I don't like surprises."

"O.K., O.K. But now just listen for a minute. I'm not committed. So hold your horses until you hear my story. All right?"

Harry Stahl had calmed down. He knew his "partner" all too well to doubt that there must be something big involved: something that must interest the bejesus out of Stanley. That was not easy these days. Grudgingly Harry said, "I ordered you a shrimp cocktail and a steak—rare, with french-fried onions."

Stanley had then told what little there really was to be told at this point. At nine that morning a fellow, who introduced himself as Omar Radazan from Beirut, had called him and asked for an appointment at his earliest possible convenience. He had referred to a man from Miami who was big in the international resort hotel business and a client of long standing of Stanley. At ten-thirty he had shown up. A dapper little bastard. Smooth as silk, polite as hell, about forty. His card had indicated that he was head of the Beirut branch of the Commercial Bank of the Trucial States, headquartered in Bahrein for Christ's sake. It seemed that all of the Arab banks have branches in Beirut. This just by the way. It had taken Radazan less than five minutes to ask Rosen if he would consider taking over the management of the investment funds of one of his friends, or clients, or relatives—the relationship was never really clearly spelled out. But the funds were. Just over $100 million. At present they were invested in a whole string of U.S. common shares, a sprinkling of preferreds, and a big block of, for Christ's sake, municipal bonds. Municipal bonds for an Arab?

Initially, Radazan had not mentioned the investment bank in New York which was handling the account, but after he pulled out the sheet listing the cats and dogs in the portfolio, Stanley had identified it immediately. Their record had been piss-poor for years. But they still lived well on their reputation, and the reputations of ex-Cabinet members, generals, and even admirals which they regularly bought in competition with other banks, aero-space companies, and management consultants in the true spirit of free enterprise. Unlike baseball, a systematic draft system had not yet evolved. But back to money and the mysterious Oriental.

Rosen had been very, very leery in the beginning. He had had enough experience in international finance to know two things. First, Arab money is 99 percent myth, or perhaps 99.999 percent. He had never met anyone who had ever really seen a major chunk of it. Second, whenever strange people start talking in terms of tens of millions of dollars, not to speak of a hundred million, the chances are a thousand to one that it's a complete waste of time—no, a million to one.

At this point Harry Stahl had interrupted. "So why didn't you kick him out of the office?"

"I'll tell you why. Because he offered to arrange immediately for first-class fare to Beirut, and $10,000 prepaid expenses. With no commitment on either side."

This even stopped Harry. "Well, I'll be damned! But Arabs! Don't they know you're Jewish?"

"He didn't ask. But what the hell, If those fellows make such an offer, they much have checked up pretty carefully before-hand."

"Do you want to work for a bunch of crazy Arabs, Stanley?"

"That's just it. I would. I mean, if those guys have somehow developed enough interest in me to make such an approach, well, dammit, I think that's pretty good. I get tired of lining up broads for most of those schnucks we've got now as clients. And tired of listening to them tell me for the hundreth time how hard their family had to work to make all that money—and to be careful with it, or else. This would be something new."

"But Stanley, how in hell are you going to communicate with these guys? Most of the people in New York can't even understand you."

The conversation had then eased into the usual kidding session. After lunch Stanley called Mr. Radazan at the Regency. They had agreed upon the arrangements. And here he was. In Lebanon, for God's sake.

Stanley decided to take a shower and then a nap. About four hours later the phone rang. It was Radazan. He suggested dinner together, but Rosen declined. They agreed that Stanley would get some more rest that night, and that Radazan would pick him up at the hotel at ten. Stanley went back to sleep.

The following morning, Tuesday October 21, Rosen had breakfast on the terrace outside of his hotel living room. The weather was absolutely superb and the view of the Mediterranean magnificent. The similiarity to the French Riviera was unmistakable.

Radazan arrived at ten on the dot, with Cadillac and chauffeur, and within twenty minutes they were in his office, in what appeared to be a spanking new twelve-storey building, of which the Beirut branch of the Commercial Bank of the Trucial States had one floor. There was absolutely no activity on the premises.

Radazan introduced Rosen to a man who was apparently his brother, or cousin, or some such thing, who did not speak a word of English and appeared to mumble a few words in French. Rosen's French was so bad that he could not really tell. The cousin had the function of chief coffee bringer. Thick, not very hot, syrupy—ugh! The only saving grace was the large glass of water that came with it. As Stanley found out, it was useless to try to gulp it down, and get the whole damn thing over with. A few seconds after you put your cup down, old cousin appeared like magic with a fresh one, ready to go for the second round. And so forth.

"Mr. Rosen," began Radazan, "first I would like to tell you how very much I appreciate your coming all this way to talk to us. We feel honoured."

"I'm really the one who should feel honoured, Mr. Radazan,"

replied Rosen. "Tell me, what prompted you to contact me in the first place?"

Stanley's thoughts in New York proved correct. They had investigated him from top to bottom. They were essentially interested in what Mr. Radazan termed his track record. Lebanese.

"Frankly, Mr. Rosen. We are not interested in your Panamanian corporations or Liechtenstein Anstalten. We don't need that sort of thing. We have no tax problems here. What my client seeks is performance, and we have not been getting it so far in New York."

"Something puzzles me, Mr. Radazan. I have had zero experience in this part of the world. But still, I do get around a bit. And I know that 'performance' was never really important here. I've been told on many different occasions that most of the investment funds coming out of here are put either into property or into bank time deposits. Period. And that one is even very fussy about the banks, with the result that such money placements are restricted more or less to the top fifty banks in the world—and that the British banks have always gotten the lion's share. So pardon me if I sound just slightly suspicious. I don't want to waste your time, and I hope you won't waste mine. I'm not a property specialist, and I don't work for Barclays."

Radazan did not appear at all upset at this show of bluntness. Quite the contrary. "Mr. Rosen, your analysis of the situation here is quite correct—or should I say, was correct until a few years ago. Also here in the Near East things change. A new generation has come into key positions, not just in Egypt or Libya but also in other countries and even sheikdoms. These younger people have, for the most part, been well educated in England or France and have quite an able understanding of investment procedures and markets. To be sure, they are by no means in charge. But they are seeking to promote a middle way between the ultraconservatism of their fathers and grandfathers and the legitimate objective of capital gains in the modern sense."

"Fine. But why come all the way to New York for professional money management? You've got enough much closer—right here in Beirut, or in any case in London, or Amsterdam, or Geneva."

"Well, I cannot answer in general; most of the money from this area does go to Europe. But in this specific case my friend tried Europe but did not get results, or at least the results he had hoped for with his 'new' approach. He then came to me for advice. I am a simple commercial banker and not able to run investment funds of this size. So I contacted some friends in New York who I thought would be ideal. You saw the portfolio that resulted. Within the last twelve months they have managed to drop almost $10 million. And this was an improvement over what happened in Europe."

There was a familiar ring to all this for Stanley Rosen. Investors jumping from the frying pan into the fire and then back into a fresh frying pan, mistaking motion for action.

"So I'm supposed to pick up the pieces," stated Stanley.

"Quite," replied Radazan. "The fee we are discussing is .5 of one percent per annum based on the assets under management, plus 10 percent of the annual gains achieved—if any. The exact formula can be worked out to your satisfaction, I'm sure, when we reach that point."

"Are you in a position to make the commitment?" asked Rosen.

"No," replied Radazan. "I think that I should make it quite clear that I am just what I believe you call an errand boy for my friend. Actually, he's my uncle on my mother's side. He's in Beirut and is expecting to see us right about now."

"What does he expect to hear from me?"

"Not just blah blah. If you have something very specific in mind that you could propose, I think it would be advantageous for all of us."

"I do."

"Fine. Then I would suggest we move right on."

This speed and firmness of decision could not have been more atypical of the Arab way of doing business. The normal pattern involved days, weeks, and months of back and forth and up and down, all with a maximum of ritual and a minimum of concrete proposals. Apparently somebody had done a magnificent job of selling Stanley Rosen to Radazan, and Radazan had done an even better job with his client. As Radazan later related to him, the process had already been going on for more than four months.

They got back into the waiting car and moved off. "Tell me, Mr. Radazan, how did you get so smart?" asked Rosen.

"You mean my English?" countered Radazan.

"That and a few other things," answered Rosen.

"Essentially from you Americans. I attended the American University here in Beirut—studied law—and a few years following graduation went to the middle management business school at Fontainebleau. They use essentially the Harvard case method, you know."

"Oh," commented Stanley, thinking that he had been right in believing that this new client would be a major step up from those jerks in Vegas and their tin-plated lawyers. This was class!

The contrast between Stanley's thoughts and the scenery outside the car window could not have been greater, for he suddenly found himself in the old Arab quarter of Beirut. The streets were crowded and dirty, the traffic a chaotic mixture of carts, donkeys, unbelievably overloaded trucks: the dress of the people was just as exotic. It was smelly. Much to Rosen's surprise, they stopped right in the middle of one of the crummiest streets of all, and Radazan indicated that they were to get out.

To enter the building that was apparently their goal, both had to almost climb over a crippled beggar that huddled in the doorway. Stanley suddenly did not like this one little bit.

Is this just one big fucking put-on? was the elegant thought which struck him as he followed Radazan up two flights of stairs—very rickety stairs.

The only door on the second floor was immediately opened after Radazan rang the bell. A bearded Arab in full desert dress ushered them in after Radazan and he had exchanged a few words in Arabic. In the large front office, if you wanted to call it that for want of a better term, similar Bedouin types were lounging around. A seventh, dressed in European style, stopped picking away on a typewriter that appeared at least fifty years old to glare at them as they were ushered through into the adjoining office.

As they entered, an almost grotesque figure arose from behind his desk, and extended his hand to Radazan. Radazan in turn introduced the person to Stanley as Ali ben Fezali, his uncle on his mother's side. The man appeared to be in his seventies, was hugely fat, dirty—a nomadic version of Sydney Greenstreet. His desk was cluttered with papers in complete disorder, some of them yellow with age or perhaps camel dung; others just plain smeared. The desk was huge, but old —and for some reason, battered. The only other pieces of furniture in the room were two plain straightback chairs, a small coffee table, and a couch—obviously of leather stuffed with horsehair.

Rosen in his life had dealt with some peculiar principals in the States—to put it mildly—but this took the absolute goddamned cake.

Radazan took his place on the horsehair couch and motioned to Rosen to join him. Fezali settled once again behind his desk. Simultaneously, the door opened, and another one— also in full robes—entered and presented everybody with the usual small cup of thick coffee. This time without a glass of water.

Fezali began to speak to Radazan in Arabic, and as he spoke it became apparent, that he was a man of humour. His huge face crinkled often with a smile as he spoke. Stanley started to relax.

Radazan, in due time, turned to Rosen. "First, Mr. Rosen, my uncle would like to apologize that he does not speak English. When he was a boy it had not been necessary. He would like to thank you for your visit. He apologizes for the lack of better facilities here but explains that he has been using this office in Beirut for the past forty years—and does not intend to change now."

Rosen mumbled the usual reciprocal words, and Radazan passed them on.

Radazan then once again turned to Rosen. "My uncle has asked me to explain his situation. He is a banker. One of the most famous ones in the entire Near East. In fact, he also owns the bank where I work."

Rosen must have shown his disbelief most obviously, for both Fezali and Radazan immediately broke out into laughter.

"I know that this is most difficult for you to imagine, Radazan said, "but it is so. Let me explain."

The story was not uninteresting. Fezali had already inherited from his father and grandfather a banking system which was in a tradition as old as the sands of the Levant, yet as modern as the drive-in-facilities which California could claim as its only important contribution to the world of finance. The Fezali family—brothers, cousins, nephews—had for generations controlled the money-changing facilities in and around Mecca and Medina. Such facilities consisted of a table and chair, covered from the burning sun, temporarily placed alongside the road or in the streets. The clientele were pilgrims from the world's Moslem countries, ranging from nearby Egypt to faraway Pakistan and Indonesia. Mecca represented the fulfillment of the most fervent prayers of all Mohammedans— ranging from the very very rich to the very very poor. They often came with what amounted to the better part of their life's savings in a myriad of forms, ranging from Maria Theresa thalers to napoleons to crumbled dollar bills. The Fezali family acted as their money changer. They conducted this type of banking with a speed and accuracy which had become legend.

The logistics of the operations were as complex as the bewildering array of monetary units in which they dealt. Couriers, armed to the teeth and always in pairs, moved the funds in and out of the Mecca area. The ultimate staging point was Beirut. The means of transportation ranged from foot to camel to horse—and today—to fast cars and jet airplanes. The rates of exchange were set daily by the head of the family himself, Ali ben Fezali, and through some mysterious system of communication extended to the last roadside table within hours. Really very little had changed over many generations.

Then came oil, and immense amounts of money which the ruling class, with the best will in the world, simply could not spend as fast as it came in—with the result that the Fezali family's ancient talents were suddenly in great demand. Stanley's new principal explained it; Radazan translated.

"Suddenly my family had to expand its operations—to Kuwait, to Riad, to Qatar, to the Trucial States, to Abu Dhabi, and even to Oman, that desert pestilence. Iraq is not for us. We do not like those maniacs. Our friends bring much money to us. But we learn slowly. We have very simple operations. We have no organized money or capital markets in most places. Even in Beirut things are very small and limited. So we have no choice but to go abroad with our money. To Lloyds and Barclays, at first. These were the only places we would leave our money, in London, in sterling at 7 percent. We still leave a lot there, but we have been hurt. Two devaluations wiped out years of interest. So we have tried Switzerland. No devaluation, but also no interest. The Swiss feel that we must be thankful that they keep our money for us at zero percent, or maybe 1 per cent or 2 per cent less never-ending fees and charges and insolence. You know what I mean."

Stanley only knew too well.

"The Dutch? Not bad. But a dull people, and a very crafty people. Born with fraudulent instincts, which, as a result of success, are encouraged as they grow older. The French we have also tried: too complicated. The Germans? Too German.

So, with the help of my nephew here, we finally decided to try the United States. As an experiment. You know, I am sure, that it is not that hard to make money. But it is very difficult to preserve it, and dangerous to make money with money. The Koran is most wise on this subject. Money changing—yes, that we can do. But capital investment—that is something we must still leave to the capitalists, until we learn the art ourselves.

"That is why we came to New York, and that is why we have come to you, Mr. Rosen. Because we have heard that you are very successful with large amounts of capital. And now, I would like to know what you would do with my capital, if you take over a part of it to manage."

It was Stanley's turn. He had given the situation most careful thought during the time which had passed since Radazan's approach in New York. He had developed an idea which, though daring and unusual, still was completely in keeping with his low-risk philosophy of money management. The only real problem had been timing. And here luck, which Rosen knew was one of the most important factors of all in financial affairs, may have appeared on the scene at just the right moment.

During Rosen's weekend stopover in Paris, on route to Beirut from New York, he had taken advantage of an invitation to a cocktail party being thrown by a friend of a friend in that city. As usual, Stanley had once again wound up leaving with the prettiest girl there. A very tall redhead who, it later turned out, had a thing for short men like Stanley. The broad was apparently unbelievably well connected as the conversation during the rather long night had increasingly indicated. One of the most talkative screws he had ever met—but a damn good screw nevertheless, obviously with lots of practice. But what had hit Stanley like a bomb was an anecdote she had told—Stanley would have guessed around four in the morning—about her "steady," apparently a most important Swiss banker. The poor bastard had not been able to come through the evening before, even though he had come to Paris for that single purpose. As the lengthy redhead had revealed, it was all the fault of the secretary of the treasury of the United States of America, and some other fellow with some international bank in Bâle—she didn't recall all the details. But she recalled quite enough for Stanley, who, in contrast to his predecessor of the preceding evening, managed to combine business and pleasure very successfully that night.

Rosen turned to Fezali. "Mr. Fezali, let me tell you my investment philosophy in a few words. I don't gamble. I take very carefully calculated risks. I do not promise to make 5 percent or 10 percent return on your money each year. But I can promise you that I won't lose half of it. I don't run either a casino or a mutual fund. I hate major downside risks. I am willing, however, to put money into anything, anywhere, provided the downside risk is measurable and acceptable and the chances of a good profit are better than 50 percent. If I am wrong on the profit, at least the capital base remains intact for the next round. Finally, I try not to work with my clients from behind a screen of mystery. If I intend to make a major move with their money, I explain my reasoning and intentions to them. If they don't fully buy the idea, I will not proceed. One last thing. I put my own money into the same projects as those which I develop for my clients."

Radazan translated all this for his uncle. Fezali was apparently impressed and in agreement.

Rosen continued. "I further feel most strongly that there is a specific time for every type of investment. There is a time to be in common stock and a time to stay completely out. There is a time for property investments, and there are periods when property should be avoided like the plague. There are times when one should be investing in Japan and others when one should be concentrating on Western Europe. I do not believe in spreading risk across the board, since I feel it is illogical to put money into things just for the sake of diversification, when you know full well that they will be losers. I believe that you must search out those very positive situations, and until you find them, park the money at a good solid rate of interest. Good

60

opportunities do not fly in through the window and hit you on the head. They are developed through hard work. The implementation of an idea demands even harder work. That's what I get paid for, and I expect to get paid well."

Radazan again translated, and Fezali again nodded his agreement.

"All right," continued Rosen. Once he got started on his favorite subject it was impossible to stop him. "I believe that I have developed one of these opportunities. To you, it will no doubt sound like bringing coals to Newcastle. Nevertheless, I'll explain it to you. If you like it, fine. We can do business together right now. If not, fine too, and no hard feelings I hope on either side."

"O.K. My idea is quite simply the following. I feel that the time is here to make a very big play on gold bullion and against the United States dollar. All the signals are go—for the first time since the early 1930s. There have been innumerable false starts on this. And the suckers have lost their shirts more than once. But this time I think it will be for real. The absolute key to success will be timing; timing is more important in this field than any other investment area, bar none. If you are wrong in your schedule, when the target date passes the only answer is to bow your head in shame, pick up your marbles, and go. Otherwise you just bleed a slow death."

Rosen paused again. Apparently Radazan was having a bit of trouble with the Arabic term for "marbles." Finally he appeared to have once again caught up with Stanley's rush of words.

"Normally, I do not like one shot deals," Stanley continued, "but this one looks too tempting. The downside risk is very low relative to the potential profit. At worst we would stand to lose a maximum of 15 percent, but more probably 10 percent. If we win, we will quadruple our money within the next two months."

Fezali, after once again listening very carefully to Radazan's repetition of Rosen's words—all the while with his eyes on

Stanley, did not exactly appear overwhelmed by the last part. Through Radazan he voiced his doubts.

"Mr. Rosen, for decades now we in the Near East have been investing in gold. To be sure, our capital remained intact. But for decades it brought us neither interest nor capital gains. Only very recently did the free market price finally move up, hardly by enough to make up for those many years of no income, but still up. The younger people in our family, our organization, came to me. They said that this was the time to get out of gold; to find new and better ways of placing our funds, so that they do not lie sterile for another generation or two. This is one of the reasons why we sought advice in America."

"The logic was right," interjected Rosen, "but the timing wrong. In fact, very wrong. Because now, right now, the price of gold could explode. It's an investment that should bring a sure capital gain, with no downside risk, or an extremely small one. My case is very simple. The American dollar is again in trouble. The reason is that nobody around the world trusts it, because since 1971 it has not been convertible into gold. The American government must do something to restore confidence if the entire world monetary system is not to break down in a way which would make what happened in 1971 look like a Sunday School picnic. The only solution will be to restore dollar convertibility. That will require a massive increase in the price of gold—to at least $125 an ounce and maybe higher. This will then represent the new governmentally guaranteed price for that metal. You can buy gold now for $74 an ounce in London or Zurich. That's what I suggest we do. After this is over, forget about gold. Permanently. Your young people I understand. But after all these years, they certainly should be able to be patient for just a few more weeks.

"One more thing. You can be sure that when the Americans devalue the dollar relative to gold they will also force through a dollar devaluation relative to the currencies of those countries which have been giving the States such a hard time in the monetary area, like France, Germany, Switzerland, and Japan.

Sure, it will hardly be anything near as drastic as with gold, but I figure that at least 10 percent is in the cards."

There seemed to be no violent disagreement thus far, so Stanley continued. "But now I come to the heart of the matter. Maximum leverage. We squeeze everything we can get out of our $100 million in cold cash. Money like that talks very loud. And I'm thinking in terms of what we back home call a double whammy. First step, we deposit our $100 million in a Swiss bank. Second, we take out a credit of a matching $100 million, and put everything into gold: $200 million worth."

He was interrupted by Radazan. "You call that maximum leverage? Remember I'm a banker, and as one from the Near East I know more than a little bit about gold. You're talking about putting up 50 percent cash margin on gold bullion. I know 20 percent will be enough—not that I'm suggesting we go that far."

Rosen cut in. "Hold on. I'm not through. The final stage of the operation is that we go massively short on the American dollar. I figure that if we block all that gold as a guarantee, we can sell at least $1.5 billion short, and maybe $2 billion in the forward market. If my calculations are correct, we would stand to make $100 million on gold, and another $200 million on our short dollar position. That's not as much as Howard Hughes made when he sold his TWA stock in the 1960s, but it comes as close as anybody else has managed since."

The two Arabs went into a huddle.

"Before we get down to the principle involved," said Radazan," I'd first like to point out that if, and I say *if*, your theories are right, we would stand to make almost the same money by simply putting everything into gold bullion. If we operate on a 20 percent cash margin, we could buy half a billion dollars worth of gold—which, you say, is sure to move up 50 percent in price almost immediately thereafter. Then we would not have to run any risks in the foreign exchange market."

"Aha," replied Rosen. "I see you're with me all the way. But you forget one little factor. The gold bullion market is a delicate one. Even the purchase of $200 million will push the price up. To try to buy half a billion dollars worth could wreck the market."

"The Libyan government did it a couple of years ago."

"Yeah. And they pushed the price up $15 an ounce in the process."

"What makes you think it will be that easy to sell $2 billion short?"

"Easy it will not be. But also not that difficult. In the forward foreign exchange market billions of dollars are bought and sold every day in the week. Sure, we might cause a flurry in the market—but only that."

Again Radazan consulted with his uncle.

"If everything turns wrong, how much would we lose?"

"On the gold, nothing. We would just have to take our time unloading, that's all. On the currency operation, about 1 per cent of the face amount. On $2 billion, that would be $20 million.

Rosen smiled. "That's the kind of game Stanley Rosen likes to play. I figure that if the entire deal goes haywire, we'll drop a maximum—remember, *maximum*—of $20 million on the foreign exchange side. It could just as well be nothing, however, and it is not impossible that we could even luck through with a tiny profit. But still, we would have a $100 million loan outstanding for perhaps a half year until we could prudently unload that gold. So that would mean, say, $5 million interest. But against that we have a $300 million profit potential. Three hundred to twenty-five—them are the odds I like at the race track, but believe me, this is not a race track."

"Fine, Mr. Rosen," said Radazan. "But that still leaves us with what you yourself termed the most important factor in this type of operation—timing. What makes you so sure you're right on that?"

"I'm not sure. But I intend to become surer. You understand me? That's what you pay me for. Right?"

"And if you change your mind?"

"I'll come back to you. This is not the only idea I've got. But it is by far the best one at the moment. Sure, I've got a complete alternative program in my briefcase back in the hotel. But let me put something real straight to you fellows. Essentially you're not buying a plan or a program. You're buying Stanley Rosen. As simple as that."

Radazan translated all of this once again for his uncle. Then the two of them entered into a dialogue which lasted a good fifteen minutes. Stanley just sat there on the horsehair couch.

"My uncle agrees to work with you," stated Radazan. "He wants us to immediately work out the contract."

Both Arabs rose, and within ten minutes, after an enormous number of handshakes, smiles, and headnodding, Stanley and Radazan were back in the Cadillac.

By early afternoon the next day Rosen was on an airplane, with a power-of-attorney over a portfolio of cats and dogs in New York worth just over $100 million, and the usual management contract appointing him—or rather one of his companies in Bermuda—as an investment advisor to the Commercial Bank of the Trucial States. For a whopping fee, of course.

Stanley was bound for Paris. He planned to spend one night there. His purpose, to use an airline expression: reconfirmation.

6

The Air France flight reached Orly at five o'clock local time, and less than an hour later Rosen entered the lobby of the George V. He asked for a suite in the north wing, facing the garden, and the hotel condescended to give him one, at the modest rate of only $135 a night, plus 22 percent service, 15 percent tax, and a $10 surcharge, the latter representing rather good value since it was subject to neither service nor tax.

Step two in Rosen's check-in procedure was to slip a $20 bill to the head concierge. Stanley also slipped him the name and telephone number of the lady he wanted to contact. Long ago he had learned that it was suicidal to try to take on the French telephone system without the expert aid of local consultants. It went somewhat against Stanley's grain to pay an average of $10 for each local call, but in this instance he felt it worthwhile in view of the millions which were at stake.

No less than three minutes after he was installed upstairs, the phone rang. It was Jean-Paul, his telecommunications aide. "Monsieur Rosen," he said, "the young lady is out, but her maid expects her back within the hour. She promised that madame would return your call at that time."

"Fine, fine," Stanley said. "Now could you do something else for me?"

"Certainly, Mr. Rosen," was the oily response.

"I'd like a table at the most expensive restaurant in Paris."

"The most expensive?"

"Yes."

"Well, I'm told that the Tour d'Argent—"

"That sounds fine. And make sure we get the best table. For two. I'll make it worth your while, Jean-Paul."

"Ah yes, you can most certainly depend upon me, Mr. Rosen. Rest assured that it will be arranged. For what time, sir?"

"Around eight-thirty would probably be all right."

"Yes sir, and will you be needing a car?"

"Now that's an idea. Sure, why not?"

"A Bentley, perhaps?"

"Great. But make sure the driver speaks English."

"*Certainement,* monsieur. The driver is a friend of mine."

"Now one more thing. I want two—no, make it three bottles of the best champagne you've got put on ice and sent up to my suite around, say eleven. I won't be back then, so just have them leave it. Understand?"

"Of course. Should I make the selection for you, Mr. Rosen?"

"Certainly, Jean-Paul. And *merci beaucoup!*"

With that linguistic flourish he hung up and went to take a shower.

Just forty-five minutes later the phone rang again. Stanley picked it up cautiously.

"Hello," was all he ventured.

"Stanley, darling, is that you?"

"Claudine! I'm so glad you could call back."

"But of course. Now tell me, what brings you back to Paris so quickly?"

"You of course."

"Oh la la," she said and sounded pleased.

"Claudine, I've arranged a table at the Tour d'Argent for eight-thirty and I'll pick you up at eight. And I won't take no for an answer."

"But Stanley, at such short notice—"

"Claudine, I only have one night in Paris. And somehow, I thought you enjoyed our last evening together."

"But I did," she replied with enthusiasm.

"Good. Then let's make it even better tonight."

There was only the slightest of pauses. "I'll come."

"That I will arrange also."

"Stanley! We're on the telephone!"

"I'll see you at eight. Until then, Claudine."

"Bye, darling."

A couple of hours later, as she stepped from the Bentley in front of the Tour d'Argent, Claudine de Beauchamp made a smashing impression. The exquisite pure white mini, and the stunning pair of legs which emerged below, flashed through the dark mink coat, leaving even the doorman somewhat breathless. Her rich red hair flowed from beneath the fur cape, as she swept through the small entrance hall into the elevator. Stanley, a good six inches shorter, trotted behind, and almost gasped when he found himself enclosed in a small red velvet cage, operated by a young person with white hair sitting on a stool beside the controls, a white poodle in his lap. A large red ribbon adorning the poodle rounded out the picture of superb decadence. Claudine chatted gaily with the person of quite indeterminable sex as the lift moved up to the first floor. She was obviously well known there. In fact, when they emerged from the elevator, the head waiter paused hardly a second before coming over to bow before Claudine. Stanley stepped forward to identify himself but was completely ignored as Claudine moved toward the windowed alcove at the far side of the room, with most eyes in the room upon her.

"This is my favourite table," she said to Stanley, as with great fuss the head waiter removed her mink and eased a chair toward her poised popo, taking most careful note of the target in the process.

The fawning bastard, thought Stanley, as the head waiter disappeared without once acknowledging Rosen's presence. But his flagging mood was immediately revived when, for the first time, he looked beyond Claudine. There, perfectly framed in the alcove windows, was the Notre Dame, its towers and buttresses glowing in a soft light. Rosen, beneath the veneer a sentimental man, choked up for a fleeting instant, for it felt good, very good, to be near so much beauty. It was, he felt, a moment to be remembered, for it was perhaps symbolic of a new and better life which was now within his grasp.

The arrival of the menus brought Stanley back to reality rather quickly, for not only were they exclusively in French, but no prices were indicated either. To gain time, Stanley ordered two dry martinis on the rocks.

"Chéri," asked Claudine, "are you hungry?"

"Yes," he replied, "but frankly I can't make head or tail out of this goddamned menu."

"Stanley darling," said Claudine, reaching out to touch Rosen's hand, "that is why I liked you so much from the first moment. You are the only honest American I've ever met, the only one who would dare admit that he knows very little of the French language, even less about French food, and absolutely nothing about French wine. Would you be terribly hurt if I did the choosing?"

Stanley could not have been more relieved. "Claudine," he said, now squeezing her hand, "go right to it, baby."

And she did. The delicate filet de sole cardinal was followed by their famous caneton Tour d'Argent and topped off with soufflé Valtesse. The 1959 white Burgundy was succeeded by an absolutely superb 1949 Haut-Brion. The cognac, from the restaurant's special reserve, proved to be as golden in flavour as in colour. The only deviation from Claudine's suggestions upon which Stanley insisted was coffee. He refused to touch the stuff. The memories of Beirut were still too strong.

The bill proved staggering, but Stanley paid it with a flourish worthy of the Aga Khan. Back in the Bentley, Claudine took his head between her two gloved hands and pecked him ever so slightly on the nose.

"That was lovely," she said, "and now let's go back to my apartment."

"No," said Stanley, "there's one place I've always wanted to go to, but somehow never made it. I know it's a bit touristy, but—"

"Not the Moulin Rouge?" exclaimed Claudine.

"No. The Crazy Horse Saloon."

So the Crazy Horse Saloon it was. Packed as usual, but as always with space for people who waved $10 bills. Stanley and Claudine ended up beside each other, jammed behind a table squeezed onto a semicircular extended settee immediately in front of the small stage. The din was deafening, the smoke in the room overpowering, and the number of Midwestern Americans with their plastic wives astounding.

"It's wonderful!" screamed Claudine, as the music started, adding yet another claustrophobic element to the atmosphere of total suffocation already pervading the place. But in spite of it all, the show was full of electric excitement from the very outset. The flashing lights, the kooky costumes, the gorgeous girls brought the temperature of the room up another ten degrees within minutes. The middle-aged woman from Little Rock pressed between Stanley and her husband, one elbow stubbornly imbedded in Stanley's ribs, noticeably recoiled when one of the girls damn near shoved her well-groomed pubic hair into her hubby's rather red nose. The man's self-control collapsed completely, as he broke into a series of violent sneezes.

Claudine thought this was hilarious and burst into pealing laughter, soon infecting the dozens of people immediately around them, especially when the nice American lady, with a touch of silver in her hair, turned to her embarrassed spouse and said, in a loud voice, "Henry! Don't make a fucking ass of yourself."

The tableaux on the stage before them changed, this time to an African pair. Soon all female attention in the room was riveted on the crotch of the enormous black man, as, with a rather noticeable swelling where it counted most, he began a relentless pursuit of his virginal partner. As the room became increasingly hushed, Stanley stiffened. For there, tugging at his zipper with immediate and complete success, was a hand. And as soon as he was totally unleashed, yet another hand took a firm hold.

"Jeezus," whispered Stanley out of the side of his mouth. "What're you trying to do?"

The only reply came from the two hands, which slowly began to move in rhythm with the pulsing drums, now providing the background to the frenzy of the increasingly entangled pair on the stage. As the climax slowly began the approach, the room went into total darkness. The two carefully prepared naked bodies reflected the ultraviolent lights which now played upon them, creating images of dark and eerie sex.

At this point the American lady on Stanley's left stirred. To his utter horror, a third hand was laid upon him. Ever so cagily it had dropped to his knee, as if by accident under the crowded circumstances. But then, purposefully, it began inching its way up. There wasn't a goddamned thing Stanley could do but sit there in awful anticipation, since he was totally wedged in by solid flesh on both sides and blocked by the table in front. The rather oversized table cloth which, thankfully, concealed Stanley's lap, started to flutter like a tent in a hurricane, as the confusion below increased. He could almost feel the anticipation of the new set of chubby fingers as they worked their way, ever faster, toward the target area. They paused, thrown into doubt as contact was made with that other set of busy French fingers. But then, with regained courage, they searched for, and found, if not all, at least the tip of the object which had developed such enormous local popularity.

By now it appeared to dawn on Claudine that something extraordinary was happening.

"Is that you?" she whispered.

Stanley was too paralyzed to reply, but words were hardly necessary since there, right on top of the table, his white cuffs —two of them—unmistakably reflected the bluish light of the ultraviolet lamps. Suddenly Claudine's hands withdrew, and with the air of royalty she leaned past Stanley and said in the sweetest of loud voices to the matron on his left, whose hand was firmly clutching its prize:

"Madame, would you mind taking your hand off my friend's cock?"

Which she did, as Stanley went into violent withdrawal symptoms that became even more accentuated when Claudine went on, equally loud, "Stanley, zip up your trousers. We're leaving."

One would think that this happened every night at the Crazy Horse Saloon, for not a head turned during the entire episode. The American lady, now primly clutching her husband's arm, did not even take her eyes from the stage as Stanley struggled to his feet and wrestled his way to freedom, with Claudine following haughtily behind. But then her giggles started again, and she couldn't stop until they had stepped outside the club onto the Avenue George V, after Stanley, in midflight, had hurriedly pressed $50 into a surprised waiter's hand.

"Stanley," she said when finally calmed down, "at least you've got to give her credit for having good taste. Although, come to think of it, she didn't get that far. Poor thing. She'll never know what she's missing. But maybe you prefer threesomes?"

Stanley was still too unnerved to either laugh or cry. But then slowly he had to admit to himself that, until Claudine had broken up things, they had been moving toward a rather interesting crescendo. In fact, the more he thought of it, of the very audacity of the situation, the more he began to anticipate the rest of the evening. By the time Claudine and he had entered his hotel suite, both were in a state of white heat. But again it was Claudine who took the lead.

"I want you, Stanley. Now!"

She flung the mink aside and pulled Rosen into the bedroom. Her urgency was so great that the white mini stayed on until both had reached a crashing climax, which left Claudine—all six feet of her—thrashing on top of him, as she came time and time again. Finally she lay still. Then breathing hard, she rose to remove the rest of her clothes. She did the same for Stanley, her hands busy with his body all the time. Suddenly she disappeared into the living room, to return carrying a chilled bottle of champagne and two glasses.

"You stay right there," she said to Rosen, as he lay sprawled across the bed. "From now on, I'm going to provide the treats."

With just a flick of the thumbs, the cork flew off. Claudine filled the glasses to the brim, handed them to Stanley, then climbed into the large bed, pulling the eiderdown on top of both in a series of easy movements. She retrieved one of the glasses and tipped it toward Stanley.

"Stanley darling. You are such a wonderful man. Except for one thing."

Rosen was startled again. He was not used to complaints in bedrooms.

"There was something wrong?" he asked anxiously. "After what that woman pulled, I wouldn't be surprised. The bloody nerve!"

"No, nothing wrong, darling" she said laughing. "Just that you would be absolutely perfect if you had a moustache."

"Aha," said Stanley, relieved. "You mean like your little banking friend from Switzerland." Now he took his first sip of champagne.

"Yes."

"But I thought, from what you told me last time, that he turned out to be a total failure on his last trip."

"Well, not total. He at least had a stiff moustache. But let's not talk about him."

"But," insisted Stanley, "I'd like to. Just for a minute. The guy intrigues me."

"How could he intrigue you? You've never met."

"Of course not, but what I mean is that it intrigues me that a guy could get so worked up about business that even you could not get him worked up in bed."

"I told you. He had something very big on his mind."

73

"How could anything be that big?"

"He said that the meeting of those two men he saw together in London could mean that something very very important was going to happen. You know, with gold and dollars and all that stuff."

"You mean the American Secretary of the Treasury?"

"Yes and that other one."

"From what bank was he again?"

"In English I don't know. But in French it's the Banque pour le . . . I forget. He called it BIZ or BEEZ or something like that." Then she paused and gave Rosen a curious look.

"But why," she continued, "are you so interested?"

"Well, I mean he is more or less your boyfriend, isn't he?"

"In a way. But not in any way that has anything to do with us."

"I'm not so sure. I mean, you can hardly be happy with a man who is impotent."

"I never said that. In fact, that was the first time that such a thing happened."

"Sure," said Stanley.

"Now you listen to me. You hardly think that I would become involved with a man who couldn't even—" She was obviously insulted.

"Claudine," interrupted Rosen, "let's change the subject. I'm sorry. You're right. It's hardly any concern of mine. I just hope that you'll be seeing a lot more of me in the future than that Swiss jerk."

The fact was that during the next four hours they saw quite a bit of each other, often from some of the most amazing angles. It was just before dawn when they sank into an exhausted sleep.

The first thing Stanley did when he woke up around noon was to look at the date on his watch. October 23. Time to get back to work.

7

Exactly six days later, on October 29, George Bernoulli had just straightened out his desk at the headquarters of the Special Branch of the Swiss Federal Police in Bern ready to leave for lunch, when the phone rang.

"Herr Doktor Bernoulli?" asked the metallic voice.

"*Jawohl, am Telefon.*"

"One moment please, Herr Doktor. You have a call from the Federal Council chambers."

The call was extremely brief. The minister of finance wanted to see Bernoulli within the shortest possible time—immediately, if convenient. It was.

The quickest way was to walk. Fifteen minutes later Bernoulli entered the office of the minister. The latter was not alone. He had two additional members of the Federal Council with him. After the usual round of handshakes, the finance minister, Jakob Gerber, took over.

"Herr Bernoulli, please accept our apologies for the short notice. But we have a problem that is quite urgent, and most delicate. I think you are the man to help us."

Gerber gave Bernoulli that super-earnest look which seems to be a prerequisite for high public office, no matter what the country.

"Thank you, sir. I would, of course, be most happy to help in any way I possibly can," said Bernoulli, the obedient servant.

"Good. Let me outline the situation. It apparently started in Rome last month, at the IMF meeting. The Germans, French, and Japanese came to a decision that if the United States was going to refuse to restore gold-dollar convertibility, they would force the issue by banding together into a gold bloc. Feelers were put out to us to join in, but in view of our neutrality we of course abstained. For this whole project would have amounted to nothing short of an open rebellion against the United States. In addition, I personally doubt whether it could have been carried off anyway. But that is now a moot point. For somehow the Americans got wind of the whole affair."

Gerber paused. He liked to formulate his thoughts quite precisely before speaking. "Well, as I said, the American delegation apparently got tipped off, and nothing short of a miracle happened. The president took the decision to restore the dollar-gold link by revaluing the official price of gold to $125 per ounce. This is extremely good news, of course. And you are probably wondering how we have come to know about it."

Bernoulli had no choice but to nod.

Gerber continued: "For good reasons, the president decided to put the secretary-general of the Bank for International Settlements in the picture. Apparently the Americans realized that it would be absolutely essential to inform Bollinger in advance —you know Bollinger, of course—since the BIS will have to assume a good share of the responsibility for steadying the foreign exchange markets, after the announcement is made. By the way, the firmly established revaluation date is November 8. In just over a week."

Gerber paused again. In contrast to the other six members of the Federal Council, who together represented the collective presidency of Switzerland, he was not a professional politician. He came from an industrial background and was known to be a man who could make tough decisions quickly. In spite of the fact that he had held the governmental post for over two years, he still appeared more than slightly uncomfortable in the company of some of his colleagues. The associate on his left, the minister of the interior, was best known for his ability to yodel at the conclusion of rural gatherings, which were much more noted for their alcoholic than political content. The man on his right, the minister of justice, was an ex-part-time university professor. He had no such claim to fame in the yodeling field, or for that matter, in any other. The law required seven men on the Federal Council, and he was simply the seventh. He could, however, smoke a pipe with a certain amount of élan.

The finance minister went on. "Obviously I still have not fully explained why we are involved. For the Americans demanded, and received, a pledge of absolute secrecy from Bollinger. Well, an accident happened. Upon his return from London, where he met with the American Secretary of the Treasury, Bollinger put his copy of the gold plan into a small safe which he maintains at his home. This was not all that unusual. Bollinger told me that he often brings documents home, especially over weekends, as we all do, I suppose. In this instance there was a special incentive for Bollinger to use his private facilities. He did not want any of his associates at the bank —most of them foreigners, as you know—to stumble upon this document, for obvious reasons.

"Somebody tampered with the safe a week later—which was the day before yesterday. Bollinger found himself in a most difficult dilemma. If somebody had deliberately taken illegal steps to get hold of the plan and maliciously leaked its contents, the result would probably be the biggest monetary explosion the world has ever seen. Even if the Americans now changed the plan, documentary evidence that it existed would produce such mass exodus from the dollar, and flight into anything else, ranging from marks to yen to lire, from Swiss common shares to South African gold mines, that possibly every bank in the free world, as well as all securities and commodities exchanges, might have to close their doors for weeks, maybe months. It would mean total chaos. I think that should be obvious. The German government leaked their exact thoughts about letting the mark float in May, 1971. The ultimate result was that in the final thirty-five minutes before they stopped accepting dollars, they took in over one billion! Just imagine what would happen under these circumstances."

The room remained completely silent.

"One possibility is that somebody is out to sabotage the dollar, once and for all. The other possibility is that this is the start of a highly organized criminal effort. You can imagine what this information could be worth to a speculator, or a group of speculators. An absolutely staggering amount. Then there is still the chance that a freak coincidence is involved. Perhaps some petty thief took a crack at this safe hoping for the best and, finding nothing of value, took along what struck him as the most impressive set of papers. For Bollinger claims that no one, absolutely no one, could possibly have known that a dossier of this importance was in his possession. But in any case, it was gone.

"After giving the matter twenty-four hours of thought, Bollinger decided not to tell the Americans. He is Swiss, like you and me. And we all know quite well that for all the good features of our friends in the United States, one talent they are not endowed with is the ability to tackle a problem with finesse, subtlety, a fine hand. This is not a criticism, mind you. Just a well-proven fact. As one of my British colleagues has often repeated, 'At the United States Treasury, every night is amateur night.' Had Bollinger told them, they would have come storming into Basel like a bunch of drunken cowboys, if you'll excuse the expression."

Bernoulli, who knew Americans well, felt that Gerber was overdoing things somewhat. But the minister of the interior, whose closest contact with America had been an occasional bottle of Coca-Cola amply laced with rum, burped his obvious approval. Also the pipe of the minister of justice seemed to be sending up positive signals. The resulting increased density of alcoholic fumes and smoke in the air did not seem to bother the minister of finance. He had apparently hardened in office. Gerber spoke again.

"The end of the story is quite simple. This morning, very early, Bollinger came to me, quite unofficially, of course, and asked for advice. I have pondered it ever since and reached the following conclusions about an hour ago. They are: First, we as a country very strongly desire that this gold revaluation plan be implemented as foreseen. It is in our national interest. Second, the fact is that the harm has already been done. The dossier is gone. Third, if we take this matter to the Americans, either a disastrous type of investigation will be started, and/or the devaluation will be called off permanently. Everybody, including the Americans, would suffer as a result. Fourth, we do not want any international institution domiciled in Switzerland to get involved in a scandal of such monumental proportions if we can help it. Thus my decision, based upon these conclusions, is the following: We will try to run this thing to the ground immediately. It may very well be a quite simple internal Swiss affair. If so, we will just squelch it. If a foreign government is involved, we will immediately withdraw from the scene, and everybody forgets everything. In any case, we as a government—and I cannot stress this fact more strongly—have no, absolutely no, knowledge of this incident. I hope you all quite clearly understand what I am saying—and especially you, Bernoulli."

"Yes, sir," replied the young man, "I understand this most clearly."

"But I don't."

Gerber was startled. Of all people, it was the ex-professor who was speaking.

"As I understand these matters, a massive revaluation of the official gold price would mean, ipso facto, a massive devaluation of the dollar."

Obviously the man had hidden, well hidden, strengths.

"I suspect, in fact I know, that this will not be acceptable to Western Europe, nor would it be acceptable under any circumstances to Switzerland."

Gerber stepped in again. "My dear colleague, in theory you are of course correct. But in fact, I am convinced the following will evolve. Most countries in the world will follow the dollar's devaluation completely. They will devalue, relative to gold, by exactly the same amount. So nothing will actually change, as far as exchange rates are concerned. It will only mean that the dollar is once again convertible into gold, at a much higher gold price. This obviously is in the interest of everyone."

"Most countries, yes. But most probably not all. And those are the ones that count."

"Indeed, this will represent a complication. Whether the Japanese, the Germans, or even the British will go all the way is not sure. You know as well as I do that the dollar outflow was not stopped by the 1971 and 1973 devaluations. They simply did not go far enough. So another adjustment in exchange rates, involving a limited number of countries, may be necessary. After all, this time we want to solve the problem once and for all."

"Are you saying that, for the third time now in less than three years, the Swiss franc will be increased in value, relative to the dollar?"

"I am merely saying that we cannot rule this possibility out."

"By how much?"

"Fifteen percent."

"Our industry will not like this."

"Nor will industry in Germany, Japan, or Britain. But we must end the dollar problem. And the time is now. Remember, this entire affair will bring a tremendous windfall gain to our country."

"How?"

"We have one of the largest gold reserves of any nation on earth: $3.5 billion worth. This will almost triple in value overnight. It will insure that the Swiss franc will remain as the hardest currency in the world for years, perhaps decades, to come. This, gentlemen, is obviously in our country's interest."

The room fell into silence.

Gerber shifted his attention.

"Bernoulli, I have decided to put you in charge of this investigation. You will meet with Bollinger tomorrow morning at eight to get all the details. He is expecting you. The best thing for you to do is to go over to Basel this evening and get some sleep tonight. You have a completely free hand, Bernoulli.

But I want you to report to me daily. By telephone, if you please."

The audience was over almost as abruptly as it began.

Bernoulli took the eighty-thirty train to Basel. At ten he checked into the Euler Hotel. Before he went down to the bar for a drink, he called his friend at the local police and asked him to start picking up all of the locally known safecrackers for interrogation. He explained the type of job that was involved and the place, but made no mention of the nature of the stolen goods. Kommissar Heinz Bucher promised to keep in touch.

Bernoulli turned in for the evening shortly before midnight.

At one the phone rang. Bernoulli was awake immediately.

"Is this Herr Doktor Bernoulli?" asked a familiar voice.

"Heinz, it's me and it's late," replied George Bernoulli.

"We've already got something. A guy that might fit. He's just in the process of being booked on suspicion of theft—for another job."

"Where?"

"At the Lohnhof." This was the city's central jail, a converted medieval convent.

"All right, get back to your fellows, Heinz. Tell them two things. First, put the fellow into an empty cell but one with two beds. Second, tell them you'll be bringing another one along in about a half hour. They should book me on suspicion of forgery with no other questions asked. Right? And then have me put in the same cell with this guy. And for God's sake, don't tell anybody, either the police or the jail people, who I really am. Use the name Salzmann for me. O.K.?"

"Agreed."

"Heinz," yelled Bernoulli. "What's the man's name?"

"Bechot. Sammy Bechot," came the answer.

"I'll be right over,' Bernoulli said and hung up.

He dressed quickly and left the hotel by the back stairs. It took him a quarter of an hour by foot to reach police head-quarters. Bernoulli, like most Swiss, liked to walk. It's supposed to be healthy. Kommissar Bucher was waiting for him outside. The jail was immediately adjacent to the police building.

The lockup proceedings were rather dreary. Tie, cuff links, watch, wallet went into a brown package. He signed his agreement that everything was duly there. Then down the corridor, through two doors of steel bars, and into a small room. He was ordered to strip. Disease check. Redressed more or less, he was handed over to a new warden and led up the stairs and then to the left. Ghastly place. Just a line of steel doors, all painted yellow. Why yellow? The door to cell 15 was closed. Bernoulli was handed two woolen blankets, two sheets, one rather worn towel, a mini bar of soap, and motioned in. The man inside had been sleeping. He barely took notice of the intruders. Bernoulli was instructed to pull down his bed, which was firmly hinged to the wall, make it, get in, and shut up. It was late.

Within fifteen minutes Bernoulli was asleep. This was not exactly the Euler, but a bed was a bed.

8

The church bells bonged. Six-thirty. A few minutes later the light in the cell was turned on from somewhere, the door opened, and a warden shoved in a broom. Door closed and locked. Bernoulli's cellmate began unwinding himself from the narrow bed, looked over to Bernoulli, and grinned.

"Bonjour!"

"*Guete Tag,*" replied Bernoulli in the local Swiss dialect.

"Aha. *Un Bâlois,*" said his roommate, who then continued in heavily accented, though excellent, German. "My name is Sammy Bechot. You new here?"

"Right. I'm George Salzmann," replied Bernoulli, "and this is the first time I've had the privilege of enjoying the hospitality of the Lohnhof."

"Don't worry," said Sammy, "I've been here before. You plan to be here long?"

Bernoulli just shrugged.

"Don't worry," repeated Sammy. "It's not bad here. But we had better get up. That's the rule here at six-thirty."

They took turns washing—one basin, cold water—and got dressed. Following Sammy's example, Bernoulli folded together his bedding and swung the cot back up against the wall. The only other furnishings in the cell were a very small wooden table, matched by a wooden bench, both firmly attached to floor and wall. At seven the door was unlocked and opened again. Two breakfasts were handed in: café au lait in huge metal cups and two pieces of black bread for each. Door closed and locked. Twenty minutes later the same ritual with the door. This time the cups were handed out, and the broom.

Shortly before, Sammy had made exactly three perfunctory swipes at the floor with it.

Then silence.

Half an hour later the door was once again swung open. The chief warden on his daily tour of inspection, continental style. For he also appeared to be chief order taker, and Sammy was ready to order: one transistor radio, shaving cream, three sausages, two large beers, 100 grams of powdered coffee, pickles. He assured the chief warden that sufficient funds were available, even though they had been forceably and unconstitutionally removed from his pockets the evening before.

Twenty minutes later the action continued. This time it was one of the trustees who arrived with a catalogue from the prison library. An extremely pleasant type. Apparently an American from his peculiar accent. Sammy wrote out a list of thirty books: 50 percent crime stories, the other half Westerns.

Thus far the two men in cell 15 had exchanged nothing further than their original introductions. Bernoulli was calculating how he could get things moving, when for the sixth time the steel door clanked open.

"Salzmann?"

"That's me."

"Kommissar wants you."

"Why?"

"How should I know. Come on, let's go."

Ten minutes later Bernoulli found himself in Kommissar Bucher's office.

"Take a chair, George, and tell me what's really going on here," said Bucher. "We had all of two or three minutes on the phone last night, and I did what you asked. But it seems to me that you are going about all this quite the wrong way. You know as well as I do that anything you get out of Bechot in this manner will never be admitted before court."

"I know that, Heinz. That's not my objective."

"Well, what is, if I may be so free as to ask?"

"I can't tell you. So there's no use to any further questions along this line."

"Fine. If that's the way it is, all right." Bucher obviously did not think it was so fine, but he had learned long ago to stick to the book when something out of the ordinary was going on.

"Where do we go from here?"

"First of all, why do you feel so strongly that Bechot might be our man?" asked Bernoulli.

"For a number of reasons. He's a pro—one of the best in the field, with a record a kilometre long. And it seems that he has recently developed some kind of a new way of getting into safes without wrecking them, right on the spot too. He used to leave them so full of holes you would hardly have believed it. But last night another safe was taken, also in a private house—on the outskirts of the city. It was the same story as you told me. No marks, no nothing on the safe. This time it was completely cleaned out and once again closed. The victim was an Englishman, a scientist, connected with the chemical industry. Among other things he lost a stack of five-pound notes. He reported the theft around six in the evening yesterday—at the local station. I got the report shortly after you called from the Euler and immediately put out a general signal to pick up any of the professionals known to us, and in the vicinity. Sammy was the first to show. And although he had nothing more than a couple of hundred francs on him, shortly before we picked him up he had apparently paid for his drinks with a five-pound note in one of those bars in the Rhine harbour area."

"Have you any reason to believe he did the other job, too?"

"None whatsoever. But I think that even you can perhaps detect that there just might be some grounds for suspecting so."

"Thanks," replied Bernoulli. "When do you plan to put him through the wringer?"

"Just as soon as you would like. But let me warn you. We've

had Bechot here before. A couple of years ago. He won't talk. Not a chance. He's a two-time loser, and he knows that if we can nail him again, the court will put him away for five years, at least."

"Right. Well, Heinz, then I'd appreciate it very much if you could give me a couple of days to try it my way. I'm here under instructions from Bern."

"I know. I know."

"So just leave him alone for the time being. O.K.? And I'd appreciate it if you could come and get me tomorrow—same time."

"Right."

"Before I go I would like to make two phone calls, please. And in private, if you don't mind."

Bucher just grinned and left the room.

The first call went to the office of the secretary-general of the Bank for International Settlements. Bernoulli apologized profusely for not making his appointment, past due now by a good half hour. They agreed to a new date, at Bollinger's home. The second call went to Bern.

Then he just leaned back and enjoyed a cigarette, fairly pleased with himself.

Now at this point I think it would be fair to point out that George Bernoulli is not in the Anglo-Saxon tradition we are all so used to. Sure, he's involved in the dark side of state affairs— but not with a revolver, although he's got one and knows how to use it. Nor with a Ferrari. He drives a standard Alfa Romeo 1600. Standing at over six feet, with dark hair and a thin moustache, he cuts a very good figure. But he dresses conservatively and is almost never without a tie. He does not even own a pair of brown shoes. He seldom turns down a drink and never fails to show due appreciation to a good bottle of wine, preferring red wines, peculiarly enough, even with fish. At thirty-four he is not married, but he is never without a girlfriend. He can outski most Swiss and spends a good part of February and

March in either St. Moritz or Gstaad. Although for some odd reason he had never learned to swim, still he spends almost all his summer vacations on or near the Mediterranean. He likes to "fool around," as he puts it, with archeology. Thus he is a regular visitor to places like French Provence, Crete, and Turkey, although for security reasons he has been forced to avoid Egypt, a fact he constantly regrets.

So he is really a rather low-key type, and that is what the Swiss government wants for men in his profession. Bernoulli's function, the government expects, is that of a quite inconspicuous backup man to the politicians, as a member of a very small espionage-counterespionage force maintained by the Swiss Federal government, an operation that is absolute chicken feed compared with the immense organizations maintained by so many other nations. The Swiss, in this as in so many other matters, prefer quality to quantity. Bernoulli meets their specifications perfectly; he has family, education, intelligence, discipline. He is ideal for this particular job. His speciality is finance and economics. Money is extremely dear to the hearts of all Swiss. So their curiosity about what is going on in the world in this particular area is, should we say, out of proportion to their interest in other areas. They like to be informed well in advance of a possible devaluation of the pound sterling, or a decision of the American government to cut off support to some developing country deeply engaged in dam or road construction. This is quite natural, since Switzerland often holds large amounts of sterling, and a number of companies key to the Swiss economy are major producers of power generating equipment and cement. Filling these gaps in the market suddenly left open by the Americans requires speedy action and often "indirect" government aid in the form of timely information. The Swiss like to think of this as "productive espionage."

Much of Bernoulli's job was spent at a desk, filtering such information and passing it along to the right place. But he had already worked extensively in the field, where his expertise in economic matters only served as a cover. For quite a period he had served with the International Red Cross, operating out of its world headquarters in Geneva. The top jobs there are reserved exclusively for Swiss, since after all the Red Cross was a Swiss invention. He had been slipped into the Number Three slot in their financial department. The spot was a good one. Thus, for instance, when in 1970 the Arabs kidnapped a couple of planeloads of people, including one Swiss DC-8, it was the International Red Cross which made the arrangements to get the people back from Jordan. The Swiss nationals, naturally, were the first to leave. Dr. Bernoulli had done a beautiful job under difficult circumstances, although it did cost quite a few Swiss francs. He was also in Biafra quite regularly, helping out the poor refugees, but also making quite sure that Swiss businessmen were put into contact with the people who would come out on top when Nigeria was reunited. His participation in the aid mission to West Bengal led to a noticeable cooling of relations between Switzerland and Pakistan, matched by a new fervour for India's development problems, at least two months before the military clash which resulted in the creation of Bangladesh and the emergence of Indian hegemony on that subcontinent.

It was not without some regret that Bernoulli agreed to his recall to that department's headquarters in Bern. In fact, he secretly hoped that he would soon be sent back to Geneva to serve the cause of humanity. Maybe success in Basel would help. And, at the moment, this did not seem impossible. For Bernoulli was convinced that, as Sammy Bechot's cellmate, he could get to the heart of the matter in a very short time, with just a little luck.

But I've got to get things moving, he thought, as he was walked back to his cell, accompanied by a uniformed policeman, who was apparently not in on the game. It had hardly been necessary, for God's sake, to put on handcuffs. Or maybe it was just a sick joke of Bucher's.

Not much time had really passed. It was just shortly after

ten when the cell door clanked closed behind him once again. Bechot was stretched out on his bed reading and barely glanced up as George pulled down his bed and also lay down.

"Hey," said George finally, "what's new?"

"Hah," replied Sammy, "what's ever new here!"

"What have you doing?"

"Reading. You read?"

"Sure, but I don't feel like it right now. You play chess?"

"Of course. But we need a chess set."

"How do we do that?"

"Watch!"

Sammy jumped from his bed and started pounding on the metal door with his fist. He just kept pounding until the door opened.

"Sammy, you know better than that," said the warden with a big grin. "What are you trying to do, impress your friend?"

"Look," replied Sammy, "you are here to protect and help us, and we need a little service. A chess set."

"Sure, I'll see if I can drum one up."

"No, no. Now," said Sammy.

"Why now?"

"Because my friend here feels suicidal. I'm trying to occupy his mind. You prefer to mop up a big puddle of blood?"

The warden looked carefully at George. You never knew in this place.

"O.K. Just calm down, Sammy."

Five minutes later he was back with a battered chess set, and left after giving Bernoulli another rather mistrustful look. Nobody in prisons likes nuts, and a quiet one like this was always suspicious. With a shrug he left again, locking the door with what seemed to be an extra flourish this time.

Sammy had the board set up immediately on his bed and soon was deeply involved in his initial moves. He played amazingly well, and George, who was very rusty to say the least, was well on his way to losing when the door clanged open again.

Lunchtime. At eleven o'clock in the morning, for God's sake.

In spite of the metal containers, the meal was astoundingly well prepared.

"Is the food always so good here?"

"The best of any prison in Switzerland," answered Sammy. "I know, I've tried a few of them and heard about lots of others. One thing is sure, if the cops are looking for you, make sure you get arrested here and not in Geneva or St. Moritz. Those places are horrible. Some people, you know, have absolutely no sense of responsibility. They let their jails run down in a way you simply would not believe."

Sammy reached under his bed, and his hand reappeared holding a bottle of beer. His supplies had obviously arrived during Bernoulli's short absence.

"You see what I mean. In the Bâle prison you get service, prompt service. It's also the only jail in the country where they let you drink."

He offered Bernoulli a pull on the bottle and was not turned down.

"Aah," gasped Bernoulli, "that really hit the spot. Sammy, you know, somehow I have the feeling that things are looking up."

"Well, I'm glad to hear it. You sure looked worried earlier this morning."

"I guess because it's my first time. You know how it is when you have absolutely no idea how the system works."

"Sure, I went through the same thing about, lemme think, yeah, about seven years ago. And that was in Geneva. Ugh. Look, just make sure you order lots to eat and drink from the outside. It takes your mind off of other things. You must have money the way you look. What did you do?"

"Bad cheque. And you?"

"Safes. That's my speciality. They know me all over. Sammy Bechot. The best in the business."

Both men had suddenly warmed to each other. Bernoulli found Sammy to be a highly sympathetic and amusing person. And obviously Sammy felt more than a bit sorry for this man who could not quite cope with a life to which Sammy had long ago become accustomed. Prison cells produce peculiar social chemistry.

In the afternoon Bernoulli followed Sammy's advice and pounded on the door with his metal cup, and when the warden appeared handed him a list of food and especially wine—good wine—that he wanted bought as soon as possible. He deliberately overordered. When the supplies came, the bulk of them was locked in a wooden cupboard right outside the cell door in the corridor. The daily ration of alcohol per day was limited to one litre of wine per head. Through some mixup, however, Bernoulli ended up with two litres in the cell. Then Sammy came up with a further brilliant idea. Nothing in the jail rules precluded one inmate from making gifts to another. He banged on the door with his cup, producing a volume of noise reflecting skill born of practice. This time the door was not opened. The night shift was just coming on and security precautions increased. The metal covering on the peephole in the door was swung aside.

"What's going on?"

"All I want is some wine for the evening."

"Sammy, don't push things too far. All you've got is beer and you damn well know it."

"But my friend George wants to offer me one of his bottles. And he thought you might be able to use one, too."

The door swung open.

"Not so loud, Sammy. For Christ's sake, you want to get us all into trouble?" He turned to Bernoulli.

"Is Sammy here telling the truth?"

"Of course."

"Well, fine. As an exception, mind you, I'll accept your offer." He unlocked the cabinet in the corridor and two more bottles appeared. He started to apply the corkscrew, hanging from his heavy keychain.

"Stop it!" commanded Sammy. "Just leave the corkscrew here."

"You know that's against the rules. I open the bottles. You drink."

"Ah, come on. My friend here is not used to drinking stale wine. Look, for God's sake. It's a 1957 Pommard. You want to ruin a thing like that?"

The warden looked at the label: in fact, he studied it with sudden respect.

"O.K., just wait a minute. I'll get another one."

"I'll come with you," said Sammy. "After all, you've had a long day."

To Bernoulli's surprise, both of them disappeared, leaving the door completely open. Five minutes later Sammy reappeared and produced not only a corkscrew but two cigars, two bottles of beer, and a candle.

"Met a buddy" was his only explanation.

At nine-thirty, exactly, the lights in the cell went out. Just as punctually, Sammy's candle went on. Bernoulli and Bechot settled down to a hard night of drinking, mingled with jokes and resulting laughter that at one time invoked a heavy banging on the cell wall. Apparently the guy next door wanted to sleep. It must have been well past midnight when Sammy started talking shop. It was an unexpected opportunity, with such an obviously literate and appreciative audience. And sure enough, when he described his new technique, it elicited a response of respect, true respect. By this time the wine was gone. They turned to the beer, which had been cooling in the wash basin, under continuously running water for hours. The occasion also called for cigars.

"Ain't this the life?" asked Sammy.

"Sure, as long as it doesn't drag on too long," countered Bernoulli.

"Well, I don't know about you, but I'm not worried one little bit on that score. I'll be out of here in less than a week— maximum."

"Really?"

Sammy meant it—really. They would not dare keep him; his

second-last job had been done for the cops themselves! One of the kommissars who had dealt with Sammy in regard to an earlier charge, which eventually had brought him twenty-four months behind bars, had set it up, and paid Sammy 10,000 francs for one of the simplest jobs he had ever done in his life. His latest little escapade would be swept under the rug for lack of evidence, and that would be that.

This was all Bernoulli needed. To press for more information from Sammy at this point would simply be too risky. With or without alcohol, Bechot was a crafty character.

They soon finished off their beer and cigars. Sammy blew out the candle and carefully hid the stump in a spare pair of socks. Obviously he knew his way around the cell, even in pitch darkness.

Within minutes both men were asleep, and in fact both slept very well in the sure knowledge that they would not be in jail much longer.

The next morning Bernoulli was again collected from his cell for interrogation. Within fifteen minutes his friend Heinz Bucher collected every dossier of information they had on Sammy Bechot. After Bernoulli's retelling of Sammy's tale of the previous evening, Bucher had turned white with anger; it had the ring of truth.

As the two men systematically went through the documentation, containing hundreds of pages of past interrogation of Bechot, they both had one single objective—the listing of every cop that had ever dealt with Sammy.

In order to maintain the façade, Bernoulli was returned to his cell for lunch. When he returned an hour later, Bucher was still on the job.

"Heinz, when are you going to eat?"

"Tomorrow."

"Look, don't take it personally for God's sake. It happens in the best police forces."

"Yeah, sure."

"Maybe Sammy's lying after all."

"I doubt it. Why don't you shut up, so that we can get this dirty work over."

By four o'clock they had the full list of police contacts with Bechot from the past. Fourteen names. As Bucher reread the list for what must have been the twentieth time, he suddenly slammed his hand down on his desk.

"George, dammit, I'll bet I've got it. That dirty son of a bitch. We'll hang that bastard up so high they'll need a crane to get him back down."

"Who is it, Heinz?"

"Probably a fellow named Rolf Lutz."

"What's his rank?"

"He has none. He left the force about four years ago. Used to be a kommissar in the fraud squad. We worked together quite a bit. Then he set up a collection agency in town. It went very well. So he branched out to Zurich and Geneva, then Lugano."

"That does not exactly fit, Heinz. I mean just because he's apparently the only fellow on your list who has left the force does not mean you have to jump to such conclusions."

"That's not the whole story. He didn't stick to collections. Two years ago he changed the name of his company to Swiss Security Consultants. Now the bulk of the business is the investigation of thefts, frauds, scandals that companies don't want leaked. His success has been fantastic. By now Lutz must have a group of at least fifty people, most of them ex-policemen, on his staff. He moved headquarters to Geneva last year—same time as he changed the name. They tell me he picked up a whole crew of communications guys down there. They'll sweep a place for you on a regular contract basis for bugs, wiretaps, or just plain carelessness. But as far as I know, he's never been caught stepping out of line. Strictly defensive stuff."

"You got a file on him?"

"No. As I told you he's been operating out of Geneva for

the past couple of years. And we've had no reason to investigate his local operations."

"What makes you feel that he would get involved in something like this? I mean, there's an enormous risk."

"Just a feeling. First, I don't like coincidences one bit. Bechot would hardly differentiate between a cop and an ex-cop. He thinks strictly in terms of us and them. Second, Lutz did not leave this place in a blaze of glory. We all get our hands a bit dirty now and then. You know that. But Lutz seemed to make a habit of it."

"So he was fired?"

"No, but nobody here was especially sad to see him go. He liked money just a little too much."

"Heinz, I'll just have to trust your judgement," said Bernoulli. "I don't have time to wait for a laborious sifting out of the other people on the list."

"But I can hardly pick him up, or even approach him, on the grounds of your story, George."

"I know, and that would be the very last thing we would want. For the moment I really need just one thing. A more complete dossier on Swiss Security Consultants A.G. Geneva must have something. The most important factor is a better feeling for their clientele."

"O.K. I'll ask the fellows in Geneva."

"But do it real easy, Heinz," stressed Bernoulli. "I don't want one speck of dust stirred up."

"I'll work it out."

"Now one other thing. I want you to try to trace Bechot's movements—all of them—on the evening and night of October 27. Check every hotel and every bar in the city. Carefully."

"Right."

By this time it was starting to get dark outside. Bernoulli was brought back to his cell just in time for the evening meal. It consisted of dark bread and thick cocoa.

"How did it go?" asked Bechot.

"Fine. It should be all cleared up by tomorrow."

"How come?"

"My father has agreed to cover the check. All one big mixup, you know. I thought his regular transfer had arrived, but it seems that he forgot it, or something."

"Oh."

"Yeah. Unfortunately this is not the first time. I had a little problem like this in Germany a while back. But there we could arrange things without me being locked up."

"Hah," said Bechot. "Do you think it's the first time for any of us here? Once they get to know you they never leave you alone. It's too bad. Now I'll probably get some damn Turk or Italian for a cellmate. But that's all right. They won't dare keep me for long either."

That evening they enjoyed another two bottles of wine together and listened to Sammy's newly acquired radio.

At nine the next morning a warden appeared to tell Bernoulli to collect all of his things. He shook hands with Sammy, bequeathed him the rest of his wine, and left.

By nine-thirty Bernoulli was back in the Euler Hotel. After a rather lame explanation to the man at the reception desk, he retrieved his key and within minutes was in the shower. It was amazing how quickly one felt permeated with the smell of prison.

9

Dr. Bollinger, secretary-general of the Bank for International Settlements, was impatiently pacing up and down his living room. It was furnished in Louis XV. Real Louis XV. A fantastic blue silk Chinese rug covered the floor of the living room. A Paul Klee, a Renoir, two Kadinskys graced its walls. It was lovely.

Bollinger was a bachelor. He was also a homosexual. It never failed to astound the girls in the bank's secretarial pool how Bollinger's colleagues managed to overlook the man's idiosyncrasy. But his colleagues knew quite well why. Bollinger was probably the most brilliantly inventive mind to appear on the international monetary scene in a decade. While all other international institutions appeared to be coming apart at the seams, the BIS experienced, if anything, growing prestige. This was due almost exclusively to Bollinger. He enjoyed the absolute trust and confidence, yes, respect, of all the important central bankers of the world. Although he had been educated at the University of Zurich, then Stanford, and finally the London School of Economics, he sported a French so abominable that by comparison even Edward Heath appeared to be a linguist. His background could hardly have been worse by Gallic standards—still the head of the Banque de France thought the world of the man. The ultimate test of all mortals.

The doorbell rang. It was Bernoulli. The two men knew each other on a formal basis. Yes, Minister Gerber had explained everything.

"Please have a seat, Dr. Bernoulli. May I offer you coffee, or perhaps tea?"

"No thanks, Dr. Bollinger. If you agree, I think we should

get right at it," answered Bernoulli. "First, where's the safe?"

"Right over there, behind the Klee."

"It's rather a large canvas for a Klee."

"He did it shortly before he died."

"May I?"

"Certainly."

Bernoulli took the painting down. It was a wall safe like thousands of others. Nothing special. Probably about ten years old. Easy. He rehung the picture and then returned to his chair.

"Aren't you going to get some people over to take fingerprints and all that?"

"No. It would be a waste of time at this point. But if you insist—?"

"Of course not. But I just thought—"

"When exactly did you notice that the document was missing?"

"Just a few days ago. On Tuesday morning when I was going to take it to the office with me. That would have been October 28."

"When had you last seen or used the document?"

"Last Monday."

"Why?"

"What do you mean—'why'?"

"Well, you'd had it here in Basel since the middle of the month, What prompted you to look for it, or at it, last Monday?"

"Bernoulli, we're dealing here with highly complex matters and a highly complex document. Do you think I memorized it?"

"Just asking," replied Bernoulli with the greatest of calm. "So in other words, it must have disappeared on Monday of this week."

"Yes."

"Where were you on Monday?"

"I spent the entire day at the office. I always lunch at the bank."

"And the evening?"

"I freshened up after five and went out to a cocktail party.

Then dinner. It was all in honour of the Belgian ambassador. He spent the day in Basel and the local government put on a do for him. I was invited along with at least fifty other people."

"You probably came home fairly late?"

"Around midnight."

"Notice anything unusual? You know, doors ajar that should not have been. Dirt on the rug. That sort of thing?"

"No. I went straight to bed. I don't have a suspicious mind."

"No? I thought everybody in the banking business had. No matter. In any case, I think it's fairly well established when it happened. Monday evening between five and midnight."

"Yes. The question now is who. And why."

"I think I already know something about the 'who' part," stated Bernoulli.

"But then why all the—"

"I said I think so. I'd rather not go into details at the moment, but we already appear to have some rather strong circumstantial evidence. A man named Sammy Bechot. Know him?"

"Never heard the name."

"Looks a little like a beatnick. Twenty-seven years old. Average height. Fairly fat. Long hair, beard. Both dark. Mother tongue is French, but he speaks German quite well, with the usual accent. He's a professional safecracker. Ring any bells?"

"Hardly."

"We guessed as much. Fine, let's try another approach now. And it's extremely important that you concentrate," stressed Bernoulli. "Do you mind if I smoke?"

"No, go right ahead."

"Let's go over your trip to London step by step. I am not particularly interested in what you did. I am extremely interested in whom you saw, whether deliberately, accidentally, or incidentally. Anybody and everybody who recognized you or could have recognized you."

Bollinger nodded.

"First, who at the bank knew, or knows, about the purpose of your trip to London?"

"No one."

"But surely your secretary or deputy must have known that you were meeting the American secretary of the treasury?"

"No, they did not then, nor do they have any knowledge of it now."

"But how was the appointment arranged?"

"Secretary Crosby telephoned me at home to make the arrangements. Right here is where I took the call." Bollinger pointed at a white telephone, neatly centred on a lace doily, which covered part of the top of an exquisite little side table that must have set Bollinger back at least a couple of thousand francs.

"Who lives with you?"

"No one. I am a bachelor, and my housekeeper, whom I've had for almost twenty years, takes care of the house during the day. She stays and cooks dinner only if I have guests. She is completely reliable and cannot possibly be involved in this dreadful thing."

"I'll accept that. So no one, absolutely no one here in Basel, knows about this document, nor about the purpose of your trip to London?"

"No one."

"But you must have had some explanation for your flight over there."

"I did give a very good one. The chancellor of the exchequer had repeatedly asked me to drop by to discuss the arrangement for unwinding the remnants of a very complex series of currency swaps which have developed over the years. I met him after my talks with Secretary Crosby, and we agreed on a most satisfactory series of steps to resolve this issue. In fact, my staff and I have been quite busy since my return with the implementation of our agreement."

"Right. Now let's concentrate on London itself."

Bernoulli continued, "As I understand it, you flew over on the one o'clock flight on October 16. That would be sixteen days ago. I think it was a Thursday."

"That's all perfectly correct."

"Now you arrived at Heathrow around two-fifteen local time. Did you talk to anybody at the airport or on the plane?"

"Nobody whatsoever."

"Who met you in London?"

"No one. I rented a chauffeur-driven car from Hertz. I always do that. It's only slightly more expensive than a taxi and immeasurably more comfortable. I went directly to the Savoy."

"When did you meet Secretary Crosby?"

"Shortly after my arrival at the hotel. We met in his suite, and after very long talks, ate dinner together in the Grill Room."

"Did you continue your business talks over dinner?"

"Yes, of course. But we had a table quite to ourselves."

"You noticed no one in your vicinity acting overly curious?"

"Of course not. Otherwise we would hardly have continued our talks."

"And after dinner?"

"We said good-bye at the elevator. I took the dossier to my room and went to sleep very early. Quite early the next morning I met the Bank of England people, as arranged."

"And you met no one else in the hotel?"

"No one."

"And you recognized no one in the hotel who might have recognized you and perhaps Crosby as well?"

"No one. Well, that's not totally correct. In fact I did recognize one man. As we were leaving the Grill Room after dinner, I had to return to the table to retrieve my pen which I had left lying there. Just by chance I noticed Dr. Walter Hofer, dining by himself of all things, on the opposite side of the room."

"Dr. Hofer of the General Bank of Switzerland?"

"Yes."

"You know him well, of course."

"Certainly."

"Did you greet each other?"

"No. I'm sure he also did not notice me."

"And did you see each other later in the hall, or perhaps the next morning over breakfast?"

"No."

By this time Bollinger was getting a bit peeved. He had expected that he would have to answer some questions after talking to Bern, but there were ways of going about such things and ways not to. This chap Bernoulli was getting just a touch too arrogant for his taste. But there was no sense in showing it. Just as long as Bernoulli stayed clear of his private life. And so far, he had. But if the Americans got involved, they would grab onto *that* first thing and never let go.

"In other words, as far as you remember, Hofer was the only acquaintance of yours who might have seen you and Secretary Crosby together?"

"Yes, if you want to put it that way."

"That's the way I want to put it."

A smart ass, that's what he is, thought Bollinger. He hoped it did not show.

Bernoulli continued. "Now I must assume that you made no mention of this whole thing at the Bank of England."

"Yes, you're quite safe in that assumption, my dear Doktor Bernoulli."

Aha, thought Bernoulli. Finally getting under his skin. That's always good.

"Right," he said aloud. "Now let's cover the trip home."

"That's quite simple. After lunch at the Bank of England, I went directly to the airport even though it was a bit early. It was the same story there. I saw no one I knew and talked to no one but the girl at the newsstand in the international lounge."

"Fine. Now let's take the flight home."

"Well, that was a bit different," replied Bollinger. "First I met Igor Melekov of the Soviet Foreign Trade Bank on the plane. We have known each other for years. In fact, we sat together for part of the trip and chatted."

"Where did you have the dossier?"

"In my briefcase, of course."

"Did you ever take the dossier out of your briefcase while on the plane?"

"No."

"What were you and this Russian talking about anyway?"

"Things which cannot possibly be of any relevance."

"Ah, so."

"After landing in Zurich I had about a forty-five-minute stopover before catching the connecting flight to Basel."

"And your Russian friend?"

"He went into Zurich."

"I see. Please continue."

"I chatted with the VIP greeter in the Swissair lounge in Zurich. He took me directly to the plane in his car. On the plane I was recognized, greeted, and spoken to by my tailor. He was just coming back from a trip to South Africa."

"Hm. Quite a tailor. And in Basel?"

"I took a taxi directly home, deposited the documents in my wall safe which you have examined, and retired for the evening."

"Fine. Well, I think that does it for today," said Bernoulli, and rose abruptly. "Say, do you by any chance know a man called Rolf Lutz? He used to be with the police department here—fraud squad."

"No."

"Have you ever had any dealings with a company called Swiss Security Consultants?"

"The bank does, yes. They make regular security sweeps. I personally find the whole idea absurd. But some of the Anglo-Saxon participants in our regular monetary meetings at the bank insisted."

"You mean the Americans or the British?"

"The Americans."

"You have problems with the Americans?"

"No more than anybody else."

"Lutz is head of Swiss Security Consultants."

"Then no doubt I have met him. Why?"

"Just wondering."

"Then we've covered what you want to know?"

"Yes. Thanks so much, Dr. Bollinger. I promise to keep in touch. If you think of anything else that might help, please call me at the Euler Hotel."

They started walking toward the door.

"Say, just one more little item," said Bernoulli, his hand resting on the doorknob. "What could happen if this document is in the wrong hands?"

"What do you mean by 'wrong hands'?"

"Let's say a government hostile to the United States."

"That's flatly impossible."

"O.K., but just for the fun of it, what if it happened?"

"If they leaked its contents, it would start a tremendous run on the dollar. No one could foresee the ultimate consequences."

"But why?"

"The world would no doubt interpret the contents of this document as the intention of the United States to make a new massive devaluation of the dollar. They would all want out— all at the same time."

"But that's not the intention of the United States, is it?"

"Technically yes, but only relative to gold. There will be another devaluation of the dollar relative to other currencies simultaneously, but it will be rather minor—15 percent. That's not what matters. We are dealing here with mass psychology. The world has been extremely edgy about the dollar for years now. This could set off the panic which everyone has been trying to avoid."

"And if it was just a private group, or person?"

"Obviously one or the other could make a lot of money."

"Or," added Bernoulli, "he could use the document to forward some private crackpot scheme. You know, bring on the death throes of capitalism or some such thing."

"I must say, you certainly do not lack imagination, Bernoulli."

"Well, I'm not a banker."

With that he left. Bollinger walked slowly back to the living room and poured himself a fairly stiff cognac.

Ten minutes later Bernoulli was going through exactly the same exercise back at his hotel. Then he got on the telephone. First to Bern to report in and then to Kommissar Bucher at the local police headquarters.

"George," said Bucher, "I'm glad you called. I'm starting to like working with you."

"How come?" asked Bernoulli.

"Because between us things happen—fast. We've already got Bechot nailed. One of our fellows, checking out all the bars and hotels, determined that he spent another five-pound note. This time at the bar of the Three Kings Hotel. It was on the same evening as the robbery. The bartender is willing to testify as a witness. We already have a signed statement from him."

"Great, but how does that help me?"

"It seems that Bechot has been coming to that bar each night, for four consecutive days, starting on Friday, October 24, and ending on the night of the robbery when he left the five-pound note."

"Uh huh."

"So we checked the hotel roster. And we turned up enough to make your hair stand on end. First, our mutual friend Rolf Lutz spent four nights there. They overlap with Bechot's visits."

"It looks like we're lucking it out, Heinz."

"Wait a minute, there's more. Five—get this—five Russians were there during exactly the same time span. I figured that if Bern is involved, this was bound to tie in somehow."

"Maybe. Anything else?"

"The Russians had reserved for the entire week. Last Tuesday they checked out suddenly—within thirty minutes. Then there's a fat little American who during the same weekend was waving around girls and dollar bills like crazy. He left something less than the greatest impression with the hotel management. Spent exactly the same period of time there as Lutz. Right across the hall from Lutz. The hallporter claims to have seen them together, very late one night. Finally there's a Brazilian. From his description he very closely resembles one of the biggest con men in the business. Interpol has had a signal out for him for years. He stayed at the Three Kings for a week and departed Tuesday morning, the night after the theft—very early. Tuesday seems to have been a big day for people to leave Basel."

"Great, Heinz. I'll come right over and get all the details."

As usual, Bernoulli walked. It was a sunny autumn day but a chilly wind was starting to come in from the east.

10

Three days later on Tuesday, November 4, snow was lightly falling as Igor Melekov left the Foreign Trade Bank of the Soviet Union. He crossed the street, against a rather brisk wind, and headed toward the main entrance of the Bolshoi Theatre, less than a hundred metres away. His Thunderbird was once again in trouble. The fleet of black Zis limousines of the bank were there for the asking, but as usual he disdained using them. They had absolutely no style. Melekov preferred to take a taxi rather than relent on such an important principle. Not that Moscow taxis had any style either. But that was not the point.

There was the normal bustle of people and traffic in front of the Bolshoi and five cabs were parked there, the drivers in the usual huddle. But no luck. They were taken. It was just one more of Mother Russia's unfathomable mysteries. As in New York, the majority of downtown traffic in Moscow consisted of taxis. But in Moscow none were ever free. Melekov did not really mind. He was in an excellent mood.

He decided to walk. It was at most a fifteen-minute stroll to the Russaya Hotel. Melekov struck a good figure. He was tall, well dressed, and moved briskly. Going up the rise to Red Square, he had to skirt the usual snaking line of visitors waiting to get a brief glimpse at Lenin's mummy. Melekov glanced at his watch, a Rolex, and then paused for a moment in front of the showcases of the Gum department store. He figured he was just a shade early. Russians were never early, and he knew that the Germans took account of every little detail, however minute, in their calculations.

He ambled now, through the rest of the huge square, heading toward the Moscow River. The Russaya suddenly loomed on his left—the largest hotel in the world. Here, he noticed, there were lots of taxis, waiting and free. The drivers knew where the dollars were buried. But, he thought, it's harmless. Let them do their little thing. Most foreigners in Moscow are much too afraid to fool around with petty black market currency deals.

He passed the hotel's Beriozhka shop and stopped again. He must remember to order another case of Black and White. The shop appeared to be completely full, as usual. It was amazing how all these people came into possession of dollars, the only currency accepted in the Beriozhka stores. One could not help but wonder who in the world had given the original consent for the opening of these operations. The best store in Moscow, offering everything from Heinz soups to Kodak film, and if you tried to pay in rubles they would throw you out. Ostensibly for tourists; amazing how many of them spoke Russian! Oh, well, that was somebody else's worry.

Melekov's worry at the moment was the Germans. Then Valentajn Ivanovich Stepanov. In that order only in terms of chronology, not priority. He could hardly wait until afternoon, and the showdown with that financial nitwit, Hero of the Soviet Socialist Republics. If only the caricaturists of the West knew how close they often came to the truth—that fellow strutting around on May Day, medals and all, had to be seen to be believed.

The entrance hall at the Russaya was huge, and it was only one of four with exactly the same design. The hotel had been built as a monstrous quadrangle, four separate but equal wings, each containing well over a thousand rooms. A Byzantine Hilton of bizarre proportions. The lines at the desk were long. It was almost as difficult to check into a Russian hotel as it was to check out of an American. But this was also not his problem.

"Comrade Melekov, the head of the German delegation is expecting you on the second floor."

Melekov's waiting assistant led the way to the elevators. After five minutes one arrived. Three giggling American girls and one slightly drunken Russian emerged.

The spread of dollars and decadence seem to go hand in hand, thought Melekov, as he rode the lift up to the second floor. The suite which he entered was Slavic Holiday Inn. Now Americans could also travel to Russia without ever having to touch foreign soil.

Hans Klausen, managing director of the Rhein-Ruhr Stahlwerk, greeted Melekov profusely in gutteral English. Melekov knew German very well, but he would still be at a disadvantage in that language. Klausen pretended no knowledge of Russian, which was of course not true. Like so many other Germans he had learned Russian the hard way, courtesy of the military genius of Adolf Hitler. Klausen's English was decent, but not as good as Melekov's. So although the advantage was slight, it was there. Melekov had learned long ago never to seek to negotiate in a language he had not completely mastered.

"My dear Herr Klausen, my people tell me that all the technical aspects of the agreement have been settled and that the contract is ready for signature," said Melekov, as he settled opposite the German on the barbarous piece of foam rubber and steel which served as a chair.

"*Jawohl*, Herr Melekov," replied the German. He was just under sixty, and known as the most aggressive man in the steel business in Europe. A self-made man. A man with no political opinions. A man who worked day and night, not for the glory of Germany, but solely for the success of the Rhein-Ruhr Stahlwerk.

"All that remains to be finalized are the financial arrangements. Even there during the past weeks we have worked out a draft agreement with your people at the Foreign Trade Bank, and both sides now feel the results are most acceptable."

He handed Melekov a twenty-page document—ten pages

109

each in German and Russian; Russian would be the binding text. Melekov settled back, as best one could with the furniture available, and began to read.

The basic elements of the transaction had been under negotiation for almost two years. It involved the purchase of just under $2 billion worth of large diameter steel pipe from the Rhein-Ruhr Stahlwerk, the biggest foreign purchase in the history of the Soviet Union. The reason for this transaction was simple. Russia's energy needs were climbing as rapidly as those in the West—doubling every ten years. Huge quantities of energy, in the form of crude petroleum and natural gas, were available in the eastern half of Russia. But these had to be brought to the refineries and to industry—and they were concentrated in the western regions of that vast country, this side of the Urals. Once brought to European Russia, there was no reason why a good part of the oil and gas could not be sent just a bit farther into Western Europe which was desperately seeking to reduce its dependency upon Libya for petroleum. Thus oil and gas could provide the answer to two essential Soviet needs—for energy and foreign exchange. Since both needs had become acute, a crash program was decided upon. Intensive calculations, part of the most detailed project planning yet achieved in the Soviet Union, had shown that during the next five years the building program would require an enormous amount of pipe for the dual lines which had to be put in. But they had also demonstrated beyond any doubt that thereafter demand would settle back to a level which just about matched the existing capacity of domestic producers. The conclusion: It did not make economic sense to build up Russian large-diameter pipe capacity to meet a temporary peak need. The investment required would be enormous, and the long-term return highly doubtful, unless a large proportion of output could be sold in world markets in the 1980s. A very expensive study, done for the Russians by Britain's leading market research organization, proved that competition from producers in Western Europe, the United States, and Japan would preclude this. So the answer was: Meet the unique high-peak need for pipe during the next five years through imports.

The problem had then reduced itself to the supplier. Which country would get this big fat contract? Everybody, of course, got into the act. All ramifications were considered: political, military, financial, technical. But this time, in contrast to earlier deals involving Cuban sugar or Egyptian cotton, the cool logic of the technocrats, who now ruled the country, had prevailed. Reciprocal trade potential, quality, speed, punctuality of delivery, price, and financial terms—these were to be the criteria upon which the decision was to be based—in exactly that descending order. The Americans out of Milwaukee would have won hands down on speed; the Italians from Genoa on financial terms; the British on price; the Japanese on punctuality. But only the German got high points in all six areas—first in quality, overwhelmingly first where potential reciprocal trade was concerned since they could probably absorb all the Russian gas and crude that would be offered and pay for it in hard cash, and second in all the rest.

The Soviets recognized that Germany once more had the most efficient industrial machines in the world. The country was just one big modern factory, led by men who attacked markets with the efficiency of Prussian generals, supported by engineers and technicians who were perfectionists and manned by workers who had no equivalent for devotion to duty, quality of work, and identification with their company, their products, and the success of both. He was a Marxian nightmare, this German worker with his Volkswagen, his colour TV, his vacations in Spain.

"I see really only one area that does not seem to be perfectly regulated," said Melekov finally, breaking the twenty-minute silence which had settled over the room as he studied the financial part of the contract.

The German stiffened. He did not like this—at all. He and his people had now spent almost seven months of hard work, haggling over the most minute details, often with second-rate bureaucrats who would not have been offered any greater responsibility than driving a streetcar if they lived in Düsseldorf. In spite of this, the entire 700-page agreement, not to speak of the thousands of items in the appendices, was already initialled, ready for final signature. Except for these last ten pages.

"What area are you referring to?" was Klausen's response. The man was obviously having difficulty.

"The mode of payment."

"But, Herr Melekov, we have discussed this matter at least a dozen times with your people. This, finally, is *your* draft, not ours."

"I am not speaking of the terms. Ten years is satisfactory. Nor am I referring to the rate of interest. Eight percent seems correct. Finally, I am not referring either to the takedown conditions or the amortization plan. What has been worked out there is quite acceptable. No, I am referring solely to the currency. We desire that the transaction be made in United States dollars and not in German marks. That's all."

Klausen had regained his cool. He did not twitch an eyebrow.

"That's all?"

"That's all," restated Melekov.

"But you surely realize that this is not just a slight change. The entire credit scheme is based upon a most complex set of arrangements between ourselves and a consortium involving the five largest bank groups in our country. Our banks are German banks. Our currency is the mark. Our product is based upon German costs, mark costs. Therefore the entire transaction must done in marks."

"My dear Herr Klausen, our banks deal in rubles. Our costs are calculated in rubles. Our workers are paid in rubles. But we adapt to the realities of international trade. When we sell you machine tools, and we have sold many to your company, we bill you in dollars and you pay in dollars—not rubles and not marks. When, or should I say if, we sell crude petroleum

112

and natural gas to you after this pipeline is finished, you know as well as I that the terms will be agreed upon in dollars—just as they are on oil transactions everywhere else in the world."

"And who will give us forward foreign exchange cover? Who will give a guarantee protecting us against currency losses ten years into the future?"

"That, my dear Klausen, is your problem, as you know full well. And it's hardly the first time you've had such a problem. But I'm sure you can solve it. You're a resourceful man. You know as well as I that you and your bankers in Germany have been deeply involved in dollar financing for many years. Availability of dollar funds should be no problem. Interest rates will likewise be no problem. At the moment long-term rates in dollars and marks are almost exactly the same. *We* prefer dollars. We do 90 percent of our foreign trade in dollars. We do not desire to make such a major exception."

Klausen's thoughts raced. This is it. Either or. Either this Melekov is serious or he has been instructed to sabotage the deal. No use stalling.

"Fine, Herr Melekov. I will give you an answer at noon tomorrow. If my answer is positive, you will agree to proceeding with the final signing of the contracts as scheduled—at five tomorrow afternoon?"

"Yes," replied Melekov.

"No other problems?"

"None."

"May I call you tomorrow at the bank? Say, just before noon?"

"Splendid," agreed Melekov. His assistant, who had been sitting on Melekov's left during the entire performance was as stunned as Klausen, but his face indicated nothing more than steadily increasing boredom. The fact that he had personally drafted the final version of the financial side of this agreement—in marks—and that both Melekov and the bank's chairman, Stepanov, had approved it was already being relegated to that particular compartment of his memory banks which he reserved for what he privately termed *Kuriosum*.

After leaving the Germans, Melekov took the lift to the top floor of the hotel and treated his assistant to a sumptuous lunch. No further reference was made to business. By two o'clock both were back at the Foreign Trade Bank of the Soviet Union. And the first thing Melekov did was knock on the door of the office of his boss, the bank's chairman—Valentajn Ivanovich Stepanov, Hero at Stalingrad, protégé of Khrushchev. A remnant of the glorious past, and a big pain in the ass. After knocking he moved right in with no further formality.

"Take a seat," commanded Stepanov, in a voice which was harsh and raspy. "How did it go?"

"Fine. I'm shifting the whole transaction onto a dollar basis."

"You're what?"

"I said, quite distinctly I thought, that I'm shifting the entire pipeline purchase onto a dollar basis."

"Are you crazy?"

"No. Hardly."

"Who authorized you to do this?"

"My dear Valentajn Ivanovich, I do not require authorization. I am in charge of the foreign exchange operations of this bank."

"But I am in charge of this bank. And such a decision is my prerogative. My God, the basic national interests of the entire Soviet Union are at stake. Have you gone mad?"

"I believe I've already covered the subject of my mental health. As to the rest, I have very carefully discussed this matter with the president of the National Bank. He fully agrees with the new policy."

"New policy? What new policy?" screamed Stepanov, who by now had risen from behind his desk and gotten very red in the face. "What new policy, I asked?"

"The new dollar policy," replied his deputy chairman.

Stepanov seemed to sense that something was going on here

that could be very very dangerous. He sat down behind his desk once again and started to fiddle with a ball-point pen.

"Melekov, I do wish you would stop talking in riddles."

"There is no riddle. As you quite well know, if I must repeat it, I am in charge of the foreign exchange operations of this bank. And it is my duty to coordinate all plans and operations in this area with the head of our parent institution, the National Bank of the Soviet Union. After all, they—not we—hold the gold and foreign exchange reserves of this country. They also control the money supply inside the country. Therefore they set the policy. We manage the day-to-day flows of money and credits to and from our country, according to that policy. I think I hardly need to explain this to you."

"Melekov, I'll ask you just one more time: what new dollar policy?" His voice had sunk to a hoarse whisper.

"It is quite simple," replied his deputy. "We have very grave doubts about the immediate future of the dollar. We think it will be devalued again, and by an appreciable amount. We have, therefore, decided to get out of that currency."

"Just like that!" was the sarcastic comment from the other side of the desk.

"No, not just like that. During the past weeks we have given the entire matter the greatest possible consideration, done enormous research both here and abroad, and reached the conclusion that we must act now, and with the greatest possible speed. We are selling our dollars on the open market starting today. But it is being done very carefully, according to a quite definitive plan."

"So, you and Roskin have worked out a 'quite definitive plan,' have you?"

"That's right. And part of it is to pay for as many of our future imports with devalued dollars as possible, allowing us a one-time discount of perhaps as much as 15 percent on everything that we have contracted for. The Soviet Union will save billions of dollars. On the pipe contract alone it will come to a quarter of a billion."

"And Germany will accept it—just like that?"

"They will have no choice, once the contract has been signed."

"Fine. Very clever. But, my dear Melekov, just who says that the dollar is going to be devalued? You? That arrogant academic quack Roskin? Hasn't the news seeped through to you geniuses that the dollar was devalued in 1971?"

Melekov sat there.

"And now, like that, based upon some crackpot thinking, you and Roskin are going to overthrow a key policy—no, *the* key policy of our bank?"

"That's right," was the cool response. "I think Roskin intends to call a meeting later this week to explain the full ramifications for the future to all of us here at the Foreign Trade Bank."

"That is most thoughtful of Comrade Roskin. And so kind of you to give me advance notice. That's all you have for me today, Melekov?" He did not wait for a reply. "Fine, fine. Then I see no reason to detain you any longer. I'm sure you have much more important matters awaiting you."

Melekov rose and left Stepanov's office without any further words. It was one of the most satisfactory moments of his career.

Five minutes later he was in the trading room of his foreign exchange department. The action was hectic. His chief trader hung up a telephone the moment he spotted Melekov and hurried over.

"I'm glad you're here."

"Anything wrong?"

"No, quite the contrary. But I must know where we go from here."

"How much have you gotten rid of?"

"About a billion dollars."

"Who are the takers?"

"We did about $500 million in both Zurich and London. We're now working on Frankfurt and Paris."

"What's happening to the rates?"

"Well, we must be putting a lot of pressure on the forward dollar. But it's holding damn well. We're being matched immediately by takers every time."

"Good. When does New York open?"

His man glanced at a large wall clock. It showed just a few minutes past three.

"Daylight saving time in the States is over now, so we're back to ten hours difference. That would mean New York opens in three hours."

"Right. Try to sell at least another billion in the United States. But mix it up. If necessary do the last part on the West Coast. But remember, keep exclusively to the forward market. Don't touch spot. And keep the rates coming to me. I'll be in the office until midnight."

"One more item before you go. We made that transfer of $500 million to Zurich as you instructed. Now what should we tell them to do with it?"

"I'm handling that directly," replied Melekov. "But I think you must be kept fully in the whole picture. We're using it to buy gold bullion."

"You mean that the Swiss government is actually selling gold?" was the response of his astonished trader.

"No. We're going to get it in the free market."

This time the only response was a low whistle.

Melekov added, "That, my friend, is for your ears only. Do we understand each other?"

The nod of agreement could not have been more emphatic. And the stride of Melekov as he left the foreign exchange trading room could not have been more confident. He was taking the biggest gamble of his entire career. But he was in his fifties and it was now or never. Such an opportunity would not come again.

Hans Klausen had not lunched at the Russaya. He had rushed to the German embassy minutes after Melekov had left.

That was the only place from which he could hope to communicate with Düsseldorf free of a few dozen curious Russian ears.

The ambassador received him minutes after his arrival, and both of them were soon in the communications room in the basement of the building. They remained there until well past midnight. The future of the ambassador's status in Moscow related very closely to the future of this pipeline deal. A sudden collapse of the negotiations—just hours before the signing—could set back his newly found rapport with the Soviets by years. He communicated this to Bonn in the strongest possible terms.

At one-fifteen in the morning, Moscow time, he had the answer. The transaction could be based on U.S. dollars. The German government would provide an airtight guarantee to Rhein-Ruhr covering the foreign exchange risk. The interest rate to be paid by the Russians would have to be increased by a token .25 percent, however. After all, prestige was always at stake.

Both Klausen and the ambassador were satisfied. They finished off the bottle of Steinhäger shortly after two. Klausen spent the night in one of the guest rooms at the embassy. He was too tired to move. And he needed to regain his strength for the closing of the contract later that day. Not that the signing would be particularly strenuous. But he knew his Russians. The celebration which would follow would last the entire night.

On this same evening, while the two Germans sat in the basement of the embassy, and while Melekov was directing the moves of his foreign exchange and gold people from his office in the Foreign Trade Bank of the Soviet Union, his boss—Chairman Stepanov—was dining at the Georgian restaurant on the Gorky street with a friend. They had met at seven and after five courses, accompanied by much vodka and a few

118

beers, they were now basking over the remnants, with cigars and a bottle of cold Crimean champagne.

The time had come to broach the subject.

"Josef," said Stepanov, "tell me something. Did the committee discuss any change in our foreign exchange policy recently?"

"No. Not that I know of. I understand nothing about financial matters. You know that, Valentajn."

"Of course. But was there no discussion about the dollar?"

"No. Of that I am sure."

"I thought so."

"What?"

"Roskin and especially that fellow Melekov are not only working behind my back but also behind the back of the committee. You've heard me talk of those two before."

"Indeed I have."

"Ambitious, ruthless, dangerous. Both of them. They are like twins in their thinking and in their history; educated for years outside of Russia; neither of them fired a shot, or even heard a shot, during the war. They consider men like you and me, Josef, to be Georgian peasants, people who must be removed from the system to make room for academic fancy-pants like themselves. That is exactly what they are trying to do now. I'm sure of it. If we let them get any further, neither you nor I will remain unscathed. It is an absolute outrage. We must do something."

Stepanov was working himself up into quite a state. But in this restaurant no one noticed. As usual the atmosphere was boisterous. The alcohol was flowing faster and faster as the hour grew later.

"What have you got in mind, Valentajn?"

"I think that you and I—both of us—must approach the committee, immediately."

"But do you really feel that it is that important?"

"There can be no doubt. A grave error is being committed."

"Are you sure of your grounds?"

"Positive!"

"I will make the arrangements, Valentajn."

"Many many thanks. Josef. You are a true friend."

The orchestra, seated on the balcony against the background of a wildly colourful mural depicting the Alpine-like scenery of that corner of Russia so dear to the hearts of the majority of guests, struck up another tune with slightly off-key gusto. The two men decided that another bottle of champagne was in order, with just a touch of vodka on the side.

11

The next morning in Zurich the banks started their foreign exchange operations as usual. On this Wednesday, business was brisk, as usual; rumours were flying, as usual. And the Swiss were making money, as usual, in what many people regard as the most difficult of financial markets. Foreign exchange comes natural to the Swiss, and for many years they have been exploiting this natural resource to the hilt.

The development of this unusual talent stems from that fact that almost every Swiss is somehow involved in foreign exchange transactions from a very early age. Living in a small country in the center of Europe, no Swiss is ever more than a hundred miles from some border—that of France, Germany, Austria, or Italy—and the rates of exchange between the Swiss franc and those of these neighbouring countries are as familiar a fact as the price of gasoline is to the average American, or the cost of a pint of beer to a Welshman. In fact, many a Swiss will be able to quite readily tell you the price of gasoline in all of his neighbouring countries, expressed in terms of Swiss francs or even dollars if you like, since, with his built-in frugality, he will always calculate very carefully whether he should fill up his tank at home, or abroad, when he sets out on a Sunday drive across the border with his well-polished automobile. In other words, he goes through constant and sometimes complex foreign exchange calculations as a matter of course in his daily life. Take, for instance, a citizen of Basel. This second-largest city in Switzerland borders immediately upon both France and Germany. It is quite natural for a Bâlois to go shopping in Germany, just across the border, in the afternoon, seeking bargains in the supermarkets, and then go

121

over to France for dinner in the evening, attracted especially by the price and quality of the wine. He does not go back and forth to the bank twice a day buying the required German marks or French francs. No, he just keeps their separate compartments in his billfold—one for each of the three currencies which are part of his everyday life.

What is unique about Switzerland is that they play *all* currencies against *all other* currencies. By contrast, in London, for example, the foreign exchange market is almost totally restricted to pound sterling–U.S. dollar transactions. In New York, it is the dollar's price in terms of sterling, the German mark, the Japanese yen, and the Canadian dollar which preoccupies traders. But in Zurich, they will be juggling yen against pounds, German marks against Dutch guilders, Swiss francs against Italian lire, and work out a fair price for black-market rubles against the U.S. dollar. They will quote you a price on the Iranian rials, including the cost of picking them up in cash form in Teheran, and converting them into Swiss francs for deposit in Geneva under a number or a phony name.

The nerve center of these operations are the foreign exchange trading departments of the major Swiss banks, always a very large room, packed with communications equipment. The traders—up to a dozen of them—sit around an oval-shaped desk of immense proportions. Each man has two telephones at his disposal, often three. Each phone has at least six separate outside lines. Thus each trader can literally be talking to a large number of people at the same time. On telephone one, line two, he may have a customer in Hong Kong. On telephone two, line four, he may have the FX desk of the Deutsche Bank in Frankfurt. On the same telephone, line six, he may have his counterpart in the bank's branch in London on a standby basis. On telephone three, line one, he could have a money broker in Geneva. And three or four other lines might be flashing, as incoming calls stack up. The trader plays his telephones like an electronic organ—pushing keys, pulling stops, and creating quite a bit of noise in the process as he yells, and even screams,

122

his instructions. The cacophony is added to by the constant clattering of Telex machines which line the walls of the huge room—often a dozen machines, all banging out information on market conditions from the various financial capitals of the world, or bringing in confirmations of transactions just completed minutes ago by telephone. Girls scurry around, tearing off urgent messages and placing them in front of the trader involved, who barely glances at them during telephone calls, signs his O.K., and passes them back. It often takes him just two seconds to finalize transactions involving tens of millions of dollars.

On the wall is a scoreboard, resembling those we are so used to from sports arenas. Prices of all major currencies, in terms of Swiss francs, are constantly being posted electronically—in line with the latest trades—thus keeping everyone in the room informed. Very quietly, in a corner, three other men pore over long sheets of paper. They post the so-called position sheets. Each trade is immediately entered, allowing the chief of the department to tell at a glance the net position of the bank. In one hour from opening, his traders might have sold $200 million and bought $210 million—leaving the bank a net position of $10 million. He tries to keep the two figures in close balance, unless of course he receives instructions to the contrary from the big guys.

It was into just such an atmosphere that Dr. Walter Hofer walked on the morning of November 5. He was accompanied by a young lady of perhaps twenty-two or twenty-three. In spite of the hectic activity, none of this escaped anyone in the room. It was unusual enough for the chairman of the General Bank of Switzerland to appear in the foreign exchange trading room. But to see him there, with a well-built young blonde— that was an event to be cherished, every minute of it.

Hofer walked directly to the chief trader.

"Herr Zimmerer, I would like to introduce Miss Mary Rogers." He spoke in English. "She is with a newspaper in Los

123

Angeles and would like to learn a little about your operations. Miss Rogers is the daughter of my wife's sister who, as you probably do not know, has been living in the States for the last thirty years. So please take good care of her. When you're finished, I would appreciate it if you could bring her up to my office. I would like to have a few words with you before the morning is over."

"With great pleasure, sir," replied Zimmerer, as Hofer turned and left as abruptly as he had come.

"Now please don't go to any great trouble on my account. I know you must be very busy," said the petite Miss Rogers, five feet two, with blue eyes to go along with her long blonde hair and a bosom which could not be totally overlooked, even if she was the big boss's niece.

"No trouble at all," mumbled Zimmerer, thinking oh my God and on a morning like this. The Swiss never have learned how to mix business with pleasure during working hours except at the highest echelons.

"Uncle Walter insisted I come into his bank today to look around, and he thought that this might be one of the most interesting spots. I know really nothing about the foreign exchange business. But I have worked on the business section of our paper for over two years now and am not totally ignorant. My mother and I are spending a week here in Zurich. It sure is a lovely city at this time of year. Are you from here?"

"Yes," replied Zimmerer.

A man suddenly shouted across the room at him. "Herr Zimmerer, the Deutsche Bank in Stuttgart wants $25 million spot at 3.40 flat."

"Sell 'em. Then everybody stop all trades. I want to know our exact positions to the franc in every currency within ten minutes. So hang up the phones and recheck everything."

If he was to see Hofer, he wanted to know exactly where the department stood, right up to the minute.

Then another call. "Hey, Zimmerer, it's Kellermann. He wants you right now. I'll switch him to your phone—line five."

Zimmerer picked up the phone, made a few notes, and hung up.

Turning back to Mary Rogers he said, "At the risk of over-simplifying things, why don't I start by explaining what we're doing here, and then give you an idea of how we do it. Would that be all right?"

She nodded.

"Good. I think the closest thing in your experience to our foreign exchange market here would be commodities. In Chicago they make markets for corn or wheat or soybeans, and many other similar products. There, like here, the market is split: they deal in what they call 'actuals' when the real product is changing hands right there and then, and they talk about 'futures' when a deal is made involving the delivery of the product at some time in the future—maybe in a month, three months, or even a year. Well, in foreign exchange it's the same. We call the here and now transactions, where the product changes hands immediately in cash form, the spot market. Just think of it as where money changes hands on the spot. We call the futures market the forward market, and here also we deal for months or even years in advance of the actual closing of the transactions. But instead of agricultural products, the products in which we deal are different currencies—German marks, American dollars, Japanese yen—all of which have constantly changing prices depending upon supply and demand for them. Follow me?"

"Yes."

"Fine. Now since we are in Switzerland, we usually go out from the Swiss franc. I mean, we usually price all the 'products' we deal in in terms of Swiss francs. Quite normal, I think."

Again Mary nodded.

"Are you sure I'm not boring you?" asked Zimmerer.

"Oh no, please go on. It's just fascinating."

I'll bet, thought Zimmerer, but plunged on anyway.

"Right. Now let's take the American dollar. As you just heard that fellow yell from across the room, we are buying dollars at the spot rate of 3.40 francs. This can change from minute to minute, but the ultimate range is established by the government. The 'most' francs you can get for a dollar, under the rules agreed to in Switzerland in spring, 1973, is 3.4535. And the 'least' you can get is 3.3015. That's what we call the upper and lower intervention points."

"What happens if everybody is selling dollars like crazy and it goes down to 3.25?" asked Mary.

"It can't. The Swiss government, through the National Bank, is obligated to buy dollars for Swiss francs at the 3.3015 limit and to keep supplying the market with Swiss francs, taking out dollars, until the market trend reverses itself."

"Why?"

"Because the world has agreed to maintain fixed exchange rates—well, almost fixed, since as you see they can vary 4.5 percent within the band agreed upon. Without fixed rates, nobody in business or banking could plan ahead in international transactions. I mean, some Swiss watchmaker might sell a million dollars worth of watches in the States. But he might first get paid in dollars after three months. If he could not be sure of approximately how many francs this would give him, when he exchanged them, he would face enormous risks. After all, he pays his workers and suppliers in francs, not dollars. Right?"

"But in 1973 all these fixed rates were changed, weren't they?"

"They were. But this happens quite seldom."

"But it happened."

"Right. And the Swiss watch exporters got smashed, at least those who had not protected themselves in the forward foreign exchange market."

"Now I've heard about that," said Mary, "but I don't understand how you can do that."

"O.K. but you'll have to follow closely," replied Zimmerer. "Now let's stick with that watchmaker. He knows that he's going to be paid a million dollars in three months, so—if he's smart—he'll come to us and sell these dollars *in advance*."

"Can you do that?"

"Sure. That, in fact, is what this whole business is about."

"You mean he's selling something that he hasn't even got yet?"

"Absolutely right. It works like this. We, his bank, make an agreement with another bank—in this case, an American bank—which says in effect: *We*, General Bank of Switzerland, promise to deliver to you $1 million U.S. in three months. You, Chase Manhattan, promise to pay us 3.35 million francs for these dollars, upon delivery. You'll notice that the dollar sells at a small discount on the current spot rate of 3.40 when it's done on a three months forward basis. That's because the market feels that it is probable that the dollar will weaken slightly in the period ahead. It's been abnormally strong in recent weeks."

"So then when the Swiss watchmaker finally gets his dollars, he knows exactly how many francs he's going to get for them."

"Exactly, otherwise he would take a risk, as I mentioned before."

"But if he did not 'sell his dollars forward,' as you put it, he might have gotten more francs in the end. I mean, nobody can guarantee that the dollar will weaken."

"Absolutely correct. If the dollar strengthened, and the spot rate went up to, say 3.45 after three months, he could sell his dollars then and get 3.45 million francs—or exactly 100,000 more than he will get by selling them ahead of time. That's the cost of insurance."

"I know you won't believe this quite, but really I now start to understand this business. It's not so complicated, is it—I mean, not when a man like you explains it. Tell me, how did you ever get into this fascinating business?"

"My uncle. I've got one, too, and he's a friend of your uncle. He might even have known your mother, come to think of it. I'll ask him. Anyway, I started at the General Bank about ten years ago, and after being trained in about ten different departments, I chose this one for a career. I like it very much."

"Can girls do this, too?"

"Well, there's no reason why not. But in Switzerland, you know, it's still a little bit different than in the States."

"Oh, I know. My mother told me. That's why she left."

"Maybe, Miss Rogers, we should try to finish our discussion on foreign exchange," said Zimmerer, glancing at his watch.

"But I really don't want to keep you if you have important things to do."

"No, no. Now, do you have any questions?"

"Well, just one and then I'll leave you alone. What about all those currency speculators we always read about? I mean, they're hardly involved in the watch business."

"No, Miss, they're really just gamblers, gambling normally on a devaluation of a currency. It's gotten to be very big business during the past five years. Lots of Americans are in it now, especially the big multinational corporations."

"How do they do it?"

"I'll explain. But then we had better go up to your uncle's office. O.K.?"

"O.K."

"Fine. Well, let's say that I'm going to speculate on another devaluation of the dollar, and I think it's going to happen within three months. A devaluation means that the old fixed rates—remember?—will be changed between the dollar and the Swiss franc, suddenly and overnight, and thereafter the dollar will be much cheaper in terms of Swiss francs. Right?

"Good. So our speculator comes to us and we sell, for his account, $10 million three months forward—dollars that he does not have. Selling short is the term used for this type of operation. So again we make a contract: We, General Bank of Switzerland, promise to deliver to you, Chase Manhattan, $10 million U.S. in three months. You, Chase Manhattan, promise to pay us 33.5 million Swiss francs for these dollars, upon delivery. We make a separate little agreement with our speculator, informing him that we are doing this transaction in our

128

name, but for his account, and at his risk. O.K., let's say that a 15 percent devaluation of the dollar takes place. Overnight the spot exchange rate would drop to, say, 2.90 to the dollar. When the three months are up, we go into the market—the spot market—and buy the $10 million which our speculator never had in the first place. This $10 million would *now*, after devaluation, cost us only 29 million Swiss francs. Follow me? Good. But then, literally one or two minutes later, we would present this $10 million we just bought to Chase Manhattan for delivery on that forward contract we had made with each other three months earlier. Chase, on the conditions of that agreement, would have to pay us 33.5 million Swiss francs. Right? So our friendly speculator has just made himself 4.5 million Swiss francs. Let me repeat, he presold dollars he did not have for 33.5 million Swiss francs, but the cost of these dollars, after devaluation, was only 29 million Swiss francs. *Voilà.*"

"Gee."

"Yeah, and the beauty of it is that if this speculator is a good customer of ours otherwise, he would not even have to put up any margin, or deposit, on this foreign exchange forward contract. At least as long as he had a couple of million in the bank or was known to us as a very solvent person."

"But why not?"

"Because it's quite obvious that a strong currency like the Swiss franc would never be devalued. It's almost 100 percent backed by gold. Thus, it would hardly ever rise above 3.4535 —the intervention point at which the Swiss government must step in. If our speculator met the worst of all possible conditions when the three months were up, he would have to cover at this rate. Then his $10 million would cost, 34.535 million francs, but he would only get 33.5 million from Chase. So he'd be out 1,035,000 francs, or about $300,000. Big clients swallow such losses without blinking an eyelash. But it is highly unlikely that such a loss would occur. What the system does is give a government guarantee to speculators, which allows him to calculate to the last penny his greatest possible loss, while on the other hand, it allows him to make enormous profits—which can be ten times larger than the maximum possible loss. That's why speculation in foreign exchange has become such a popular sport. As one American put it to me last week, 'It's the best game in town.' And that's why we, as a bank, run very little risk when we do such transactions for our clients, even when very large numbers are involved."

"And you say Americans can also do this?"

"Why not? Of course, lots of people think that it's not very nice to speculate against your own currency, and in recent years it's the dollar that has always been getting into trouble. But I've been told that American multinational corporations cleaned up about $3 billion profits on their foreign exchange contracts made prior to the last dollar devaluation in 1973. I guess a lot of people figure, correctly, that what's good for General Motors must be good—period."

"Do you also speculate for the bank, Mr. Zimmerer?"

"Well, we're actually not supposed to talk about that. You know, then it starts that 'gnomes of Zurich' thing all over again. Better ask your uncle."

"Zimmerer!" Another interruption came from across the vast trading circle.

"Foreign Trade Bank Moscow. On the Telex again. They're offering to sell $50 million three months forward this time. Shall I give them a rate?"

"No. First, I want the positions. Tell them we've stopped trading for an hour. They should come back then."

He turned back to the young lady.

"Miss Rogers, would you mind taking a chair. I have to get some figures together for your uncle. I'll be with you in a few minutes."

And he was. "Ready to go? I'd like to talk a lot longer to you, but I think your uncle is probably waiting for us."

"That's all right. I think some of this stuff is getting a little too complicated for me anyway."

They began walking toward the door when Zimmerer took

Mary's arm. "Say, would you like to look at just one other place real quick?"

"Sure," she replied. "What is it?"

"Well, it's another part of our department—the gold bullion trading section."

"Oh yes, that would be just fascinating."

"Don't expect to see any gold bars or anything like that."

They entered another room. It was not nearly as large as the foreign exchange trading center. Only three men were at telephones and three others were obviously doing clerical work.

"What's the morning fixing?"

"74.25 an ounce."

"How much volume this morning?"

"Quite a bit. Somebody's stirring things up, but we don't know who yet."

"Well, we'll have to stir it up a bit more. Kellermann just called me. He's got a very big order for a private client—to buy $200 million in bullion."

"Wow. Who is it?"

"Don't know. A numbered account. Kellermann said he would send down the written order after lunch, but we can start now. There are no limits. Just buy at the market. But for God's sake, be careful. We don't want this to get around. Say, I'd like to introduce you to Mary Rogers. She's Dr. Hofer's niece. Maybe you could explain what this is all about."

Zimmerer turned to one of the other traders while the explanation was going on. As usual it started with the prices chalked on a big blackboard. They indicated the so-called morning and afternoon fixings of the gold bullion price, in London and in Zurich, during the past days and weeks. The world gold bullion price is set in a most peculiar, in fact, unique, fashion. In both financial centers, at almost exactly the same time of day—ten in the morning and three in the afternoon—the world's chief gold dealers sit down, four in Zurich and five in London, to compare the buy and sell orders which have come in prior to the meetings. Then they "fix" a price at which all the deals are made. If there is an excess demand, they bump the price up and meet the excess from their own stocks of gold. If an oversupply of sell orders results, they mark the gold price down and replenish their own inventory. They act as the middlemen in all gold transactions. And, of course, they always rig a nice spread between what they buy at and what they sell for. Often, as a result of five minutes' work, between ten and ten-five they will make millions of dollars in profits, by just matching large buy and sell orders and taking their slice in the middle. In London it is a clan of venerable merchant banks, who control this market. Of course, Winthrop's was one of them, and in fact, it was said that since many years they have really controlled things in the London gold pool. In Zurich it was the General Bank of Switzerland who called the shots in the gold game, due to the fact that it was they, and especially their clients, who accounted for the largest part of the volume. Not that they ever revealed what the volume of gold trading was on any day, or even during any month or year. Among themselves, the banks in London and Zurich had decided that such knowledge would contribute nothing to orderly trading, and that the speculators of the world should be protected from any unnecessary worries which might arise from their having anything better to go on than rumour. But Mary didn't know this.

"How much gold do you buy and sell here each day?"

"I'm afraid I can't tell you. It's one policy of this bank which is totally ironclad," was the gold trader's answer.

"Can you give me a hint?"

"Well, in recent years the amount of *new* gold, coming from the mines in South Africa and sometimes Russia, amounts to about 40 million ounces. At recent prices, that's almost $3 billion a year. But then you must remember that there are about another 200 million ounces in the hands of private speculators —in Switzerland, or France, or the Near East especially—and

132

they are constantly buying and selling. So that might give another ten billion changing hands each year. Some put it a lot higher—a whole lot."

"And all that business is done from this little room?" was Mary's response.

"No. But let's say this: we do more than our fair share, by quite a bit. And that's thanks to your uncle. He probably knows more about gold than anyone in the world today. He knows everybody in the business too—from South African mine operators to the big smugglers who run gold by the ton into India from Dubai on the Persian gulf. By comparison, that fellow Goldfinger in the James Bond book was nothing."

"I didn't know that."

Zimmerer now broke in. "Please, Miss Rogers, for goodness sake don't mention any of this to him. He doesn't like publicity of any kind—especially where gold is concerned."

All of a sudden Zimmerer seemed to be in a hurry. He said a few words in Swiss German to the men at the gold-trading desk and then left with Mary. After taking the elevator up three floors they entered a quite different world. The clatter and confusion of the foreign exchange department was suddenly replaced by the complete silence of a deeply carpeted, soundproof corridor. A uniformed guard rose to greet them after they had taken just a very few steps.

"Dr. Hofer is expecting us," said Zimmerer. The eyebrows of the guard rose just slightly.

"This is his niece." They fell back to normal.

Dr. Hofer's office was immense and impressive: the oak panelling, the soft paintings, the huge rugs, and even the very faint scent of cigar smoke which must have represented the lingering memory of Cuba's best. They crossed the room toward Hofer's desk—he never greeted anyone at the door to his office but merely signaled them in by means of an electric "Please enter" signal outside his door—and were waved toward a group of chairs that was about twenty yards away, on the other side of the room. The two young people waded through

133

the rugs and sat down. Neither dared to talk at first, but it seemed that Mary's nature could not stand that for long.

"You know, Mr. Zimmerer, you're awfully young to have such a position at the bank. Are you married?"

"No, Miss Rogers, I guess I've been too caught up in my work to get around to that."

"Oh, come on now. You can call me Mary, you know."

"Fine. I'm Werner."

"That's a very stern name."

"Well, it's rather common in Switzerland."

"Werner, do you know any nice place to go dancing in Zurich? You know my uncle; my aunt is no different. And Mom is hopeless. So I can hardly ask them."

"Sure, there are lots of places. But it depends on what you want. I mean like everywhere, I guess, you have to be a little choosey."

"I've got an idea," said Mary. "Why don't we two go out somewhere together this evening. Maybe a place where we can have dinner and then dance. I'll treat. I mean, if you're not too busy or something. After all, I do owe you something after this morning."

Zimmerer thought. Very nice long hair, cute little nose, and she sure looks great in that white blouse and blue skirt. Probably have to be careful though. He decided.

"I think that's a terrific idea, Mary. But are you sure your uncle won't mind?"

"Of course not. After all, I am twenty-two."

"Are you staying at his place?"

"Yes, but that's way down the lake. Can't we meet somewhere so you don't have to go out and back?"

"No. That's no trouble. What time should I pick you up?"

"Would seven be all right?"

"Perfect."

The deal was cinched. The career prospects of Herr Zimmerer had suddenly taken on a new dimension. And after a full week—no, eight days—of nothing, Mary's rather active sex life was suddenly returning to normal. This would be her first Swiss. She had noticed that generally they were rather short, compared to American boys. But maybe that did not make any difference.

"Well, Mary, how did it go?" asked her uncle who had suddenly joined them, interrupting their introspective silence.

"Just fine, Uncle Walter. You were right. It is a fascinating business."

"Good. Your mother's waiting downstairs. I'll take you. Herr Zimmerer, please wait here for a few minutes, if you don't mind."

Mary solemnly shook hands with Zimmerer, winked at him, and disappeared. A few minutes later Dr. Hofer returned.

"Herr Zimmerer, I'm glad we have this chance to talk to each other in privacy. I hear that there is a bit of commotion at the foreign exchange desk this morning. What's going on?"

"Herr Doktor, it's really too early to say. But there's big volume and some downward pressure on the dollar again."

"Where's it coming from?"

"Hard to say."

"Any unusually big sellers?"

"Really only one that we've noticed. The fellows in Moscow. They were very big on the selling side yesterday, and they're back at it again today."

"For this time of year that is peculiar. They are almost always big net buyers of dollars in late fall to pay for agricultural imports, if I recall correctly."

"That's right, sir. But, of course, this selling could very well be just concentrated on us for the moment. They might just be doing a lot of trading, playing us off against Frankfurt or London, or more probably Budapest, Bucharest and Prague. All those fellows in Eastern Europe have gotten very big in the foreign exchange game during the past couple of years. Would you like me to check all this out in detail to see if something really unusual is going on?"

"Yes. Please do, Zimmerer. But do it carefully. And do not mention any of this to your associates. Now another thing. What's our net dollar position?"

"I have brought the latest figures with me, sir. Right now we are slightly short, on balance. About $40 million. That's well within the standing limits I've been given, sir, for the bank's own position."

"Of course." Hofer paused and then went on. "Right. Now I want you to adjust our dollar position very carefully. From short to much shorter. You have authorization to go up to two billion short—as quickly as the market will take it. Stick to short maturities—three months maximum."

"You mean $2 billion or Swiss francs equivalent?"

"Dollars."

"You said, as quickly as the market will take it. Do you mean today?"

"Yes."

"Well, there could be a problem. I just received a customer order to short exactly that amount on almost exactly the same basis—all one-month maturities if possible, but three months will be acceptable."

Hofer appeared startled. He asked, "Within what price range?"

"No price limits were given. It's an absolutely open order."

"Who gave you the order?"

"Direktor Kellermann."

Hofer frowned. Zimmerer continued. "And there's something else. Kellermann told me to start executing a huge buy order for gold bullion. Same customer."

"Who is it?"

"I don't know, sir. Kellermann just said it's an important numbered account."

"I'll check this out with Kellermann. In the meantime, just carry out my instructions, Zimmerer. Thank you."

After Zimmerer had closed the door on the way out, Hofer picked up the phone and dialed four digits.

"Kellermann?"

"*Jawohl*, Herr Doktor."

"Please come up to my office. Now!" He hung up.

The moment he hung up the phone, Hofer regretted his abruptness. Kellermann had a big future with the General Bank of Switzerland. Hofer had personally handpicked him for his current position, the one which Hofer himself had filled for ten years before taking over full command of the bank. He knew that Kellermann did not have it easy.

The big private numbered accounts—that was the bailiwick of Kellermann, as inherited from Walter Hofer. The system was simple. All transactions for such accounts were done under a number only. Even where cash withdrawals were concerned, the client—in the utter privacy of an upstairs conference room —signed for it with his number, written out of course, like "One Hundred and Thirty-five Thousand Six Hundred and Three." That's Swiss for John Doe. Only two men in the entire banking organization could identify the name of the account owner with the number of his account: the account executive who set up the arrangement and Kellermann who maintained the master file of these privileged clients. The papers which contained the matching names and numbers were kept in a special safe—a huge one—solely under Kellermann's control. It was as burgler- and fireproof as modern technology would allow. But, as still a further safeguard, completely matching documents were kept in another vault, buried deep in an Alpine cavern in a small town in the Gotthardt Pass. It was literally bombproof. The key importance of the system lay in the fact that no internal spy, who, experience had taught long ago, could easily slip into a banking organization, could get at this strategic information. For strategic it was. As a group, the people behind these numbers kept assets totalling $20 billion at the General Bank of Switzerland. Brazilians, Frenchmen, Germans, Argentines, British. They were the old hands in the use of this system. But since the 1960s countless newcomers, from New York, Miami, Las Vegas, Washington, Seoul, Bangkok, Saigon, Taiwan, Hong Kong, had joined the ranks. And then there were the ex-Cubans, the ex-Algerians, ex-kings, ex-finance ministers, ex-presidents, ex-gangsters, many of doubtful nationality not to speak of residency, who regularly enjoyed the traditional hospitality of Switzerland.

The motives of all of these people were essentially the same. They sought protection from immoral intrusions into their private affairs. What could be more private than money? Nothing, said the Swiss, absolutely nothing. And they really meant it, with evangelical fervour. Sure, perhaps some of this money which sought refuge from prying eyes was untaxed. Perhaps it had been illegally smuggled out of Latin America or Asia into Switzerland. Maybe it was stolen. This was not Switzerland's concern. If nations insisted upon introducing unreasonably high taxes or foreign exchange controls limiting one of man's God-given freedoms to do what he likes with the money he amasses, that was their fault. Also a crime in Chicago was not necessarily one in Zurich. History had always proved that in money matters the Swiss were right and the rest of the world had been consistently wrong. Little did the world realize the benefits it accrued from this attitude. For it was banks like the General Bank of Switzerland which took what the incurable cynics insisted upon calling "black money," bleached it, and put it to work productively; money which otherwise would have remained hidden and idle. Thus Switzerland was able to mobilize capital, lend it to industry, and raise the living standards of the world. Its banks regularly told their clients to buy World Bank bonds for their numbered accounts, thus truly helping—in concrete terms—those underprivileged in the developing countries. It was Swiss banks who opened the way for prudent men to buy gold, as a warning to those governments who sought to undermine the currencies of the world through reckless spending programs, which only led to inflation and the indirect confiscation of the hard-earned savings of countless numbers of the aged and afflicted. It was banks like the General

138

Bank of Switzerland which offered the facilities enabling people from all countries to buy stocks and contribute to the survival of the free world in its fight against communism. The job, though difficult, was truly rewarding.

Due to misunderstanding, to envy, one could never be too careful, however. Even vis-à-vis one's own employees; pathetic but true in these days of long-haired clerks and gum-chewing secretaries. Even the young officers of the bank could no longer be trusted. They were all too often the products of chaotic universities, of confused professors who did not realize that making money with money represents the very heart of the system which has finally given dignity to a good part of mankind. The numbered account system, which in Hofer's mind represented capitalistic perfection, the ultimate response to challenge in the area of finance, was only as good as its guardians. In this regard, Kellermann was perfect. Well, almost perfect. His devotion to the Roman Catholic Church was often disturbing. He did not have to advertise it as he did. After all, the General Bank of Switzerland was a Protestant bank, like almost all of its sister institutions in Switzerland, or for that matter, also in the United States. This was so for good reasons. It was upon the Protestant ethic that all this was built. There were standards to be maintained, confidence to be preserved. To be sure, there was much to be said for ecumenical progress. As long as it did not go too far. Hofer had been one of the first financial leaders of his country to embrace the movement. But he saw himself as a pillar of moderation. More than once he had had to raise his voice in restraint to point out that the moral strength of Zurich stemmed from Zwingli, from Calvin, whose teachings were hardly compatible with the machinations of a Leo or a Gregory, not to speak of the hypocrisy of a Pius. To be sure, they were part of the past, but the Jesuits were obviously very much part of the present. The Swiss Constitution still banned them from the country. Correctly so. It may well be that their tactics had changed, but had their basic philosophy? The confusion of ends and means. This was not the Swiss way of approaching things, and every enlightened Catholic must also realize this. Or be convinced. One stood up for what one knew was right and, if necessary, died on the battlefield like Zwingli for one's faith and country.

The buzzer startled Hofer. He seldom got caught day-dreaming in this manner.

Kellerman entered the room and approached Hofer's desk.

"Glad to see you back, Dr. Hofer," he said. "I hope your trip to Johannesburg was satisfactory."

"It was. Please be seated. I've just had a brief talk with Zimmerer of the foreign exchange department. He tells me that you gave him a very large open order to buy gold bullion and sell the dollar short. For a numbered account. What's the story on that?"

"The client is an American. A certain Mr. Stanley Rosen from New York. We know him well. That is, our branch in Basel knows him. He's been a major depositor there and has done a lot of securities business with them over the years. In fact, he's high volume all around. Rosen was one of our first overseas clients to make major Euro-currency placements. Our Basel people tell me that they have had as much as $200 million outstanding for his accounts at one time—all on the usual trust basis."

"It is hardly his money."

"No, sir. Our people in New York have provided us with some background information on the man. It would seem that he has rather irregular types of people for whom he manages money, if you know what I mean. But this is no concern of ours. To date he has been absolutely correct in all of his dealings with us. Very exact, but very correct. Of course he receives no correspondence from the bank. He comes over and goes through the dossiers on his accounts with Widmer over in Basel about every other month."

"If he has always worked with the Basel branch, why are you all of a sudden handling his business?"

140

"Yesterday he came up with this very large operation. It's too big for any of our branches, including Basel. So Widmer sent him directly to me. He, of course, operates exclusively with numbered accounts. His instructions are quite simple. He wants to buy gold bullion at the market for just a shade under $200 million. He put up $100 million in cash. Then he wants to use the gold as collateral for a very substantial short sale of U.S. dollars against the Swiss franc. From our standpoint it makes good sense. We will make at least $1 million in commissions on what is essentially a very simple operation. Our exposure is nil. Of course, there is risk from his standpoint."

"He realizes this?"

"No doubt. He has one of the fastest minds I've ever seen among our private clients. Obviously a very professional money manager. I feel that I can completely assure you, Dr. Hofer, that he will not turn into a crybaby and pester us to death if the operation goes wrong. He's not a troublemaker. So also from that standpoint, our exposure is essentially nil."

"I still don't like it," stated Hofer. "At all. Has he come with good funds?"

"Yes, sir. He had the entire $100 million delivered in T-bills a few days ago in New York. The people at our branch there checked out their validity. No problem. They are authentic, not stolen. In fact, they were sold yesterday, and the proceeds have already arrived here. So he's working from cash."

"No idea where the Treasury bills originated?"

"No, sir. They're bearer instruments, you know. No way of really checking back. But still, there is something. He opened up an entirely new numbered account for these transactions. He maintains about twenty accounts in all with us—in Basel, except for this one. There is a co-signature on all the new account papers. A certain Ali ben Fezali of Beirut."

"The same one we work with in the currency business?"

"Right. We get shipments of assorted bank notes, and I do mean assorted, about every other week. We buy them from him at rather special rates, and then clear the notes, or most of them, back to the country of origin. He usually employs the proceeds for the purchase of gold and silver coinage. I would guess that we make large return shipments to him at least once a month. He maintains excellent sight balances with us, and has for many years. All in all, he's one of our better clients in Lebanon."

"Did he show up with Rosen yesterday?"

"No, sir. Apparently Rosen had all the account papers made out and signed a week or so ago. He had a habit of keeping a few sets with him. As I said, he maintains about twenty accounts with us and keeps opening up more all the time. So that's hardly unusual. Of course we've got countless specimens of Fezali's signature, and everything checks out there also."

"Isn't Rosen a Jew?" asked Hofer.

"I assume so," replied Kellermann. "But I would not attach too much importance to that element. After all, we have seen a lot of stranger combinations around here."

"Has Rosen ever done anything like this before?"

"No. He's never touched either gold or currency futures. Actually, Widmer over at our Basel branch told me that this operation is completely out of his usual line. Apparently Rosen's a type who plays things very carefully, never plunges, takes profits early, never tries to squeeze out the last drop. A rather ideal type of client. He never blames us for giving him bad advice, like so many of our other American customers. He relies completely upon himself and his own ideas. He's often not too happy about the delays and errors in our accounting. But that's not new. All Americans are very fussy in that regard."

"The more I hear, the less I like it," said Hofer. "Look, I don't want our bank to be dragged into something that could bring us up against the American authorities. You know it's illegal for an American national to deal in gold bullion. Sure they overlook all the little fishes, but a couple of years ago they tried to get at Bernie Cornfeld and IOS for an alleged gold purchase they made way back in 1968—a big one. This could mean big trouble, and that could bring big publicity, especially in those damned American newspapers. One Helga Hughes affair was enough for Zurich in this decade. And I have a funny feeling that there's something wrong here. Kellermann, you tell our people in New York to get everything available on this man. Right away. And stall Rosen in the meantime. I want a reply on my desk no later than eight tomorrow morning. The fellows in New York have almost all of a working day left to get what we need."

Kellermann frowned. This was not normal, and Kellermann did not like abnormal things. He lived a very orderly life. He prided himself that once his word was given, that was it. And he had given it to Rosen. As far as he was concerned, the bank was committed to carry out Rosen's instructions, as received.

"Dr. Hofer, I'm afraid that it's a bit too late to change things very much. I have accepted his order to buy the gold and to start building up his short position in dollars."

"Verbally?"

"Of course. But he will expect to be able to go through the confirmations of these transactions from his dossier before the week is out. He's staying in Zurich for that express purpose. As far as I know, Zimmerer's men must have already arranged to accumulate part of that gold in this afternoon's fixing session, and no doubt they are also selling dollars as instructed."

Hofer thought this over.

"Kellermann, what's done is done. That's clear. But now I want you to do something. Immediately. Get hold of Rosen and tell him that we cannot proceed further with his orders unless we get 50 percent more cash margin. If that doesn't stop him, it will at least slow him down quite a bit. Very few people can raise $50 million in cash quickly."

"Yes, sir."

"Now tell me, Kellermann, have any of your other big clients started to move in the same direction?"

"Nothing on the order of Rosen, but things have greatly heated up during the past few hours. Everybody was expecting an unusually large sale of Russian gold this week through the

Bank for International Settlements. But nothing happened. Apparently they withdrew it at the last moment, without any logical explanation. Reuters had a speculative type of story on the wire just before I came up here. Apparently they got to somebody at the Zurich airport who claimed that the gold was actually shipped in last week but is just sitting there in the bonded warehouse out at Kloten. A thing like that alone could produce a lot more action today, especially in a market which is already on the move. One thing is for sure; these days the speculators do not lack either money or crazy ideas."

"Kellermann, keep in touch with the gold department and the foreign exchange people. If anything really unusual develops this afternoon, I want you to stay personally on top of it. Something's going on." Kellermann knew when he was dismissed. Hofer simply no longer recognized his presence. This often proved highly offensive for executives new at the Hofer game. But Kellermann had gotten used to it long ago. He closed the double doors protecting Hofer's office from any possible audible intrusion from the outside world, and walked down the corridor to the bank of elevators. He was perturbed. He did not like Hofer interfering with his clientele. Especially after he was already committed. More than just Hofer was involved here. It was the integrity of the bank, and of himself. His instructions were clear. If Rosen could produce the additional cash margin, as far as he, Kellermann, was concerned, the deal was on. If not, it was strictly Hofer's responsibility, and he would have to explain it to Rosen. On that, he would insist.

But first he had to give the good news to Rosen. He proceeded to do so, in the briefest of telephone calls.

12

"So we will need an additional $50 million in cash before we can proceed further, Mr. Rosen."

"Fine, Herr Kellermann. I'll see what I can do."

The telephone went dead for a few seconds.

"You did understand what I said, Mr. Rosen."

"Completely. I'll be back to you this afternoon. Let's say after lunch. You'll be in?"

"Yes, yes."

"Fine. Good-bye."

Stanley burped, put on a pink shirt, a green tie, a blue suit, brown shoes with black socks. He placed a call to New York and went down to the Grill Room for a steak, well done, and some french fries on the side.

He actually enjoyed his lunch, while he mulled over Kellermann, the General Bank of Switzerland, and $50 million. So what else was there to expect? Everybody has to look after himself. And the aristocrats of the world were the first to learn this. That's why they became aristocrats. To himself, over lunch, Stanley had no qualms about thinking of his big customers in the States. Sure, they were Mafia. But they were the aristocrats of their chosen line of business. They were the best surviving capitalists in the United States. They believed as fiercely in the system that made America what it is, as did the Rockefellers, the Harrimans, the Kennedys of past generations. Swiss bankers were cut of exactly—but exactly—the same cloth.

They used the cloak of piety plus the bank secrecy laws in the same way as the Mafia used bribes and the threat of secrecy or death. Both provided services that a greedy and essentially anti-law public wanted. Neither group of twentieth century capitalists could survive and prosper to that degree if vast numbers of people, in both low and high places, did not want and need them. The type of power that resulted by merit of their holding the keys to many different kinds of financial kingdoms was as close to invincible as you could get. There was no use fighting it. Bow your head, accept it for what it is, roll with the punches. Cooperate. Since you can't join 'em, don't be stupid enough to try to lick 'em. Just have enough money to keep up with them. Power and money. That was something that both the Mafiosi and the gnomes of Zurich respect. And money Stanley had. That's why he enjoyed his lunch. In spite of the fact that his stomach was not exactly in A-1 shape.

The tummy trouble had started with that bender the week before. After fooling around in those bars in France and Germany right across the border from Basel until four in the morning, how could it have been avoided? That guy from Geneva sure had known them all: all the places, all the girls. And could he drink. Brother! Funny that the stomach business was hanging on so long. But still, it had been worth it. Anything would have been worth getting away from that hotel in Basel. Christ, what a stiff dump. And the manager! Boy, if looks could have killed when we turned up with those gals. Probably a fairy.

"Hey."

The head waiter stared at him.

"Hey. Gimme the check, will you?"

The head waiter approached.

"Sir?"

"Look, just gimme the check. I'm expecting a phone call upstairs."

Ten minutes later he got the check, and as he entered his suite, slightly peeved, the phone was ringing.

"Your party in New York," said the operator.

"Stanley, is that you? It's me, Harry Stahl."

God, thought Rosen, that guy will never learn that you

146

don't have to yell to be heard across the Atlantic. Typical New York jerk.

"Yes, Harry, it's me. Now just talk normal, will you. I can hear you fine. How are things going?"

"Fine, fine," screamed Harry. "How come I haven't heard from you? I was worried sick that something bad had happened."

"Harry, you worry too much. I've always told you that. And stop screaming into the phone."

"O.K. Stanley, don't get worked up. Did you do the deal with the Arabs?" Harry pronounced it A-rabs.

"I sure did. Fantastic thing. I'm onto something very, very big, Harry. The biggest idea yet."

"Like what?"

"Harry, I don't want to discuss it on the phone. You understand. Just do one thing for me, right away. Have the First National Bank of Nassau transfer $50 million to the General Bank of Switzerland, head office in Zurich, attention Kellermann."

"Wait a minute. Attention who?"

"Kellermann." He spelled it, with one n, and then continued. "Get the guys in Nassau on the phone and stress that it has to be a cable transfer. I want no screwups. The funds have to be good here not later than eight tomorrow morning, Swiss time. That gives you almost all day to arrange it on your side of the ocean."

"Fifty million?"

"Fifty million."

"Out of what accounts?"

"Take five million out of our personal one, Harry. And do the rest pro rata from some of the other really big ones. The guys from St. Louis should be good for five. The Las Vegas group's account should be good for another five. Just use your judgment. We've got lots of cash sitting around in the Bahamas."

"You sound awfully sure of yourself this time, Stanley.

Shouldn't I, perhaps, come over quick, so we can talk this over?"

"Look, Harry, I'd like to. But this must move fast. It's not the sort of thing we can sit around debating about. But don't worry. I know exactly what I'm doing."

"That's going to put every one of our operations pretty short of cash."

"I know. But not for long. This is a quick in and out. And it will involve zero downside risk where our Bahamas money is concerned. I just need that for a very short-term, very high-interest loan, to back up the operation here."

"Well, remember, Stanley, it's both our necks. Rumour has it that some of our clients play pretty rough if something gets screwed up where their money is concerned."

"I know," was Rosen's only response, although he did have to admit to himself that Stahl had a point.

"Where are you calling from, Stanley?"

"The Baur au Lac in Zurich. But I'll be checking out of here on Friday. Moving back to Basel for the weekend. Usual place."

"O.K., Stanley. If anything gets messed up in Nassau, just call me. When do you expect to be back?"

"End of next week."

"O.K., Stan. Take care, and believe me, I really mean that!"

"Bye, Harry. And thanks, buddy."

He hung up. Great guy, that Harry Stahl. A worrier though. Still, he's a guy who will stick it out, even if he doesn't have a clue as to what's going on. He picked up the phone again.

"Fräulein," he said, "give me the General Bank of Switzerland, head office. I forget the number. I'll wait."

Why these idiots don't install direct dial phones in hotels was an eternal mystery.

"General Bank of Switzerland."

"I'd like to speak to Director Kellermann."

"Just one moment, please."

Come on. Come on.

"Kellermann," came the deep voice.

148

"Herr Kellermann, this is Stanley Rosen. You'll have your $50 million in good funds tomorrow morning."

"Well—"

Rosen interrupted, "So I expect you to start proceeding on my orders immediately."

"But Mr. Rosen—"

Again Stanley cut in. "I don't think there is room for any more 'buts,' Herr Kellermann. You agreed to accept my order, and you further agreed to start immediately on the bullion purchases and short dollar sales. Frankly, you broke your commitment when you asked for the additional cash margin, but I understand your position. I'm producing the extra cash. Now I expect you to keep your word."

Rosen, unknowingly, had hit upon Kellermann's weak spot: he had given his word.

"Agreed, Mr. Rosen. I shall proceed."

"Fine. The funds will be coming by cable from the First National in Nassau. If you don't have them by nine tomorrow morning, call me up. I'm at the Baur au Lac, Room 718. In any case I'll be keeping in touch the next few days."

And that was that. Now Beirut. He placed the call and then undressed and stepped into the shower.

The shower dribbled, like most European showers. Probably because, when you come right down to it, these birds over here still have an aversion toward water—at least too much of it at one time. That's why the bidets, probably. And the looks of horror when you order some ice water in Paris on a scorching hot summer day. At least the towels were big. Huge in fact. The phone rang. In the bathroom.

Why not? thought Stanley Rosen and picked up the dainty pink receiver.

"Your call to Beirut, sir. You did place one, didn't you?"

"That's right. I'll hang on."

A minute went by and Rosen still hung. Onto a pink telephone, in the bathroom of a Swiss hotel, calling an Arab, to talk about buying gold and selling the dollar, by the millions. It had been a long way from New Jersey.

But, he thought, it was time to drop New Jersey, and Miami, and Las Vegas, and the rest of it. Very, very slowly and very, very carefully. Because in the investment business there is no such thing as lasting success. There were merely high points—and then nothing. That's the lesson the go-go boys in the fund business, the hot-shots in the brokerage game, the hot-wind artists in the savings and loan industry would never learn. So after three or maybe five years, they ended up on the same pavement they started from. There is a very definite cycle to success in any business. Rosen was convinced of this. It was obvious to any fool in industry. From the transistor to the colour TV to fast-back car to miniskirts. They started as an innovation, soared to unbelievable heights within a short time, and ended up overproduced, market-saturated, and ordinary. As time progressed, the life cycles were becoming shorter and shorter and shorter, from sensational birth to ignominious commonplaceness. The same was true with ideas in the financial business. Growth, hot new issues, performance—the gospel of a bright new generation, the obvious solution, the modern way of life—if one expected to live for three years. Capital preservation, yield, interest—the new philosophy of a new permanent approach to investments. Life expectancy: two years. International diversification, natural resources, ecology—the magic formula for the next well-spring to eternal financial success. Interest span: eighteen months. The problem was, as Stanley so well knew, you had to sell the clients on something. And no sooner were they sold, the something was passé. But if you did not sell them, somebody else right in the middle of the current product cycle would, and no more clients. A rat race.

Stanley had, with the rest of them, tried them all on. Now he was down to gold, devaluations, tax havens. Arabs. Perhaps the shortest life cycle of all. And for what?

And then there was the even bigger problem. Jersey, Miami, Vegas, and all that.

150

Maybe the answer was so simple it might work. Just cut out. Move to Switzerland, Bermuda, even London. With maybe $30 or $35 million there could be no doubt that he would be accepted, maybe not by the people right at the top of the heap, but still accepted by most people for what he represented: money and brains. Then he would manage just a very few clients—to keep his hand in. All offshore. No more monkey business.

Stanley Rosen had reached that ominous stage of almost forty-five years of age; the point of no return. What he wanted to find above all other things was something that had totally passed him by thus far: a period of real happiness and simple contentment. He had first really sensed that such an unbelievable goal might still be achievable not so very long ago. In August he'd spent three weeks doing absolutely nothing on the island of Sardinia, with a young girl of twenty-four from Norway. They had met at the Copenhagen airport and had taken the same taxi into town. They had dinner outside in the Tivoli. Corny, but fun. Then five days later, off into the blue together. Totally unplanned. To Sardinia. The Calle di Volpe. A hotel built for no more than sixty guests; Frenchmen, Belgians, Swiss, British, Italians, Germans. All well to do. Some even titled. Clubby. But they had accepted Stanley. They had asked his advice. They had invited him onto their yachts for a supper. And nobody had asked him for a loan. He had even accepted the invitation of a pair from Brussels to drop in on them at home afterwards. It turned out he was in the Cabinet. Yet Stanley Rosen was accepted as an old friend, a guest of honour. Sure. Rosen knew that they knew. That he had a great deal of money. But somehow, almost like sleight of hand, it was never mentioned. He knew that they knew he was an American "primitive." But they seemed to regard this as merely curious; his Jersey accent as rather cute; his mannerisms as "natural." Rosen was no fool. But he knew that here was a world that he must eventually pay for on the open market. He knew that the question of price would inevitably come up. But it would be worth it. Then the crude pigs from Chicago, the show girls from Las Vegas, their drunken brawls in Nassau, the nit-picking little Jews from Jersey: all this could be buried and forgotten, just as his parents had buried their memories of their ghetto in Poland. Through the simple process of emigration across the Atlantic. Thank God he had his divorce well behind him. For with her, her ghastly makeup, her shrill voice, her girlfriends, her canasta parties, the whole idea would have been absurd. But with somebody like that girl from Bergen, with a clientele in the Near East, with the credentials of a stunning success during the Great Dollar devaluation, it was possible.

The pink telephone finally came alive again.

"*Hallo, hallo, qui est là?*" came the voice.

"This is Stanley Rosen calling from Switzerland, I would like to—"

"*Hallo, hallo. Je ne parle pas Anglais, Monsieur.*"

"Oh my God," came Stanley Rosen's reply. He clicked the receiver rather frantically, hoping to hell that the connection would not be broken.

"Operator, operator" he yelled.

Nothing. And then more than nothing. The other end hung up. So did Stanley. "Son of a bitch," cursed Stanley Rosen.

Well, nothing to be done. It would take at least two or three hours to get through again. Forget about it until later.

The phone rang again.

"This is the operator, Mr. Rosen. Was your call to Beirut satisfactory? It was rather short."

"Yes, operator. Perfectly satisfactory. Thank you."

No sense in making an absolute ass of himself. This was certainly one thing he had to correct and quickly. A quick course in French and perhaps one in German. Mr. Stanley Rosen would soon be as European as Grace Kelly.

Shower completed, Stanley decided to take a nap. He was satisfied, satisfied with the future now that the biggest action of his lifetime was underway.

13

Historians who later reconstructed these happenings during this first week of November determined that the real action started around two-fifteen on that Wednesday afternoon. The dollar was hit by the biggest wave of selling thus far experienced in the twentieth century. It dropped 3 percent in value within a matter of two hours against every major currency in Western Europe, led by the Swiss franc. Around three o'clock it looked as if a recovery might occur, but then came the news of the afternoon gold fixing. The price jumped $4.10 in one session. It meant that the gold pools in both Zurich and London were unable to cope with the sudden burst of demand for the metal. After that, the situation of the dollar worsened by the minute.

Secretary-General Bollinger of the Bank for International Settlements was sitting alone in his office, poring over the Telex reports that had been flooding in since lunchtime. He looked slightly sick. He had instructed his secretary to put through no further calls, with two exceptions: the American secretary of the treasury and a certain Dr. Bernoulli.

"What now?" he asked.

The almost man-sized carving from New Guinea staring at him from across the room could hardly answer.

Just two more days to go, and all hell was breaking loose. And of all bloody people, the Russians. If the Americans found out the whole sordid story they would crucify him—at best. *Ausgerechnet die Russen!* This morning when the president of the German Bundesbank had called him, he had thought, had hoped, that it was just a coincidence. The Russians could have had a million reasons for shifting over to dollars on the pipeline purchase. Nor had the Germans been overly perturbed. They had just thought that the BIS should know. It would mean that the future demand for dollars in the Euromarket would now be higher than had generally been anticipated. That's all. It might push the long-term rates up. Maybe by .25 percent. But the people in Frankfurt did not know what he knew. And now everything was starting to tie together. First Melekov, then the delegation from Moscow pulling out, then the pipeline switch, and now the foreign exchange and gold markets going all to hell. Before it was over it could cost the United States billions—three, five, who knows—and the whole financial world would blow sky high in spite of this cost. Money thrown right out the window. Knowing the Americans, he knew that they would defend the dollar right up to the last second, rather than lose face to the Russians.

His secretary opened the door, but she just stuck her head in. She knew when the storm warnings were flying.

"Herr Doktor Bernoulli just called from the lobby downstairs and asked if he could come right up."

"Tell him to come ahead."

Bollinger was close to panic. For he was a man of total integrity, completed devoted to the immense responsibility which had been entrusted to him. He was one of those few international civil servants with enough courage and foresight to go out on a limb and do what he felt was right, regardless of the possible political consequences. He had seen no better path of action than that which he had undertaken in this terrible situation, better for all the governments concerned, including the United States. Bollinger was anything but devious. His approach was analytical; his actions were based upon logic, not tactical or strategic considerations. The circumstances now defied analysis. Events had gone underground, into a world which Bollinger had never experienced, and before which he found himself helpless . . . and increasingly bitter.

Bernoulli entered his office.

"Please excuse me for visiting you so unexpectedly, Herr

154

Bollinger, but I'm afraid that events are moving very swiftly. I must try to keep up with them."

"No problem. Please be seated."

"I think we have made excellent progress. We know now exactly the chain of action which led up to the theft. We know the two men responsible for the organization and implementation. But we still do not have the answer to the key question: Who was the final recipient of the red dossier? And what does he intend to do with it—if anything?"

"I see."

"Now I don't want to frighten you, but we've heard about the visit of that Russian delegation. The stay in Basel of your guests from Moscow coincides exactly with the period of the theft. More than that. They stayed at exactly that hotel in which the two men responsible for the physical action were seen together, more than once. The coincidence is almost overpowering, if you know what I mean. This is not the only coincidence, however. I'll come to others later. But first, let's deal with the Russians."

"I frankly think you are running so far behind the events, Herr Bernoulli, that before I let you continue, I should bring you up to date on a few things. It will save you from wasting any more time on this matter."

Bernoulli didn't like this. His eyes drew closely together. His hands clenched. And his healthy brown was suddenly tinged with more than a trace of red.

"What's that supposed to mean?" Bernoulli finally asked, after a long stare across Bollinger's desk. His voice was tight. Being upstaged by an amateur at this point was not to his liking.

"I like the word 'coincidence.' Let me add a few more, and then I believe that you will get my point."

"Go ahead. That's why I came to see you, you know."

"First, the Russian delegation. They came here to finalize arrangements for the sale of a major shipment of gold. This is by no means unusual. We have been handling the marketing of the Russians' gold for many years now. The reason is quite simple. We ourselves are a very large owner of gold. In fact, we are the only financial institution in the world which has its total capital and reserves in the form of gold. Thus we have the capacity to immediately absorb, if necessary, complete major shipments, which otherwise would overwhelm the free market and cause dangerous price fluctuations. The Soviet Union can get a firm price from us—for every last ounce. They like that. We also like that, since it gives us another means for intervening in—tampering with, if you like—the free market for that metal. Fluctuations in the gold price in the past have led to currency speculation. We try our best to avoid the latter at almost any cost."

"Thanks for the explanation, Herr Bollinger. But I'm afraid it does not bring us very much further." Bernoulli was already on his second cigarette.

"Now easy does it. Back to coincidences. The Russians came here especially to finalize the arrangements for the sale of 20 million ounces. They negotiated at the usual Eastern European pace with the head of our gold department. Everything was finally agreed upon. The days after the disappearance of the dossier from my safe, the negotiations halted just this side of being signed. Nobody spoke of any cancellation of the sale. They just said that they had to get the final authorization from Moscow and would come back to us within a very short time. They left town that same day. We have not heard from them since."

"Where's the gold?"

"In the Zurich airport."

"Why didn't you tell me this before, for God's sake?"

"Because it has happened before. It was by no means out of character. I believe that it would only have been grossly misleading if I had attached undue significance to such an event—and led you down the garden path."

"Then why do you attach such significance to it now?"

"Because of coincidence number two. For almost a year the

Russians have been negotiating with the Germans for an immense purchase of line pipe. Also here the negotiations reached the signature stage. At the very last moment, contrary to all prior indications, the Russians insisted that they would pay only in U.S. dollars."

Bernoulli got the point.

"But now comes the clincher. Since late yesterday afternoon, Eastern Europe has been selling dollars—both spot and forward. Today it has become serious. The spot rate in Zurich has been pushed down to 3.33 from 3.40 within two hours. In the foreign exchange field this is an unprecedented change. Like the Dow Jones falling 100 points in one trading session."

Bernoulli then asked, very quietly, "Herr Bollinger, what do you intend to do?"

"I'm waiting to see what happens in New York. The markets are now closed in Europe. The next moves will take place across the Atlantic. If the selling continues, we must start to act. The president of the Swiss National Bank and the finance minister will be consulted. I brought you fellows into this, much to my great regret. I must try to be fair with you right to the end."

"And what about the Americans?"

"I'll have to deal with them in my own way."

"This could get pretty bad before the weekend, I imagine."

"Yes. So if you'll please excuse me, Herr Bernoulli, I really must get back on the job."

"Just one more question. Do you really think the Russians would pull such a brazen, naked attempt to disgrace the United States?"

"A few years ago I would have said no. But the young Turks are starting to take over in the Soviet Union. They're anything but Stalinists. But they are also not of the Khrushchev school. They calculate. They recognize that the best weapon at the disposal of the Soviet Union is not the Red Army of Stalin, or their rockets, but the immense economic potential of their country. And contrary to Western countries, they have absolute central control of their economy. They can direct its energy like a general his army. But the weak point has always been the ruble. Or to put it another way, the dominating role of the dollar. Downgrade the latter, and you automatically upgrade the former in many areas of the world. Destruction of faith in the dollar system cannot help but be a major policy objective of anyone at odds with the United States. De Gaulle recognized all this years ago and took the initiative. He did not succeed. The Russians are in a quite different class, of course.

"But the risk."

"What risk? The United States has absolutely no means of retaliation. And on the dollar issue, it also has very few allies. On gold, none. The power of the dollar is a greater source of resentment throughout the Western world than any other element of American foreign policy, even right here in Switzerland."

Bernoulli rose and shook hands with Bollinger.

But as he was leaving, he got in one parting shot. "To my simple mind, this all seems just a little too pat. In any case, if anything new develops, we'll probably see each other again."

As Bernoulli left, Bollinger picked up his phone and called the foreign exchange desk of the bank.

"What's happening in New York?"

"It's continuing, sir. The bid price on spot francs has now dropped to just a shade under 3.31 cents. As you know, under the term of the 1973 monetary agreement, the Swiss National Bank must intervene at this level. They will have to start buying dollars. What do you want us to do?"

"Nothing at the moment. But nobody goes home this evening until I say so. We might have to stay on right through Tokyo tonight."

He hung up and redialed. "Joan, get me the President of the National Bank in Zurich, please. Right away."

The call was through in less then thirty seconds." "This is Bollinger. How do things look to you?"

"We don't like it a bit. Where's all this selling coming from?"

Bollinger thought carefully before he replied. "Seems to have started in Eastern Europe. Then Zurich, Frankfurt, Paris, it would seem."

"What are you fellows going to do?"

"I'm not sure. Maybe it will start to correct itself in New York."

The National Bank president did not seem to buy that one.

"I'm not so sure. Funny damned thing. It came out of absolutely nowhere. We've more or less got used to these currency speculators crawling out of the woodwork every fall, but normally you can see them coming. This thing has all built up within twenty-four hours."

"You've heard about New York, I suppose. The dollar has dropped below the 3.31 level. Will you start to intervene?"

"We're having a meeting in about fifteen minutes on that subject. My guess is that we'll try to hold it here for the rest of the day. A slight turnaround in Europe tomorrow could produce a surge of covering of short positions. Then we would be out of the woods. That's my thinking at the moment."

"Thanks. That's very important for us. We will probably also be in the market in New York within a short time, trying to stop this thing. I'll keep in touch."

"What are the people in Washington saying?"

"I don't know. I expect to hear from them any moment now," replied Bollinger.

"Right. Thanks for the call."

Although already five o'clock in Switzerland, it was only eleven in the morning in Washington. The secretary of the treasury was just entering the White House grounds in his limousine. As he stepped out of the car another government vehicle rolled up right behind him. It was the secretary of state. Both cleared the security people together, and were immediately met by one of the president's assistants who took them directly to the Cabinet room.

The chairman of the Federal Reserve Board was already there. Less than a minute later the president arrived and asked them all to be seated.

He turned first to Secretary of the Treasury Henry Crosby.

"Henry, what's going on? I got word from the Intelligence people less than an hour ago. They report that massive selling of the dollar has set in in Europe, and that the gold price has gone sky high. What's more, they claim that the Russians started it all. How is that possible, for God's sake?"

"I don't know. I just know that it's a fact."

"When did it start exactly?"

"Yesterday. During the afternoon in New York, and then at the tail end of the banking day in San Francisco. Nothing startling, but steady selling was there. Then during the European business day today that's just ending, it really started to pick up steam. The last hours have seen nothing short of a mass movement out of dollars and into the Swiss franc, the German mark, the guilder—you name it. The speculators seem to have joined in with full force only today."

"How can you tell?"

"All of a sudden the rates of future dollars began to plummet. And the gold price shot up $4 within one hour. What has everybody worried is that suddenly this has taken on all the characteristics of a highly organized effort."

"What do you propose to do, Henry?" As so often in the past, it was to Crosby that the president turned for advice when faced with a crisis situation.

"Well, we must be careful not to repeat the mistake the British made in 1967."

"And that was?"

"The circumstances were very similar to those right now. Somehow the word started getting around on a Tuesday or Wednesday that the pound was going to go on the weekend. By Thursday every last bank clerk in Europe knew about it. Instead of facing the fact that the news had leaked, the Bank of England intervened to protect the pound right down to the wire, not only in the spot market—they also were buying everything that was being offered by speculators in the forward markets as well. They lost £1.5 billion in two days that way, until even they had to give up around noon on Friday.

"The entire exercise had proven futile. Their losses could be peanuts compared to what it could cost us this week should the buildup against the dollar continue. My guess is anything between five and ten billion."

"What's the answer?"

"We've just two alternatives. Close the banks now, before this develops into total chaos. Or bluff our way through, cost what it may, knowing we may make fools of ourselves in the process."

The president had listened carefully to every word. Then he turned to the secretary of state.

"Charles, what do you think?"

"First, I disagree with the diagnosis. We are still a long way from what Henry terms total chaos. The rates have barely fallen to levels where government intervention becomes necessary. This has happened before. In fact, since 1971 it must have occurred a dozen times. We bluffed our way through then, and I'm sure we can do it again now. After all, we only have a few more days to go."

The secretary of the treasury shook his head as he listened to these comments, but the secretary of state continued without taking notice.

"But all this is really beside the point. Even if Henry is correct, and even if it would cost us five to ten billion, still in my judgment we have no choice but to defend the dollar right up to the weekend. What if we don't? The whole world will witness what they will thereafter believe was a forced tripling of the price of gold by the United States, in spite of all prior policy statements to the contrary. And much of the world would be only too happy to accept that it had been the Russians who engineered the whole thing. Imagine what would happen to future faith in the dollar. Look at what happened to Britain. Once the world lost faith in sterling, its influence in Asia, in Africa, and even in Europe proper went to the lowest levels in history. All within just a few years. Oh, no! To follow such a path of action would be political suicide. That we must raise the price of gold and once again make the dollar convertible is clear. But we must do this according to *our* plan, and *our* schedule."

The chairman of the Federal Reserve Board then spoke up for the first time.

"We could always change the plan, you know."

The president sighed. For years the man heading the Federal Reserve Board had been pushing for a restoration of convertibility of the dollar. It was he who had insisted that this could only be done through a massive increase in the official gold price. It was he who pressed the urgency of the problem. Until the president had decided to follow that advice. This, now, apparently made the entire concept suspect. Unbelievable what happens so often to reasonable men who develop illusions of greatness when in office.

"Frank," said the president, "I think we can forget that idea. It's too late to turn back at this point. What could we possibly gain from it? Irrespective of what happens in the markets during the next day or so, the fundamental problem remains. We must restore convertibility of the dollar. What's happening today only proves how urgent this is. Either we act now, or the world will act against us."

"But—"

"Look, the point that the secretary of state made is a valid one. The overriding consideration now must be the preservation of the prestige of the dollar. That is, after all, the whole objective of this exercise. We not only want to put the dollar back onto a realistic basis, but just as important, we want to regain once and for all the respect of the world for the people who manage the dollar—and that means, ultimately, the people in this room. People don't trust managers who panic. Nor do they trust people who let themselves be taken for a ride by either the Russians or the speculators."

"I'm afraid I'm being misunderstood," said the man from the Federal Reserve. "I am not for abandoning the objectives of our plan. My position on that is quite well known. I am referring to the method employed to achieve that objective. Nobody says that we must raise the price of gold to $125 overnight. Nobody says that we must, in our God-given wisdom, decide that the dollar must be devalued by 15 percent this weekend. We can let the dollar find its own level. And the same for gold. Turn them loose. Let the markets decide. Go back to floating."

Henry Crosby interrupted, "Frank, we've been over that subject at least a hundred times. You professors, or ex-professors, always toot on the same note. But 1971 proved, once and for all, that floating does not work. Everybody cheated last time, including ourselves. It would be folly to attempt that again."

The president had heard all this before. He recognized the merits of both arguments. But now he was convinced that Crosby was right. The world of commerce wanted stability; businessmen wanted to work with knowns, wanted to know where they stood not only today, but a year from today. If the United States could not give them a stable dollar based on gold that would meet their needs, they would use something else. And the Common Market would just love to give it to them. He did not want to turn this into another debate on economics. He had attended two semesters on that subject in college. And that had been quite enough.

"Gentlemen," he said, "we shall stick to the original plan. And the methodology and timing already agreed upon. But we are going to have to prevent a panic. I'm prepared to intervene in the markets right now. From what our intelligence reports said, if we let the rates slip any further a real run could start immediately. Is that right?"

The other men in the room indicated their agreement with this analysis. Again the president turned to his secretary of the treasury, Henry Crosby.

"Henry, how much will it take, and how should we go about it?"

"Mr. President, I figure that we will need as much as $5 billion to ride out the next twenty-four hours—up to noon our time tomorrow. I would not want to venture even a guess beyond that point."

"How will we work?"

"Quite simply. We will go into the market as a seller of francs, marks, guilders, yen—whatever comes pouring in at us. This way we will keep their rates relative to the dollar inside the IMF limits. Otherwise, we would be faced with a progressive de facto devaluation."

"Have we got enough of those currencies to do the job?"

"No, but we can borrow almost unlimited amounts through the Bank for International Settlements. Thank God we brought Bollinger into this plan ahead of time. I'm sure he's right on top of the situation and will be able to work out a swap arrangement in Europe immediately. We'll swap dollars for a bushel basket of those other currencies and have lots of ammunition to work with. There's one hooker here, however. The BIS will no doubt demand an insurance clause on behalf of the countries putting up their currencies. In other words, we will have to bear the risk and cost of the dollar devaluation. I am sure that once we have demonstrated such a firm stand, the Europeans will not just stay idle but also help us ward off the speculators. Between us, we should be able to withstand enormous pressure. Of course, there are always limits. That's why I say, let's try it for twenty-four hours, and then look again."

The president appeared fully satisfied with Crosby's proposal.

"What do you think we should do about the gold price?"

"There's absolutely nothing we can do. After all, we're hardly going to sell any gold from Fort Knox at current free market prices when we know that from Saturday on it will be worth

$125 an ounce. I'd say, let's just ignore gold and concentrate on stopping the run out of the dollar."

"I'll buy that," said the president. "Now, what do we do about the Russians?"

"Scare the bejeezus out of them" was the advice of Henry Crosby.

"How?"

"Give 'em a bit of their own medicine," said Crosby.

"I don't think we have that kind of medicine in stock."

"Oh, yes, we do. Wheat. They've just gone through the biggest crop failure in Russia since the revolution. They need our wheat desperately. Look," said Crosby, now in full command, "it's no longer the good old days over there. Their people won't accept going back to bread rationing, or anything near it. But if we stop all grain shipments, that's what will have to happen. The Canadians are sold out, and so are the Australians. That's why they originally came to us. Well, we'll just tell them that we've changed our minds; that we're putting an immediate embargo on all food exports to Eastern Europe. And tell them that their own foolish actions in the currency field, which are doomed to failure anyway, are responsible."

"And if the public hears about this?"

"Not a chance. We'll use the hot line to Moscow. The news won't get beyond this room and the Kremlin. Believe me, the Russians will keep quiet while they think things over."

"And if they escalate?" interjected the secretary of state.

"Then we'll escalate," replied the president promptly. "But let's move one step at a time. Everybody agree?"

They did.

The president turned back to his secretary of state.

"Could you start drafting that message right away? I'll want to review it very carefully before we send it off. But it must go out no later than this evening."

And then to Crosby. "Henry, you'd better get onto that fellow in Switzerland before things get out of hand over there."

With that the meeting was adjourned.

The secretary of the treasury hurried back to his office, and had Dr. Bollinger of the BIS on the telephone within two minutes.

"Dr. Bollinger, this is Henry Crosby."

"Yes, Mr. Secretary. Actually I tried to phone you a while ago, but your people told me you were unavailable at that time. It does not look too good, does it?"

"No. We're going to have to ask you for some help. We want to have an immediate standby facility of $5 billion equivalent of European currencies, on a swap basis. We are going to stop this thing in the market. Right now."

"This can prove enormously expensive."

"We know it. The president has just made the decision."

"But the plan is still on?"

"Yes."

"I see."

"Bollinger, now what about that swap?"

"As you know, almost all of this has been discussed previously. I shall have to finalize the arrangements immediately, but that should be possible within the hour. You realize, of course, that everyone will require an insurance clause. Along the lines agreed to by the British a number of years ago."

"We agree. Put everything through to me directly as soon as you have the package together. I'll not leave my office until I hear from you. Thank you very much, Dr. Bollinger. We won't forget it."

One hour and seven minutes later, the swap arrangement had been formally completed. It was the biggest single financial transaction ever made.

By three that afternoon the foreign exchange markets in New York had reached the boiling point. The United States government had pumped in almost $3 billion in foreign currencies to hold the dollar against the stampede of speculators who seemed hell-bent on bringing Uncle Sam to his knees. It was with the greatest possible relief that the banks in that city finally closed their doors. In Chicago and San Francisco they

166

played it cute. The banks there had always had only a marginal involvement in international finance and especially foreign exchange. On this day they either refused to make a market or just shut off the telephones in their trading departments. Their attitude: Let the Japanese handle this hot potato next.

About the same time as the American banks had closed their doors to the public after a hectic day, Dr. Walter Hofer was finishing his coffee in his home, high above the Lake of Zurich. The first snow of the year was just starting to fall outside, and his wife had decided to light the fireplace to mark the occasion.

"What's Mary all excited about?" he asked his wife.

"She's got a date. Her first in Switzerland. With a young man from the bank, I forget his name."

"Where's her mother?"

"Walter, it's not her mother, in that tone of voice. She's my sister."

"Well, I prefer to think of her as Mary's mother, if you don't mind. That super-American act of hers gets on my nerves every time she shows up here. She was born and raised right in Brugg just like you. Why in the world we have to speak English with her is beyond me."

"Now, Walter. Thirty years in America is a long time. And you have to admit, she has done a very nice job in bringing up Mary."

"Fine. Then where's your sister?"

"She went to the theatre."

The doorbell rang and Mrs. Hofer immediately rose. A minute later she returned with the young man. It was Zimmerer of the foreign exchange desk, scrubbed a healthy Swiss pink and embarrassed as hell.

"Walter, won't you look after Mr. Zimmerer for a moment. I want to go up and tell Mary he's here."

It was not exactly Hofer's style to entertain department heads of the bank in his living room, but he accepted the challenge fairly gracefully. Zimmerer turned down his offer of coffee but gratefully accepted a cognac.

"Well, well, Herr Zimmerer. Apparently my niece and you have found a common interest in foreign exchange."

Zimmerer grunted something rather inaudible and took another slug of cognac. Hofer continued, "Actually, it's very good that you dropped by. I hear that all hell broke loose in New York during the past couple of hours."

"Yes, sir. The rumours that the dollar is under steady attack from Eastern Europe seem to be proving out. Now everybody's getting into the act. I'm not sure how long the Americans can hold the dollar. Apparently, they have been massively intervening in the market all day in New York, but if the selling keeps up, it's hard to say what will happen."

"What do you think?"

"I really don't know. I can say, however, that the bank's in good shape. On balance, we are now about $2 billion short, just as you instructed, sir. But I'm afraid that we could not fill all the orders for some of our customers with the same idea. The markets were simply too hectic, and some of our major partner banks have simply stopped trading for the moment."

"Is the word out that we've been selling a lot of dollars?"

"I'm afraid it is, sir. You know how these things work. When four or five banks keep getting selling orders from us, in time their traders start talking to each other. Very gossipy bunch, you know."

"Fine, Zimmerer. Now until I say differently, I want you to stay right on the fence from now on. No more selling of dollars. But also no buying. Just keep trading within very very narrow margins. Come to think of it, if necessary buy more dollars than you sell tomorrow morning. And make sure everybody notices it." He paused. "Now tell me about gold."

"Well, Kellermann insisted we start executing those buy orders for that numbered account. And at the same time, the fellows across the street also came into the afternoon fixing with a very big purchase. The result was inevitable. The price had to be pushed up over $4 an ounce, unless somebody wanted to intervene."

"And tomorrow?"

"It can only go higher. Much higher."

"Well, I don't want it to go higher. I want you to use the bank's own gold stocks to meet every buy order tomorrow. I want the price to be kept below $80 an ounce. I'm holding you personally responsible for this."

"Yes sir, I'll be at the gold fixing meetings myself in that case. But although we can control the Zurich market, at least for a day or two, I'm afraid that there's little we can do in London."

"Let me worry about that, Zimmerer. You just carry out your instructions here."

At this point, Hofer's niece appeared. In contrast to her mother she thought Switzerland was just great. She had donned a white lace blouse and the type of dirndl so popular in the Alpine countries. Hofer, who had no children of his own, liked the young lady immensely and went out of his way to compliment her on how nice she looked. He escorted her and the young man to the door and even lingered a moment, watching them descend the stairs to the car parked below, chattering together.

"Walter," called his wife, "please come back in. You'll catch cold standing out there."

Soon he had returned to his usual chair near the fireplace.

"Troubles?" said Martha.

Hofer did not even glance up. He was gazing into the fire.

"Walter!"

"Yes, Martha. What is it?"

"I just asked you if you have troubles. You've been about ten kilometres away ever since you came home this evening."

No reply.

"Now, you know it's always better to get things off your chest. Otherwise you just sink deeper and deeper into yourself, and soon all we will be doing is grunting at each other."

"You're right, Martha. It's not so pleasant at the moment. The same old story. You do X, and the next year everybody expects you to do X plus one. And the year after, plus two. And so forth. One has to run faster and faster just to maintain the appearance of infallibility, of never making a mistake. Every year, deposits must grow 15 percent, profits 20 percent, bad loans zero percent. At this point, just one slight stumble and the word will be out that Hofer is over the hill. It's not always so easy."

"Why don't you think slowly about giving it up then? There's really nothing much more that you can hope to add to that which you've already done. You know that you get very little thanks for all you do anyway. Why go on and on and on, until something happens?"

"Not yet. Maybe in two or three years. But not now."

"Why not?"

"Martha, you know that I never like to go into details about the bank. But still, I'll try to explain very generally. Due to this craze for growth and for profits during the past ten years, we've been slowly building up a group of loans that we should have been writing off the books but didn't. It wouldn't have looked good. The competition would have laughed themselves sick. Not that they don't have the same problem. But try to prove it. Now we are faced with three new loans that must join the crowd. It's no real problem, when you consider our overall picture. None. But if we wiped that whole slate clean, it would also nearly wipe out our profits for a year. Maybe two. Then everything would be shipshape again for the next ten years."

"Well, if it's got to be done, I would not worry about those fools who have been envious of you for God knows how long. You always have the last laugh, Walter."

"It's not that easy. If I did it that way, the shareholders would be yelling for a younger man immediately. I know those birds. No, I've got to work it out during the time I've got left."

"Now Walter, you're not exactly eighty, you know."

"Still, I want that place perfectly clean before I leave. I

170

don't want anybody moving into my chair who would whisper around town about the mess he inherited from old Hofer. Oh, no! But don't worry, I have something in the works that may solve the problem right away. What bothers me is that the thing I was betting most might be blowing up in my face."

"You mean all that stuff on TV about gold and the dollar?"

"Martha, you old fox. And you always tell me that you can't tell the difference between a mark, franc, and lira when we go on vacation."

"Walter, things always work out, you know. They always have. You'll find the way. Come now, let's have a good bottle of wine together. I'll go right down to the cellar and get one of your favourites."

And she did. They sat talking until almost eleven. Then Martha's sister came home. She insisted on explaining in slangy American English the entire plot of the play which she had just seen staged in German. Hofer could only take so much of that and soon excused himself.

The moment he reached his bedroom, he picked up the phone and dialed twelve digits. He was through immediately.

"Sir Robert, this is Walter Hofer in Zurich. Sorry to call you so late."

"Not at all. In fact, I'm very happy you called. What's going wrong?"

"We're not quite sure, but this we do know: Two major buyers hit the gold market simultaneously at the afternoon fixing session. Both are here in Zurich. One we know: It's a private client of ours. The other may or may not be the Russians. We don't know. Another bank is involved and they're not talking."

"Did you make the deal in Johannesburg?" was Sir Robert Winthrop's next worried question.

"The final signing will take place tomorrow·here in Zurich."

"Tomorrow?"

"Yes."

"Well, how do you propose we cope with this situation?"

"I'll cope. But both of us must insure that the gold price stays below $80 tomorrow. We have to meet every buy order with a matching sell order. As simple as that. We'll just have to stop these fellows cold."

"Yes, but could this not ultimately mean that we will have thrown good money after bad if they refuse to sign tomorrow?"

"Sir Robert, you know as well as I that there are high risks in the gold market. We knew that from the very beginning. And we made our commitments in that full knowledge. I think I need hardly remind you that when I make a commitment it is met. Just today our people told me that we have already taken the entire $35 million of your bogus Transcontinental Airlines notes off your hands. It took us less than two weeks."

"Walter, I know that, and I will be eternally grateful. I have no intention of backing out on anything we agreed upon. I'll be in the gold market with everything we have tomorrow."

"Good."

"What does David Mason think about all this?"

"He totally agrees with the strategy. He was with me in Johannesburg, you know. He's got almost $500 million on the line in this deal. So all three of us are totally committed."

"Well," said Sir Robert Winthrop, "at least we're doing great on the dollar. Our fellows pulled out all the stops today, and I figure we must be ahead a good $25 million since lunch. I assume David has been pursuing the same course."

"Yes, but Robert, remember we've all agreed not to overdo it."

"Right. We shall stick to our agreement right down the line. Anything else?"

"No. Just remember to do everything in your power to keep the lid on the gold market tomorrow."

14

Thursday, November 6. Two days before the Great Dollar Devaluation. As a result of the decision of somebody, maybe Bishop Usher, that one day ends and the next day starts in the middle of the Pacific Ocean, the first metropolis to enjoy the new dawn was Tokyo. The excitement in the financial world had moved with the sun. In Japan it took on new dimensions. The Tokyo stock exchange was struck by a wave of buying unprecedented even in its confused history. The orders had been stacking up at the brokerage houses the entire preceding night, coming first from Zurich and Frankfurt, then from London, the process culminating in a massive influx of buy orders by telephone, Telex, and cable from New York, Chicago, San Francisco, and Los Angeles. It seemed as though everybody was counting on the Japanese yen as the best money haven on earth and the purchase of Japanese stocks as the easiest way to buy a currency insurance policy. Thus, during the first hour of trading, the Japanese equivalent of the Dow Jones Industrial Average rose 226 points.

This was in complete contrast to what had happened the preceding afternoon in New York. There the Dow Jones—the real one—had literally collapsed in the last hour of trading. Prices had been retreating and volume rising gradually all day long, so that by two o'clock the DJI was down just a shade over twelve points and volume was 15 million shares. Then the panic started. The session closed 42 points down, and the final volume stood at 32 million shares. The odd-lotters had the biggest day in the history of exchange. The story that afternoon was the same in every brokerage house on Wall Street. Instructions to get the hell out. Liquidate, sell—don't worry about prices—and then got the proceeds out of the country. Put them into something solid: Swiss bank deposits, German railroad bonds, South African gold mines, British consols. Anything not denominated in dollars. Tokyo, due to its cunning location, was the first beneficiary of the flight from the dollar. The result was near chaos that morning.

But already by midday profit taking, Japanese profit taking set in. The temptation for Japanese banks and brokerage houses to unload their cats and dogs and squirrels into the laps of the great wise men of the West ultimately proved too great. Shares that had sunk into obscurity months, even years, ago were dusted off and these marvelous discoveries grudgingly passed into foreign ownership. One Oriental wit calculated that within three hours 20 percent of the ownership of Nippon Gold Corporation, an obscure little company in the dental materials business in Sapporo, had been transferred to a group of clever investors from San Diego, California, all ex-navy. All this was reported with pride by the early editions of the afternoon newspapers. For it demonstrated beyond any doubt that Japan had been accepted as being eligible for full-fledged participation in a worldwide financial panic.

Financial panics are a funny thing. They bring out the lemming in the human race as no other event does. Sure, wars, especially invasions, do a pretty good job in the panic field. The flight from Paris in 1940 or the flood of Germans who moved west before the Red Army in 1945 demonstrated this quite amply. The plague could also move people rather smartly in the Middle Ages: a few bodies in the street, and whole cities would be temporarily abandoned. Earthquakes also make good people movers. But in all such cases—wars, pestilences, natural catastrophes—panics tend to be local affairs. It takes money, or rather the fear of the loss thereof, to panic people on a worldwide scale—as on this November day.

Lots of nervous money, lots of greed, lots of fear, no government interference. Together they meant that once again the necessary components for a great financial panic were present.

It just required somebody to really get it rolling. The Russians seemed predestined for this role, as the sun, having left Tokyo behind, brought a new day to Moscow.

The lot which boarded the Moscow subway on that morning was not much different than that one could meet at the crack of dawn in the Paris Métro or the London Underground. The scent of alcohol and soap joined forces, as the drunks and streetcleaners crossed paths.

Comrade Melekov, though undoubtedly an eager beaver, did not exactly fit into this early morning crowd. But there he was, Bally shoes, Pucci tie, Rolex watch, Cuban cigar, and all. It was not the first time that he had smoked a Cuban cigar at this hour. But that was when he was moving in the other direction, after a hard night out. Right now he was on the way to the office.

He was deep in thought, as he swayed back and forth with the movement of the train. Obviously that Ford dealer in Helsinki was a complete bust. After three telegrams and two telephone calls the new gas pump had finally arrived. It did not fit. Melekov did not intend to start commuting by subway. Nor was he going to revert back to one of those automotive marvels of Soviet advanced technology. The only answer was to switch makes. An Oldsmobile 98. That should be just about right. A Mercedes would be in bad political taste. A Cadillac would be going too far. He had heard from a number of fellows in the Foreign Ministry that the General Motors service in Finland was excellent. But what about the Thunderbird? A bit racey for most of the government people. Hockey players or football stars—that's obviously where the second hand market lay. They had the dollars, and had learned to appreciate such things. He decided to get immediately in touch with GM that very same day. Must get the brochures and start working on the extras. This time the stereo tape recorder had better work.

Shortly after seven Melekov emerged at the Bolshoi Theatre station and a few minutes later entered the Foreign Trade

Bank. The two porters just inside the seedy entrance barely looked up as he started to climb the stairs. That's one thing he would change. One of the most important banks in the world, and it didn't have an elevator. Even the stairs creaked.

It was going to be a full day. The contract signing formalities with the Germans had, of course, not taken place on schedule yesterday afternoon. But, as usual, it was not the Germans' fault. Some jackass in the Ministry of Technology had apparently insisted on some last-minute change. Melekov hoped that that had been settled and that the whole deal could be put to bed before the weekend.

Melekov unlocked his desk and took out his agenda. The weekly meeting of the management was scheduled for eight-fifteen. That would give him ample time to check all the closing positions from the night before.

His secretary, dressed as usual in brown and getting fatter every day, brought in his coffee and the bundles of tear-offs from the Teletype machine.

Melekov started reading. Fantastic! The summary of the coverage in the *Times* was especially good.

His phone rang.

"Melekov," he automatically answered.

"Good morning." It was the big boss himself. "About the management meeting this morning, it's been decided that we will move it over to the National Bank. The people there feel that a joint consultation on the situation is required between our two institutions. So nine o'clock on Radislovstreet, third-floor conference room—you know, the big one. See you there." Bang.

Aha, thought Melekov. The big play. Fine. The timing could not be better.

"Comrade Lofkin to see you. Will you receive him?" asked his secretary from just inside the door leading to her adjoining office.

"Sure. Send him right in," Melekov answered.

The young man appeared immediately.

"Lofkin, have a seat. Care for a cigar?"

"Don't mind if I do. Unbelievable, huh?" said the head of the bank's foreign exchange department.

"Absolutely fantastic. Have you got our closing positions from last night with you?"

Lofkin had. He moved his chair around closer to Melekov and explained the key numbers on the sheets he had brought along.

After a minute Melekov interrupted. "Look, why don't you just sum it up."

"All right. If I take the total position of the bank into account, we at the present time have a net short position on the U.S. dollar of $3.16 billion. I've tried to really spread it around. I would guess that Paris, Frankfurt, and Amsterdam took about the same amounts. We did the bigger volume over in Zurich, London, and New York, of course. Especially New York. Boy, we really dumped there."

"On what average basis?"

"Almost all of it is in the form of three months forward contracts. And the prices are damn good. I figure if we covered this morning, we would already be ahead a good $100 million. Not bad, is it?"

Melekov puffed away on his cigar. "May I keep these sheets for the time being?"

"Sure. What now?"

"Nothing. Just sit absolutely tight. We're having a management meeting over at the National Bank within less than an hour. I'll let you know right after that."

"If you don't mind, I'd like to get back to my office. Our fellows are absolutely buried in paper work after yesterday. I don't want there to be any foulups on the confirmations. Not the way we're sitting right now."

"Go ahead. Tell me one more thing, though. Do you think the dollar can hold through today?"

"Well, my opinion is that there's not a chance in hell. We should know around lunchtime. If the Western Europeans decide to really dump, that will be it."

"See you later."

Melekov returned to the position sheets after his assistant had left. No doubt Lofkin was right. Melekov knew that there were at least $40 billion in private hands in Western Europe. When one thought just of the immense number of Eurodollar bonds which had been sold to the European during the past ten years—probably $15 billion right there. The aftermarket for these bonds could not be thinner. Even in quiet times the sale of a block of a couple of million dollars of such bonds was a big deal. Dumping in that market would provide no solution. The only protection would be in the foreign exchange market. Sell dollars short against the box, as they said in New York. This could be unbelievable. Nobody would buy another dollar bond for the next ten years.

Melekov picked up the phone and called the head of the National Bank. "Roskin. Melekov here. What do you think?"

"By God, I think you've done it. I always knew you were a smart son of a bitch, but this is really something. You've heard about the meeting."

"Right. At your place," Melekov answered.

"Yes, but that's not what I mean. Both Litnovich and Slavic from the Central Committee will be there. I got a call very late last night asking me to make the arrangements. My friend, we've shaken them right to the top. How's our position look?"

"I just checked. We're just a bit over $3 billion short. At the closing quotes in New York we're already about $100 million ahead, Lofkin tells me. And we picked up 5 million ounces of gold at an average price of $78 an ounce in Zurich."

Roskin appeared to hardly know quite what to say. Then he proceeded. "Melekov, have you given some thought as to where we go from here?"

"Well, I think we have made an excellent beginning in the

markets. Now must come the massive followthrough. With all we've got. It must be quick and perfectly coordinated."

Roskin, who was a good solid banker of the old school, had known for years that he had never been in the same class as his younger colleague at the Bank for Foreign Trade. But he was cunning enough to know a good ally. A man with a future. So he had decided to establish a relationship over the head of Melekov's boss, or behind his back, depending upon the point of view. With Melekov as the brain, the chief theoretician, Roskin had no doubt that the two of them would end up jointly controlling the Soviet financial system. This coup would put the seal on it. When Melekov had approached him a couple of weeks ago with the plan, Roskin had at first been shocked. The daring of it, the risk involved—all went against his banker's grain. Because there was no precedent.

Russia had always been ultraconservative in the area of international monetary affairs. To be sure, this stood in great contrast to the country's aggressive use of its economic power in other ways. High Aswan dam, the Cuban sugar arrangements, the gas and oil contracts with Iran and especially Iraq, those loans to Indonesia, the support of Chile, and of Indira Gandhi in India. And most important of all, the silent war of attrition on the economic stability of the United States through the eternal prolongment of the Viet Nam conflict, a project that had been successful beyond belief. But it had taken a Melekov to realize that now was the time to take advantage of the weakened position of the United States through a spectacular attack on its soft underbelly—the international position of the dollar. Roskin had seen Melekov's point immediately, and when Melekov had demonstrated a completely atypical cocksureness on timing, he had decided to back the man. The results thus far had confirmed his confidence. But—

"Roskin, are you still there?" asked Melekov.

"Yes, I was just thinking," replied Roskin. Then he continued. "How do you propose to present all this at the meeting?"

179

Melekov answered: "The key is that the world must witness the annihilation of the dollar. Not an orderly retreat, not a negotiated adjustment, but a total route. This must be seen as the inevitable result of the policy of American dollar imperialism—the revolt of its captives all around the world. The next step must be to propose a replacement immediately, a non-imperialistic instrument of commerce. Yet one which can gain immediate international trust. My proposal is a gold-based ruble. As simple as that. Initially, we will have to control its use down to the last gold kopeck. Expand the ruble area slowly, so that we don't run into the same kinds of problems that first the British with their sterling zone, and then the French with the franc zone, and finally the Americans with their global dollar inevitably faced. We don't want to be the bankers for the world, Roskin. Only for a good part of it. But we cannot fail. As surely as the dollar replaced sterling in country after country in the world after World War II, the gold ruble can start displacing the dollar. There's an old saying about a banker's biggest capital being the trust people put in him. The United States was, until this week, the supreme banker of the world. This can now be changed."

Roskin listened most carefully to all this. And he again could not help but agree. He said. "Tell me, Melekov, do you propose to put these ideas on the table right at the outset of the meeting this morning?"

Melekov replied, "Of course. When you say *a*, you must also say *b*. We must now attack. With all the economic weapons at our disposal. And for all the world to witness!"

"Stepanov and his friends in the Central Committee might not buy it, you know."

"We'll see. Roskin, I've got to clean up just a few things here. See you in about fifteen minutes."

Melekov carefully gathered his documentation in preparation for the meeting and, after packing his briefcase, leaned back to finish his cup of coffee. After telling his secretary to expect him back around noon, he descended the stairs.

The porter at the exit indicated that a car was waiting for him. Melekov had not ordered one but stepped in anyway. It was too late to search for a taxi.

The National Bank of the Soviet Union was housed in a much more impressive structure than its sister institution. After all, this was the home of the ruble. Marble stairways. And even an elevator. Melekov did not bother to announce himself to the inevitable crew of watchdogs at the entrance. They knew him. He took the elevator to the third floor and strode down the corridor to the very large conference room at the end. He had expected many of the executives from both of the banks to be there but found that the only man awaiting him was his friend Roskin.

"Am I too early or something?" he immediately asked.

"No," replied Roskin. "It's scheduled for nine. Maybe I should take a look where everybody's hiding."

But as he entered the corridor, it was only to see a group of men heading in his direction.

"Here they come."

To be more exact, three men entered the conference room. Ivan Litnovich, the man who had moved into the Central Committee only a few years ago and who had almost immediately pulled all the strings of the Soviet financial world right into his own lap. If the Soviet Union had ever had a financial czar, it was Litnovich. He was followed by Slavic, one of the oldest hacks on the committee. He had survived three leadership changes in the Kremlin and was known for his cunning and primitiveness. And finally, Melekov's boss—Stepanov, a Soviet functionary of the standard type. All three really had only one thing in common, thought Melekov fleetingly as they entered the room: All were Georgians.

Litnovich immediately took the chair at the head of the table and indicated to Stepanov that he should close the door. There was a peculiar absence of the usual handshakes.

Litnovich spoke.

"Comrades, let's get right down to the business at hand."

Roskin immediately interrupted.

"Don't you think we should wait for the others to arrive?"

"No," replied the man from the Central Committee. "They have been advised to stay at their desks. For the time being, we have everybody here that is necessary."

Roskin glanced very briefly at Melekov.

"Comrade Melekov, the chairman of the Foreign Trade Bank of the Soviet Union has informed us in the Central Committee that you have wildly embarked on a radically new program, without his knowledge and approval. That you have exceeded your competence limits in a completely unprecedented fashion and have endangered the international financial position of the Soviet Union. I expect an explanation."

Melekov was shocked to the core. Roskin had assured him that his back had been covered. Perhaps it had been done at the very top. After all, in spite of his meteoric rise, Litnovich was still Number Four in the country at best.

"I do not really understand this accusation," said Melekov in a strong voice, perhaps a trifle too strong. The echo in this huge almost empty room was resounding. "My job is to oversee the entire foreign exchange operations of the Foreign Trade Bank of the Soviet Union. With this authority comes enormous responsibility for the welfare of our country. I have been trying to meet this responsibility to the best of my ability—and as you will see, quite successfully."

He reached for his briefcase and started to extract the various documentation he had so carefully prepared.

"I disagree," interjected Litnovich harshly. "My colleague Slavic disagrees, and your chairman, Stepanov, disagrees."

"Gentlemen," said Melekov, "you cannot disagree with irrefutable facts. I have the facts here." He waved the position sheets he had received less than an hour ago from the foreign exchange desk.

"We are as well informed on your facts as you are, Melekov.

Thanks to Chairman Stepanov. If he had not had the acute sense of responsibility which he fortunately has, and if he had not the courage to come directly to us after he had discovered your 'facts,' I am afraid that the leaders of this country would have not even received a hint of what has been going on in the Foreign Trade Bank of the Soviet Union during the past few days. Have you gone absolutely mad, Melekov? Are you trying to run a gambling casino? Or are you trying to totally undermine the image of the Soviet Union, an image it has taken us fifty years to build? We are today regarded as the most reliable trade partner in the world. Why do you think that we have literally unlimited credit everywhere? Why is a contract with the Soviet Union regarded as the most eminently bankable piece of paper there is? I'll tell you why. Because we are serious financial people. Because we always keep our word, regardless of unforeseen circumstances. Because we pay exactly on time, always. Because we do not try to hedge or cheat. Because we are a socialist country and not a pack of speculative capitalistic wolves. That's why."

Melekov was now angry.

"Now just a minute. It's very easy to throw around words like 'speculation,' 'capitalistic wolves,' and the like. But let's see whether the glove fits or not. The truth is much different. We have based our entire foreign trade with the West on the U.S. dollar. The U.S. dollar is not safe. It is going to be devalued. It would be total insanity not to recognize this. It would be greater insanity not to protect the Soviet Union from the consequences of this. And it would be folly not to seek to take advantage of this. Even my chairman should be able to follow that simple logic."

"So, so. The dollar is going to be devalued. Just like that," said Litnovich.

"Of course," answered Melekov. "Don't you realize what has been happening during the past twenty-four hours? Didn't my chairman tell you about the run out of the dollar and into gold

183

in Europe, the start of a panic in New York, the resulting chaos in Tokyo? These are quite visible symptoms of what is going to have to happen. I am not just guessing, I—"

"That's enough, Melekov," shouted Litnovich. "Just one hour ago I received a complete intelligence report on the entire situation. I know all the facts, and perhaps more than a few that you do not know. This is a trap. You hear? A trap. All the Americans were doing was looking for an excuse to cut off those wheat shipments. Which they now have done. Do you know what that can mean for our people? And for this government? The Americans know. And that's why they're cutting us off. And you've provided them with a perfect excuse. Because you fell right into their primitive trap."

"But surely you must realize that they're using this wheat thing as a bluff. Don't you understand that it is you, not I, who is falling into a trap, stupidly missing the opportunity of a lifetime. Surely—"

"Melekov! Shut up!" yelled Litnovich, "I'll do the talking from now on. And the deciding. I hope this is quite clear. I want no further interruptions. None." He pounded his fist on the conference table to emphasize the last point.

"Now you listen to me. They started this thing, quietly, subtly. With the help of their friends, of course. And you jumped on this fake bandwagon just like a greedy wild-eyed greasy speculator right out of the textbook. I know how smart you young fellows are. I know all the fancy tricks you learn in London and Zurich. Well, we don't want any part of such stuff. As a result of your megalomania, the world now thinks that *we* started this; that *we* are trying foolishly to hit the Americans right where their greatest strength lies—smack in the middle of their dollar. And when it doesn't come off? Who stands as the idiot in the eyes of the world? We will. We, the Soviet Union. And the Soviet people, who will have to stand in bread lines for the first time in twenty-five years. All because of *you*, you stupid son of a bitch. Can't you remember

184

a small incident not that many years ago on a little island in the Caribbean called Cuba? It set us back God knows how many years. Just because another maniac thought he could outbluff the Americans with his rockets. And now you, of all people, little unknown jerk Melekov, have decided to confront the world with your super-weapon, the ruble. Absolute total insanity!"

At this point Melekov made up his mind. Fine. O.K. Your funeral.

Litnovich continued, but now in a very soft voice, barely audible to Melekov who was sitting no more than five metres away. "You, Melekov, are suspended from your position at the Foreign Trade Bank of the Soviet Union. As of right now. You may leave. A car is waiting for you downstairs. You will return to your apartment, and you will remain there."

Without a word, without a glance at his "friend" Roskin, but on unsteady legs, Melekov rose and started to repack his papers.

"The papers and briefcase remain here, Melekov."

Melekov left the room.

"Now, Comrade Roskin. What has your role been in this whole scandal?" Roskin had had time to think a bit ahead. His reply was deliberate, measured—correctly measured, he hoped.

"Comrade Litnovich, I would be the last to deny that Melekov has talked to me about this matter. I can also not deny that his logic concerning the growing inherent risks which we are running in the dollar was quite convincing. Therefore I decided to take certain defensive measures. I suspended a major sale of gold last week. I agreed that it made sense to put the German pipe purchase onto a dollar basis, in the hope that we could pay for the deliveries in devalued dollars. That's it."

"But didn't you realize that Melekov was selling dollars like a maniac on the foreign exchange markets in every major Western city during the past forty hours? Didn't you know that he has built up a short position in dollars exceeding—imagine!—$3 billion? Don't you know he just bought 5 million ounces of gold for over $300 million?"

"Of course not. This is quite outside of the range of our normal discussions. We confer with each other on matters of principle, not those of operation."

Litnovich fixed Roskin in a deliberate stare. Roskin returned it quite calmly and without the twitch of an eyelash. To survive as the head of the National Bank for so long had required strong nerves more than once.

Finally Litnovich resumed. "We'll have further talks on this subject, Comrade Roskin. Right now, we have more important things to accomplish. But get this—and get it quite clearly. We want this thing stopped absolutely dead and right now. We want these stories of the Soviet Union trying to destroy the dollar in an open fight to be squelched, completely and immediately. And I want this nonsense with gold to stop—right now. By you, personally."

Five minutes later the meeting had ended. It was only ninethirty Moscow time.

The chairman of the National Bank was the first to be back at his desk. He only had to walk a few steps down the corridors from the conference room to get there. He picked up the phone, and placed an emergency call to Basel, Switzerland, for eleven-thirty. That should catch the gold people of the BIS right after they got to work. That done, he made a very careful set of notes based upon his recall of the conference which had just ended. He sought total recall. Every word would be important at some later date. Especially the exact words which Melekov had spoken.

Ten minutes later Chairman Stepanov of the Foreign Trade Bank of the Soviet Union had also returned to his office. The first thing he did was also pick up the phone.

"Get me the head of that German delegation on the pipeline deal."

His secretary replied, "Yes, sir. What's the name, and where is he?"

"Dammit, how should I know? Just get him, and now."

Obviously the place needed a bit more discipline. He'd given that man Melekov far too much authority and freedom in the place. With the best of intentions, all the good will in the world. And look what happened. He, Stepanov, would now have to pick up the pieces. That goddamned liar over at the National Bank, Roskin, had better be bloody careful, too. His position was hanging on a thread. Just one more incident and—bang! Litnovich would see to that!

The phone rang.

"I have Herr Klausen of Rhein-Ruhr Stahl," said his secretary. "Hold on, I'll connect you immediately."

The phone clicked a few times as phones always do in the Soviet Union.

"Klausen," suddenly came roaring out of the receiver.

"My dear Herr Klausen, this is Chairman Stepanov of the Foreign Trade Bank."

"Who?"

"Stepanov. Foreign Trade Bank of the Soviet Union."

"I'm afraid I have never met you. I've always dealt with Melekov."

"That's right, Herr Klausen. Unfortunately Mr. Melekov is out today, and therefore I have taken over some of his tasks. I'm his chairman."

"Fine, but Mr. Stepanov, let me tell you something. I am not at all sure that there is any task left to talk about. I had been assured that the signing of our agreement was firmly scheduled for five yesterday afternoon. At four-thirty I get a most peculiar telephone call from the Ministry of Technology that it had to be postponed. Technical difficulties was the explanation. I know damn well that we mutually agreed on every single technical detail weeks ago. Now, I suppose there are also new financial difficulties?"

"But Herr Klausen—"

"Excuse me, but I would like to finish. I have been sitting here in Moscow for almost two weeks waiting to sign an agreement, the contents of which we had all agreed upon a long time ago. I was told that the last change was the switch from German marks to dollars as the unit of account. Fine. We agreed to the change in less than twenty-four hours, even though it was not at all easy. Now comes something new. Mr. Stepanov, I intend to fly back to Düsseldorf this weekend, with or without a signed contract. Now, you were saying?"

Stepanov was not exactly accustomed to being addressed in this fashion, but as one victim of that crazy Melekov to another, he could certainly sympathize with the German in his anger.

"That's just it, Herr Klausen. I'm afraid that there has been a terrible misunderstanding in our bank. All our fault, and none of yours, of course. I fully sympathize with your feelings at this moment. Perhaps we could meet any time it might be convenient for you, perhaps at your hotel?"

"Not necessary. I'm sure we can come to the heart of the matter right here and now on the telephone. Just two questions. Who is finally authorized to approve this contract, or not approve it as the case may be? When will I get a straight answer, yes or no, from him?"

Klausen had been through the Eastern European game of musical chairs at the conference table more than once before. The other side always started with the third or fourth team and slowly worked their way up the ranks until the big boss himself finally appeared. But this was ridiculous.

"I can answer both questions. I have been authorized by Comrade Litnovich, who as you know is a member of our Central Committee, to inform you that he will personally appear for the final signing at five this afternoon. He has, however, requested that I seek your approval to just one change."

"That is?"

"That we go back to the original financial arrangements, as foreseen before my colleague Melekov asked you to change them."

188

"You mean, you want to put the whole thing back on a German mark basis, with exactly the original terms and conditions?" asked Klausen incredulously.

"Precisely."

"Done."

"Fine. If you agree I will personally pick you up at your hotel at four, shall we say, and then we can proceed directly to the Ministry of Finance in the Kremlin for the formal proceedings."

"Agreed."

"Until then, my dear Herr Klausen."

After he had hung up, Stepanov immediately buzzed for his secretary.

"Get Lofkin to my office. Right now."

There was another case: Lofkin. He knew all along what Melekov had been up to. As head of the foreign exchange desk, he had to execute every single sell order. But not even a peep to the man who was chairman of the bank.

"You asked for me, Comrade Stepanov?"

"Yes. I asked for you. Don't bother to sit down. It won't take long," said Stepanov. "You recognize these sheets?" He held up, between finger and thumb, the foreign exchange position sheets which Lotkin had delivered to Melekov not much longer than an hour ago.

"Yes, sir. These are our—"

"My friend Lofkin, I know quite well what they are. I'll now tell you. They are the results of the work of two raving maniacs—Melekov and you, you insolent little bastard."

He proceeded very slowly and deliberately.

"Now, do you know what we are going to do? Well I'll tell you. We are going to buy enough dollars in the forward market to cover every open short position you have. And then some. Do you hear! And we are going to start buying this morning. And we're going to start in Zurich. They're three hours behind us. This means they open for business in about one and a half hours. I want you to be in there right at the opening. And we are going to finish the job before you go to sleep again. Do you also hear that? I want a progress report every thirty minutes. By you. In person. In writing. Now get out of here."

Lofkin got out of there.

The first thing he tried to do when he got back to his office was to get hold of Melekov. He was informed that Melekov would not be back in the bank for the rest of the day. Then Lofkin got his staff together and gave them instructions. That done, he felt sick to his stomach. He reached into the bottom drawer of his desk, got out a bottle of kirschwasser—a gift from Melekov after his recent trip to London and Zurich—and took a large slug.

15

In Switzerland it was still a bit early for kirschwasser—even in the Alps it would have been unheard of at seven in the morning. But at least two people there thought they could have used a drop on this morning of November 6—Dr. Bernoulli because he was as frustrated as he had ever been in his life and Dr. Walter Hofer because he was as worried as he had ever been.

Bernoulli's frustration was understandable. He had gone through his whole story with the Swiss minister of finance the previous evening. He had been positive that something was not making sense. After leaving the office of the Bank of International Settlements in late afternoon, he simply could not accept the story about the Russians. Because it was too pat; too much of a sinister international plot to be true.

"Hell, things just don't happen that way," he had told the minister. Then he had given the details about Mr. Stanley Rosen. The facts were clear. First, Rosen was in the Three Kings Hotel the entire time both before and after the theft of the red dossier from Bollinger's safe. Second, Rosen was actually seen in company with the man who had organized this theft, ex-policeman Lutz, head of the Swiss Security Consultants A.G. They had staggered their way through almost every known bar within twenty kilometres of Basel—in Switzerland, France, and Germany—finally to bring back two prostitutes who were refused entry to the Three Kings. Third, the reports which the minister had received from New York confirmed beyond any doubt that Rosen was connected with the Mafia—and with the top people in that organization.

And then there was our fine Herr Dr. Hofer, chairman of

the board of the General Bank of Switzerland. He was the only man to have seen the secretary of the treasury of the United States and the secretary-general of the BIS together in London. He was not exactly a fool. He could add two and two faster than anyone in Zurich. He probably also knew the work habits of Bollinger: The fact that, as a bachelor, he spent almost every weekend working and always took an enormous briefcase of papers with him to his house. And then back to the Swiss Security Consultants A.G. Who was their most important customer? The General Bank of Switzerland. Bernoulli did not for one split second doubt that a member of the Swiss banking community was capable of organizing such a project.

But the minister was not interested in such theories. The behaviour of the Russians was no longer in the realm of theory; it was a fact, a confirmed fact.

It had been difficult for Bernoulli to argue with this logic. The Russians had an obvious motive. They had had the opportunity to organize the theft in Basel. And they were following through consistently and brutally.

But then should they not pick up the head of Swiss Security Consultants, Rolf Lutz? Under sufficient pressure, surely he would confirm what had truly happened and settle the matter once and for all. The minister of finance said no. "If it is the Russians, we simply do not want to know." Fair enough. Lutz was taboo because the Russians were taboo. But for Bernoulli that still had not been the end of it. During the long night after this conference, the problem had kept turning over and over in his mind. He could not dismiss Rosen and Hofer with such ease. In fact, the more he thought of Hofer, the more suspicious he got. If the Russian thing was too pat, maybe the Mafia thing was equally so.

Bernoulli had the advantage of coming from a banking family. They had come to Switzerland as Huguenot immigrants in the seventeenth century. Their French love of money plus Calvinism had soon produced family prosperity in their new homeland, and prosperity had led to the foundation of a private bank, a family bank, in 1796. His father was the ninth Bernoulli to head the institution. Now, as then, the only sign identifying the premises was a gold plate—24-karat gold— about the size of a calling card, mounted discreetly to the left of the massive oaken door leading into the building. It was marked with nothing more than an engraved B. To be sure, the letter was capitalized.

His father had been anything but pleased when George had chosen government work, instead of staying within the family fold. But he had never openly criticized George for his choice. There had remained no doubt in his mind that the blood which flowed in his son's veins would only endure so much humanitarianism, or whatever it was that George was trying to accomplish over in Geneva and Bern. The true calling of practicing benevolent capitalism would inevitably take hold in time.

But George knew all about this kind of benevolence. He had, after all, heard it over the dinner table year after year as a boy. That's why George Bernoulli went into government work. And that's also why he watched all bankers with a totally jaundiced eye, including the good Doktor Hofer. More than once he had met Hofer at his parents' home. How anybody could be five feet five and still look down on the entire rest of the world was beyond George. But Hofer managed it. And George's father put up with it, because Hofer was, even then, at the top of the heap in Swiss banking circles. Big profits, always bigger than everybody else's in the business. Never a setback. Uncanny, in fact, thought Bernoulli, impossible.

For there were some things that just could not find a logical explanation. For instance, metals. The General Bank of Switzerland had always specialized in precious metals. Unlike American or British banks, Swiss banks could be all financial things to all men. They were not only commercial banks, but also underwriters, stockbrokers, commodity dealers—the list was almost endless. They were the ultimate financial supermarkets. But even the big ones had their specialities. In the case of the General Bank, it had been gold, silver, platinum, palladium.

The 1960s, especially the latter part, had been great years for precious metals. During the entire period the General Bank was bullish and invested both their clients and themselves heavily. It was said that Hofer was behind this, and Hofer was never wrong. Sure enough, by 1968 all four metals reached record highs. The General Bank continued to be bullish and continued to buy, in spite of the temporary lull that followed. But, as time proved, there was nothing temporary about it. Month after month, year after year, prices of precious metals slid down. Silver went from $2.80 an ounce to $1.50. Platinum fell from $450 to $95. Palladium collapsed completely. Only gold held. Rumour had it that in the early 1970s Hofer's bank had been forced to sell. Their continual attempts to prop up all four markets almost singlehandedly had simply eaten up too much of their liquidity. The losses must have been monumental. But what happened to them? Not a word in the annual reports. Not a clue in the balance sheets. In fact, profits kept rising consistently, year after year, at the rate of 20 percent.

Then there were those loans to Chile, Egypt, Algeria, Pakistan, Rhodesia. Together they must have involved at least $250 million. Big publicity when they were announced. But since then, not a word. Their repayment was quite obviously impossible. Their amortization could not be avoided.

Yes, there could be no doubt that a big, big killing in the gold and foreign exchange markets would come in mighty handy for Dr. Walter Hofer.

But what about this fellow Stanley Rosen? There could be absolutely no doubt that he was managing the biggest pool of illegal money ever to be packaged in the history of the United States. He was big! But he was apparently also extremely successful. This was very well known to the American authorities. Bernoulli knew; they had sent him a dossier on Rosen that was almost 200 pages long. A summary. Rosen had been investigated at least twelve times during the past five years. Almost every federal and state agency that could possibly find an excuse had already been through his shop. But there was nothing to find. Rosen did only one thing. He served as an investment advisor, on a fee basis, to some twenty-five or thirty offshore investment companies. All quite legal and completely in line with the regulations laid down in the 1940 investment act. His partner, Harry Stahl, ran a small brokerage company, with seats on both the New York and American exchanges, and recently also on the Pacific Coast exchange. He would accept brokerage business from the general public only when they almost forced their way through the door. That sort of stuff was just a nuisance. He was strictly interested in one client only—Stanley Rosen.

The whole system stood or fell with one link in the chain: the movement of the funds out of the United States. For once they were out, that was it. They disappeared into anonymous corporations in the Caribbean or other weird little countries spotted around the world, places to which the United States authorities had no access.

In the early days of Rosen's game, it had been simple. Anybody could walk into any commercial bank in the country, make a transfer to a foreign bank, and the money was gone forever, without a trace. Year after year, billions of dollars had been leaving the United States completely unnoticed. They finally appeared, laconically listed under "Errors and Omissions" in the balance-of-payments statistics of the Department of Commerce. The country which was the ultimate beneficiary of most of such "Errors" was, peculiarly enough, Switzerland. Uncle Sam played into the hands of people like Rosen and his friends for years before catching on. Then things changed. First, the banks had to start reporting all major transfers out of the country. Then the Internal Revenue Service required a listing of all foreign bank accounts as part of the regular income tax return. Finally, in July, 1972, anyone carrying more than $5,000 in cash with him out of the United States had to report it in detail. Suddenly the risks for international financial engineers like Stanley Rosen had become immeasurably greater. That, thought Bernoulli, may be the explanation for Rosen's Beirut connection. He wants to get some reinsurance in the form of non-American clients. And he must prove himself over here. Make a spectacular showing. Then the clients from the Near East, from Europe, would flock to him, just as the Americans had during the past decade. But in the future, as in the past, it would no doubt be shady money. And in the future, as before, fellows like Rosen would need the secrecy cover of Swiss banks to do their thing. Here was where they were a menace to Switzerland. Their blatant abuse of the facilities offered by Swiss banks could undermine the entire system, a system upon which Swiss prosperity had been built. If it turned out that Stanley Rosen had organized the theft of the gold-dollar plan of the United States government, and if it was discovered that his criminal machinations had been carried out through numbered accounts in Zurich, the Swiss banking system would be dealt a mortal blow. For Bernoulli also knew America. They would not stand for any more of *that* kind of crap.

Bernoulli decided that it would definitely not help anybody if he stayed in bed any longer. There was one way in which he might be able to cut right through the dilemma facing him: by employment of the most honoured of European police tactics—the confrontation.

First, he would have to tackle Walter Hofer. Then Stanley Rosen. And finally, confront both of them, separately of course, with Rolf Lutz of Swiss Security Consultants. He would get to the bottom of this yet.

Dr. Walter Hofer had also not gotten up immediately after waking on that Thursday morning. For he also had things to think about. His was a position where real difficulties, not to speak of downright public failure, were unthinkable. They had to stay unthinkable. Unfortunately, in recent years the possibility could no longer be dismissed as totally absurd. The men at the top of Rolls Royce had found this out. So had those of Penn Central. Hofer had known men from both companies. They had his sympathy. But his own position was even more difficult. He was a banker. And one thing bankers never do is make a mistake and admit it. They always find a way out. So must he. Well, he thought, I'll know a lot more in just a few hours.

"Walter," came his wife's voice from downstairs. "Will you be ready soon?"

"Yes, Martha. I'll be down in five minutes. Please go ahead. I'll join you right away."

As usual he took an almost cold shower and also as usual donned a dark blue suit. Except for vacations and formal affairs, Dr. Hofer inevitably wore a blue suit. He had twenty-one in his closet. He also wore blue socks, black shoes, and tended toward dark shades of red in his ties. His wife always picked his suits out for him before he rose in the morning. Also his ties. In fact, she also bought them all. The ties, that is. The suits came at the rate of two every month. His tailor brought them up to the house for the last fittings. Martha supervised that part of it. The results were always good.

Within ten minutes Hofer was at the breakfast table.

"Aren't you going to drink some orange juice this morning?" his wife asked.

"No, just coffee and a sweet roll, Martha."

"You do feel all right, don't you Walter?"

"Of course. Just didn't sleep too well last night. Probably the *Föhn*. Anyway, its getting near the end of the week. Maybe both of us could just take it easy this weekend. Stay at home and relax. What do you say?" Hofer drank his coffee black. During the past ten years he had not gained a pound. His tailor had told him more than once that he had never seen a man who held his figure so constant for so long.

"Oh yes, Walter. That would be nice for a change. But there is one thing. You must give that talk on Sunday evening in

Altdorf to the Ecumenical Society. But I know you always enjoy those meetings. So I'm sure it won't take much preparation."

"I'd forgotten about that. You're right, though. I should be able to draft that out on Sunday morning. Tell me, do they expect a good crowd?"

"I'm sure so. You know how curious people are about you. Many cannot understand how you find time for church affairs with all the other things you must attend to. Probably some are jealous and come in the hope of seeing you make a fool of yourself."

"Now Martha. But I must be going. Is Heinrich waiting?"

"Yes, he pulled into the driveway just before you came down."

"Fine. I must go. I'll see you around six."

Walter Hofer gave his wife the usual peck on the cheek and, with a final wave of the hand, disappeared into the back seat of the bank limousine.

The early morning traffic up the right bank of the Lake of Zurich was extremely heavy and the road narrow.

"And how are you this morning, Heinrich?" Hofer asked his chauffeur.

"Couldn't be better, sir. Won exactly 526 francs in the football pool yesterday. Hit ten out of twelve correctly. The wife and I went out last night for dinner to celebrate. First time we've done that during the week for years. You ever try the pools, sir?"

"No, I'm afraid not, Heinrich. I wouldn't even know how to fill out one of those coupons," said Hofer, laughing. "Anyway, just imagine if I hit the jackpot and it got all over the papers. That wouldn't do at all."

"No, you're right, sir."

"Quite a bit of fog, this morning. When do you expect to get to the bank?"

"It'll thin out as usual within a kilometre or two. We'll be there in about fifteen minutes."

In exactly fourteen minutes they passed the front of the massive entrance to the General Bank of Switzerland and, after rounding the corner, disappeared into the huge underground parking facility.

"Will you be needing me this morning?" asked the chauffeur as Hofer stepped out.

"No. I'll see you down here around five-thirty this afternoon. And don't worry about the weekend, Heinrich. I will be staying at home, so feel free to work out anything you might have in mind with the family."

"Thank you, sir, I'll do that. I think I'll take the boy to the football game on Sunday. Quarter finals in the European Cup, you know."

But Dr. Hofer had already turned his mind to other things as he walked to the elevators.

"*Guten Tag*, Herr Doktor."
"*Guten Tag*, Herr Doktor."

The morning ritual. Hofer merely tipped his hat to his people.

"*Guten Tag*, Herr Doktor." This time it was Kellermann.

"Herr Kellermann. Say, would you perhaps join me for a moment in the elevator."

When the next elevator arrived, the growing group of incoming executives waited respectfully as Hofer waved Kellermann into the lift. No one else joined them. It was an unwritten rule of the bank that Dr. Walter Hofer always went first class, in splendid isolation.

Both men stepped out on the fourth floor.

"Tell me, Kellermann, what's developed on the fellow from New York?"

"I expect we'll have a full report waiting for us on the Telex. But I'm afraid that the news will not be good. Late yesterday afternoon I received a call from the Basel police, asking about Rosen."

"What did they want to know?"

"The usual questions about his relationship with us. A kommissar named Bucher. He was quite firm about it. Said that if necessary he would get a court order. I felt that there would be no sense in going through that, so I did confirm that he was a client of ours and did an extremely large volume of business with us."

"Did they want details?"

"No. But I'm positive that we have not heard the end of it by any means."

"Is it really any worry of ours? After all, we did put a stop to him by asking for that additional $50 million margin."

"Not exactly. The margin arrived first thing this morning."

"And what did you do?"

"Well, what could I do? We made our conditions and he met them. We have been proceeding on his instructions."

"Sometimes, Kellermann—" Hofer decided not to finish his thoughts aloud. Instead he turned abruptly without any further word and moved down the corridor to his office. It was seven forty-five central European time.

His secretary appeared the minute he reached his desk.

"Dr. Hofer, there are dozens of people who have already been trying to reach you this morning. At least half of them from the press. What should we do?"

"The usual. Tell them I'm not available. You know whom to put through if it's absolutely necessary."

"The *Times* man has been especially insistent. They have always been quite decent toward us, you know. He's on the line right now, again."

"All right, put him through. But that's all. No other press for the rest of the day."

Almost as soon as he had settled behind his desk. the phone rang. He lifted the receiver carefully, as he always did.

"Hofer speaking."

"Dr. Hofer, this is Fred Hastings from the *Times*. I guess you know why I'm calling."

"I've a fairly good idea, yes."

"Well, I know that you hardly want to make any statement under the circumstances, but I would very much appreciate your thoughts on what might happen today. There are very strong rumours that you people are going to suspend foreign exchange trading this morning. Is that correct?"

"No, sir. That is incorrect. Frankly, I think you are talking to the wrong bank in the wrong country. The current problem is a dollar problem, not one of the Swiss franc. The issue is one facing the United States, not Switzerland. If trading is suspended, it will have to be the New York fellows who do it. We are open for business. All day."

"Is it true that you people, along with those in Eastern Europe, have been as responsible as anyone for this sudden run against the dollar?"

"Hastings, you ought to know better than to ask a thing like that. Every time a currency gets into trouble, we in Zurich get accused by every boulevard paper on earth. You at the *Times* know that is simply preposterous. We are a very small fish in a huge pond. My position on the dollar is quite well known. I have said for years that it must be made convertible into gold. But I have always stated that this must be done in an orderly fashion, in cooperation with all the major countries in the world. These waves of speculation help no one."

"But it is true that you would stand to make huge profits, on gold, for example, if such a decision were taken?"

"That is also not true. We maintain a stock of gold, just like our partner banks, because we make a market in gold. It's quite logical that you can't make a market in anything if you don't have something on the shelf. But we have our risk in both directions as a result—as you yourself have pointed out in more than one article, Mr. Hastings."

The *Times* man knew better than to press too much on this subject.

"Well, let me ask something else. If I walked into your bank right now and asked you to short a million dollars for me, would you do it?"

"It would depend upon the reason. We are not here to promote speculation. If you could show us a good commercial reason, or could demonstrate that you needed to hedge your private holdings, and if you were a client of our bank of long and good standing, we certainly would try to do our best for you. So would any other bank in the world. Whether we would advise you to do it at this time is another thing. The statement out of Washington yesterday was quite clear. If you short the dollar right now, it could turn out to be a very expensive bit of insurance, you know."

"I deduct that you are quite sceptical concerning a dollar devaluation at this time?" asked the *Times* man.

"I am always sceptical about any devaluation rumours. Especially where the dollar is concerned."

"May I quote you on that, Dr. Hofer?"

"You may. Now, Mr. Hastings, I'm afraid that I must go."

"I understand. Thank you very much, sir. I appreciate your talking to me."

As he hung up, Dr. Hofer's secretary again entered the room.

"There's one thing which I feel I should bring to your attention," he said." A certain Dr. George Bernoulli called very early this morning and left a message. He would like to see you, very urgently, on a private matter this morning. He suggested that he would be here shortly after nine and would appreciate it if you could receive him for just a few minutes."

"That must be the young Bernoulli boy. All right, I think I can fit it in. Just send him right in when he arrives. I'll be spending the next half hour or so getting up to date from the market reports stacked on my desk. Remember that at ten I expect the people from South Africa. After that I don't want to be disturbed by anyone. Lunch should be sent into my office for all of us. And there must be absolutely no mention of this conference and the people involved to anyone in the bank. The only executive who will be involved is Kellermann. He will be here shortly before ten. Just have him come right in also."

He turned his attention back to his desk.

Three stories down, in the foreign exchange department, the phones had just begun to light up. At eight forty-five twenty traders went into action simultaneously. The Deutsche Bank in Frankfurt was offering $25 million spot. The General Bank agreed to take them at the rate of 3.3015, the absolute floor price for the dollar, a level that had never been reached before. The Deutsche Bank accepted. The Crédit Lyonaise in Paris offered $50 million. They did not like the price. They would come back in ten or fifteen minutes. The Banque de Bruxelles wanted to sell $35 million three months forward. The trader consulted Zimmerer. They decided to put a 5 percent discount on the forward dollar: they offered Brussels the corresponding rate of 3.136. They did not even hesitate but accepted immediately. Two minutes later the Banca Nazionale de Lavoro was offered the same rate on $40 million. They also accepted. The traders huddled with Zimmerer. They decided to drop the three months forward rate another full percent. Then came the break.

"Zimmerer, come quick. It's the Foreign Trade Bank, Moscow. They want to buy—buy!—$100 million spot and another $100 million three months forward. What should I do?"

"Gimme the call."

He argued for a full five minutes before settling on a rate. He looked completely puzzled as he hung up the phone.

"Zimmerer, it's Budapest. They want to buy $50 million spot. But they want a better rate."

"Offer them 3.31."

A pause.

"They want 3.3050."

"Done."

"For Christ's sake," came a scream from across the room.

"It's the goddamned Deutsche Bank in Frankfurt again. Now they want to *buy* $50 million. I offered them 3.33 and they took it. What the bejesus is going on?"

During the next fifteen minutes the dollar rose steadily in strength, minute after minute. After starting at 3.3015 on the first trade, by a few minutes after nine it was up to 3.3645. At five minutes after nine a girl brought Zimmerer a flash from the Telex. He stopped all trading to read it to the room. UPI reported that the German-Russian pipeline deal was to be signed and that the Russians agreed to switch from dollars to German marks as the basis for payment. Within the next five minutes the dollar was up to 3.38. It had become obvious that all the professionals in the business were covering their short positions; the only sellers of dollars left in the market were the suckers, still way behind on news, still believing that the events of the previous day would continue. Zimmerer was in a bind. The General Bank was $2 billion short. During the past twenty minutes, the book value of this position had gone down in value by a full 90 million Swiss francs. He picked up the phone and asked for Dr. Hofer. He accepted the call immediately.

"Zimmerer here. Look, Dr. Hofer, I think it would be good if you came down here. The market has completely reversed itself. The dollar is up to 3.38 and gaining. We're down a good 90 million francs on our position and it's getting worse every minute. I think we should cover before we have a real catastrophe."

He listened for ten seconds, and hung up.

"I sure hope he knows what he's doing," Zimmerer muttered, and then stood up to put on his jacket. He had to prepare for the gold fixing at ten. That was forty-five minutes off.

At nine-fifteen on the dot Dr. George Bernoulli entered the immense office of Walter Hofer. Hofer rose to greet him. Bernoulli was a full eight inches taller than Hofer, who had to look well up to meet the younger man's eyes. Which he did, for Hofer was known as an eye-to-eye man.

"George. I do hope you don't mind me calling you that. But I've used your first name since you were a rather small boy. How is your father?" Hofer led Bernoulli over to a chair and offered him a cigar.

"No thanks, Dr. Hofer. Father is, as far as I know, quite fine. Actually, I haven't been home for a number of months now. But at least I can say that I've heard no bad reports."

"How is your work coming along in Bern, anyway? I've heard that you are moving right up the ladder."

"I'm quite satisfied. Would you mind, sir, if perhaps we got right down to the reason for my call. Actually, it concerns the government, but if you agree, I think we should be able to keep it on a quite unofficial level. I realize this may seem a bit unorthodox to you, but I think you are quite accustomed to a touch of that from our family."

Hofer chuckled. He had heard about George Bernoulli's cockiness from more than one side and had in fact witnessed it on one occasion in the house of his parents more than a few years ago.

"You just go right ahead, George. What's the problem?"

"Quite simple. What do you know about a man called Stanley Rosen?"

"He's a client of our bank. Has been for years over at the branch in Basel. Works with large sums of money for investment purposes. He's identified with at least twenty-five or more closed-end investment companies, all domiciled outside the United States. It is said that he may be connected with the Mafia. We have no proof of it."

"I appreciate your candor, Dr. Hofer. We know that he has been visiting the bank here regularly during the past few days. May I ask for what purposes?"

Walter Hofer's eyebrows rose. He looked George squarely in the face and for a moment did not reply. Even a member of the Special Branch of Federal Police required a court order to ask such questions of a Swiss bank, and both of them knew that quite well.

"Well, George, it's none of your business at this stage, and you know it. But I'll tell you. He wants to buy $200 million of gold bullion and wants us to use it as collateral for selling an immense amount of U.S. dollars short. He's obviously speculating in a very major way on a fundamental change in the status of the dollar and gold."

"When you say, very major, what do you mean?"

"He's talking in terms of a billion and more dollars. Short."

"And you?"

"We don't like it."

"Why do you think this man is taking such an immense plunge? There is absolutely nothing in his background that suggests that he is a currency expert."

"I have no idea. But from what I've been told, he's extremely sure of himself."

"Is it possible that he has some inside information from somewhere?" asked Bernoulli, perhaps not quite as shrewdly as he would have liked.

"My dear George. You've been close enough to your father's business to know that everybody thinks he has some kind of inside information. I really can't answer that one. I've never met the man. I've heard about him strictly secondhand from our man Kellermann. If you like, I can ask him up."

"No, I don't think that will be necessary. I guess you would not be able to tell me who else, if anybody, is also involved with Rosen's accounts?"

"You are right, George. Actually, I've gone much too far as it is. I'm afraid that you'll have to go through official channels if you want that sort of information. What's up? Are the Americans after him?"

"No. We think he may be involved with the theft of some documents from the Bank for International Settlements." Bernoulli's eyes followed Hofer with the intensity of a laser beam as he spoke these words. Not a flicker of response.

"Aha. In connection with the dollar perhaps?" This time Hofer was the man who had his partner under the most careful observation.

"Perhaps." replied Bernoulli. He continued, "Why do you ask that?"

"Now George", chuckled Hofer. "I know that you think that both your father and I are two completely senile old men. But we can still add two and two together, at least before noon during week-days."

"Well, you're right. There might be some connection. If there is, Dr. Hofer, I'm sure you are quite aware of the fact that this would not be good for your bank or for the entire banking community here in Switzerland."

Hofer nodded. "I think I see the point. But perhaps you could be somewhat more specific, George."

"Well, I'll try to be. We are not sure, but it may be that some strategic American documents were stolen from the home of the secretary-general of the Bank for International Settlements. At least they seem to be missing. It happened about ten days ago. A week or so after Bollinger returned from a trip to London. I believe that you were in London about the same time."

"What was that?"

"I said, I believe that you happened to be in London at the same time, and in the same hotel as Bollinger. I think you know each other quite well."

"Of course we do. But I still don't quite get the implication. You say that Bollinger and I were in London in the same hotel some time last month. What's that supposed to mean?"

"It's not supposed to mean anything. It's just a fact."

"Now, George, I don't think you raised the subject just to make a bit of conversation."

"Well, there is something more perhaps. Did you notice whether Bollinger was perhaps in any way acting out of character in London? Or perhaps was in the company of peculiar people? You know what I mean."

"Now, Bernoulli. Do you mean that you suspect that Bollinger might have been involved in some sort of hanky-panky? That is totally ridiculous."

"I'm not indicating we suspect anything or anybody. We just know that some documents seem to be missing and that the explanations are either too pat or too wildly improbable. Thus a rather simple question about Bollinger."

"Well, I did see Bollinger very fleetingly in the Grill Room of the Savoy, yes. He was, I believe, dining with one of the monetary officials from Washington. But it was merely a fleeting impression, as I just indicated. They left together shortly after I noticed them. We did not even greet. Haven't seen him since."

"Tell me a bit about Bollinger's character. I believe that you have had rather close relations with the man, both professionally and privately, for quite a number of years."

Hofer said. "Well, I think 'close' is the wrong word. We dealt with each other on a regular basis, yes. Also, we have more than once ended up sitting beside each other at various dinner parties and the like. I can tell you this without any doubt. He's the best man in Europe, and maybe the world, in the field of international monetary matters. Absolutely tops."

Hofer's phone rang. "Excuse me, George," he said, and then listened very carefully for a full minute before hanging up.

"Unbelievable. The dollar is being bought all over Europe. The short artists appear to be running for cover."

Bernoulli's face showed his astonishment. "Come again, Dr. Hofer? I've been on the train during the last hour. What's happened to the Russians and all?"

"Amazing thing. I know, since I have been closely watching the activity in our foreign exchange department all week. For obvious reasons. Around eight forty-five the Eastern Europeans apparently switched from the major sellers of yesterday to major buyers. The Germans followed a few minutes later. Then the news came out about the Russian sales of gold, and the tide now seems to have turned."

"The Russians are selling gold?" asked Bernoulli, incredulously.

"Yes. It's been confirmed, according to our people. Am I disturbing some of your theories, George?"

Touché.

"Right now I'm not quite sure. You might be. It seems I keep changing theories about every other hour. The latest one popped up on the train on the way over. Maybe it should pop right down again."

"The Bollinger theory?"

"I would not exactly put it that way. But let's say, I'm interested in knowing a bit more about Bollinger. What are his political views?"

Hofer reached for the cigar box, a delicately designed Persian piece, gold filament superimposed upon thin silver, with the usual enamelled patterns.

"He has none. But I see what you're driving at. Maybe Bollinger and the Russians have been working together, against the dollar. Not a chance. And the events of the past few minutes obviously prove it."

"I agree."

"It would seem to me that our Mr. Rosen is a much better candidate."

"I also agree there. Do you know a man named Rolf Lutz of Swiss Security Consultants A.G. in Geneva?"

"Now, what was that again, George?" answered Hofer.

"Lutz. Security Consultants. Do you know him?"

Hofer replied, "What in the devil does that have to do with Bollinger or Rosen?"

"I'm not sure. You do know him, I assume."

"Know him?" replied Hofer. "I would hardly put it that way. I've dealt with him on more than one occasion, yes. We use his company for various problems which we unfortunately have as a bank. Increasingly so during the past few years, I'm sorry to say. His people are good. The best in the country, in my judgment. That's it."

"Right", said Bernoulli. He stood up.

This caught Hofer a bit off balance. That was normally quite difficult to accomplish.

"So, George Bernoulli—master policeman," came his sarcastic comment. "I'm not sure you carry it off all that well."

Bernoulli was not in the least perturbed. "Dr. Hofer, I've heard that quite often before."

Both men started walking toward the door.

"Say, tell me, how is silver doing these days, Dr. Hofer?"

That one struck home. Hofer turned directly toward Bernoulli and gave him a look that indicated the strongest possible warning that enough was enough. The façade of etiquette splintered.

"Ask your father, George" was Hofer's reply.

His handshake was the briefest possible as Bernoulli left. The great man was offended.

As Hofer returned to his desk, he was furious. "That impertinent young jackass" he said aloud, and in an ugly voice.

At ten o'clock the South Africans arrived. They were met by Hofer and Kellermann. After lunch Hofer instructed his secretary to send in a large cold bottle of champagne. At two forty-five the South Africans left by the garage entrance, just as they had come.

Within the next fifteen minutes Hofer had talked to both Sir Robert Winthrop in London and David Mason in New York. Both agreed to meet Hofer in Zurich two days later. At the Grand Dolder, for lunch.

At three o'clock new massive buying of gold bullion occurred in both London and Zurich. The price which had fallen to $74 an ounce following the news from Russia suddenly shot back to $77 an ounce. The dollar, which had recovered almost all of the ground it had lost during the week of massive speculation, followed by panic short-covering, suddenly began to fall once more. This time nobody could put the finger on any one source of this action. It seemed to be happening simultaneously in Zurich, London, and New York.

At three forty-five Herr Kellermann took a call from Stanley Rosen. Yes, the funds had arrived from Nassau. Yes, the bank was proceeding on Rosen's instructions. No, there was nothing more Rosen could contribute at the moment. Yes, he would note that Rosen was going to Basel early the next morning. Indeed he would keep in contact with him over the weekend if necessary. At four o'clock Kellermann reported all this to Dr. Hofer.

At nine that evening Dr. Bernoulli was received by the Swiss minister of finance. The great relief that both had felt during most of the day had totally disappeared as news of the new flareup in the gold and dollar markets spread. The meeting was short. At eleven-fifteen Bernoulli received an anonymous telephone call. He, in turn, was on the phone to the minister minutes later. Finally, a course of action was set.

16

"That will be $396.50, Mr. Rosen. It includes the phone calls. By the way, did you have any extras with breakfast this morning? That information always takes some time to reach the cashier."

"No. In fact I did not have breakfast. I'm planning to have it on the train. There will be a dining car, I hope."

"Where are you leaving for, sir?"

"Basel."

"On the seven forty-six?"

"Yes."

"It always has a diner."

Stanley gave the man $400 in travellers cheques and carefully counted the change when he received it.

"You would like a taxi, Mr. Rosen?"

"Yes, if you please."

Fifteen minutes later, after a torturously slow taxi ride, he alighted at the Zurich Bahnhof. Just half-past eight in the morning and the place was teeming with people. All grim as the weather outside, where grey clouds swept across the sky pushed by a cold wind that seemed to be everywhere, including the Bahnhof. Rosen bought a ticket and then hurried to gate 12 where his train was waiting. He must have walked past at least ten cars before he found one marked first class. It was divided into the usual continental compartments. Stanley chose a nonsmoker. He swung his massive suitcase up onto the rack but kept his coat on. It was icy. He began his search for the dining car, passing through another half dozen second-class cars, mostly crowded with Swiss soldiers dressed in a sickly green and all packing machine pistols. None appeared older than eighteen. At last the aroma of coffee met Rosen's grateful nose. Not only that, but the car he entered was warm, very warm.

Surprisingly, the diner was full of gayly chattering people. The contrast with the dismal hordes which had been plodding through the station only minutes ago could hardly have been greater. And then Stanley noticed why. They were almost all young Americans, full of zest and jokes even at this hour. The atmosphere made Stanley feel good, and suddenly he was touched with a bit of homesickness.

Minutes later a steaming canister of coffee arrived, accompanied by a basket of superbly fresh croissants. Stanley took his morning copy of the Paris *Herald Tribune* out of his coat pocket, and settled down to the first breakfast he had ever had on a train.

The front page of the *Tribune* was full of the monetary events of the past twenty-four hours. The wild gyrations of both the gold and dollar prices in the international markets were featured in a black headline running completely across the front page. The dollar, which on Wednesday had seemed on the edge of collapse, had made a remarkable recovery on Thursday morning. Simultaneously, the gold price had gone through the biggest one-shot fall in the history of the metal. But by late afternoon, the speculation seemed to have started all over again. The commentators all agreed that Friday morning, this morning, would tip the scales one way or the other. And all eyes were on Switzerland, since that was where the speculators were.

Stanley's face was wreathed in smiles as he took all this in. He deliberately read slowly, to get maximum satisfaction out of every written line. He asked for a second pot of coffee and even ordered a cigar. He did that maybe twice a year. Almost without notice the diner suddenly began to empty. Rosen glanced at his watch and hurried back to his compartment, lurching badly in the process.

At eight forty-four the train arrived in Basel. Rosen was the last to leave his car. Two men immediately approached him.

"Stanley Rosen?"

"Yes."

"You are under arrest. Please make no trouble, otherwise we will have to put handcuffs on you."

He was taken firmly under each arm. The man on his left grabbed his suitcase. They jostled him down the stairs, then up a ramp into a waiting black car. A Volkswagen. The suitcase was thrown into the front seat. Rosen was pushed into the back seat and joined by one of the men. Neither spoke a word. The car pulled away with the usual loud VW whine. Rosen, his face the colour of ashes and both hands and legs trembling beyond control, finally spoke. "What's this all about?"

No answer. Both men, the driver and the somewhat smaller man beside him, looked straight ahead. The car soon moved out of the main roads into a series of winding, narrow, medieval streets. After three minutes they passed through a massive gateway, bordering on a tower with a large golden-faced clock. Two uniformed and armed police saluted as the car moved through. They stopped. Rosen was pulled out, this time roughly, and pushed through a door leading into a long grey building. He was led up two flights of stairs into a large rather barren office and given a chair.

"Sit down, and empty all of your pockets." Rosen did as he was told.

The suitcase was placed next to a desk facing him. Suddenly two men entered the room, both well-dressed and well-shaven. The others left. One of the men sat down behind the massive desk. It did not have a piece of paper or a speck of dust on it. His colleague remained standing by the doorway.

"Cigarette, Mr. Rosen?"

The question suddenly struck Stanley as the final touch to a situation which was absurd beyond belief, for he was still clutching his cigar, long since dead, in his left hand. It was moist with perspiration.

"No," said Stanley. It was barely audible.

"My name is Dr. Weckerlin. I am the chief prosecuting attorney of the canton of Basel-Stadt. We know all about you and I can only suggest that you cooperate to the fullest extent. It will only be in your interest to do so."

Finally Stanley calmed himself sufficiently to speak again.

"I would like to make a phone call."

"I'm sorry, that will not be possible."

"I want to consult a lawyer, immediately."

"That will also not be possible until we say so."

"Then I insist on being able to speak to the American consulate."

"In due course, Mr. Rosen. I think from the very outset you must realize that you are not in the United States. Our laws vary quite considerably from yours."

"Don't I have any rights, for God's sake? I thought this was a civilized country!" Stanley shouted, for now he was full of anger and fear to a degree never before experienced in his life.

"Until we are certain that there is no danger of collusion between you and any other parties, you will be held in the fashion we consider proper."

"And what about habeas corpus?"

"This concept is not part of the Swiss legal code. Mr. Rosen, I think that the best thing for you to do is to settle down now and tell us the truth."

"About what, for God's sake?" replied Stanley.

The man who had been standing beside the doorway suddenly moved. He picked up Rosen's suitcase and laid it on the desk.

"Is this the key?" he asked, pointing to one of those on the chain which Rosen had deposited on the desk.

"Yes."

The suitcase was opened, clothes thrown aside. The two Swiss suddenly glanced at each other.

"Stand up", said Weckerlin. Rosen did not respond.

"When he says stand up, then you stand up," said the other

man, and yanked him to his feet. Then he grabbed Rosen by the back of the collar and pushed his head into the suitcase.

"This is your suitcase, isn't it?"

"Yes," replied Rosen weakly, as he crouched over the suitcase, firmly in the grip of the man beside him.

"And what do you see at the bottom of your suitcase?"

"A red dossier. But I've never seen it before in my life."

"Come now, Mr. Rosen", replied Weckerlin, motioning to his colleague to release the American back into his chair. "That sort of nonsense will get you nowhere."

"I tell you I've never seen that dossier in my life."

"Fine, Mr. Rosen, if that's the way you want to play it. I'm afraid that, in that case, we're going to be spending a lot of time together in the next days and weeks. Would you like that?"

No answer.

Weckerlin suddenly produced a brown folder and opened it.

"You were born in Brooklyn, New York, on January 17, 1929. Your full name is Stanley Salim Rosen. Your father's name was David, your mother's Sarah, née Stein, Right so far?"

Still no answer.

"You are a Jew. Is that correct?"

"What in God's name has that got to do with this?"

"Nothing in particular. You are a Jew, aren't you?"

"Is that against the law in Switzerland?"

"No. We have no prejudices here."

"Well, that's nice to hear. Yes, I am a Jew."

"Good. It seems we are finally making progress. Would you care for a cup of coffee, Mr. Rosen?"

"No."

"As you like. By the way, we will require your tie. Please take it off."

He took it off.

"And your cuff links. And watch."

He took them off.

"What prompted you to buy $200 million worth of gold

216

through the General Bank of Switzerland this week, Mr. Rosen?"

A stunned silence.

"I asked you a question."

"And I will give you an answer. What I do with the General Bank of Switzerland or any other bank in this country is none of your business. I assume you have heard of the bank secrecy law." Stanley was slowly regaining a bit of form.

"You deny it, then?"

"I think you heard me."

Weckerlin picked up the telephone. "Give me Dr. Walter Hofer at the General Bank of Switzerland in Zurich. I'll wait."

The room was silent again.

"Dr. Hofer? Yes, well this is Weckerlin in Basel. I think Bernoulli telephoned you earlier and mentioned that I might be calling. Just one question. Can you verify that a certain Mr. Stanley Rosen of New York placed an order to buy $200 million of gold bullion through your bank this week? You can? Thank you. Sorry to have disturbed you. Yes, you will be hearing more from us."

After he had hung the phone up, Weckerlin just sat there looking at Rosen.

"You see, Mr. Rosen, when I tell you that we know all about you, you must believe me."

He reached into the suitcase for the red dossier and continued. "Now, let me tell you why you ordered $200 million worth of gold bullion. Because of what's inside this dossier." He waved it in the air.

"I tell you, I've never seen that package of papers in my life."

"Where's Lutz?" was the next abrupt question.

"Who?"

"Come on now, man," this time in a harsh voice. "Stop trying to play stupid games with me. Rolf Lutz, general manager of Swiss Security Consultants."

"I've never heard of him."

"Rosen, look, we know. Do you hear me, we know. You both were staying at the Three Kings Hotel. We have witnesses to prove that you were seen together drinking at innumerable bars across the border on October 26. The manager of the hotel saw you two—"

"Oh, him! Sure I know Rolf Lutz. But why in God's name do you keep beating around the bush like this. Has this guy Lutz done something? If so, believe me, I saw him but once in my life. We met by chance in the Three Kings and joined forces for a one-night stand. I've never seen him since, and have had absolutely nothing to do with the man."

"Come now, Mr.—"

"Now, *you* come now, goddammit. I want to know—*now*— what's going on here. I want to know right now why you have arrested me and what I am being charged with."

"All in due time, Mr. Rosen."

"Now."

"If you insist." Weckerlin rang a buzzer and almost immediately a girl appeared with two rather small white pieces of paper. Weckerlin waited until she had left.

"I have here a formal charge against you, Mr. Rosen. It says acute suspicion of economic espionage in violation of article 273 of the Swiss Federal Criminal Code. I must ask you to sign it; you may retain the copy."

"I refuse to sign any such thing. This is preposterous. Who made this charge?"

"I ask the questions here, Mr. Rosen. And if you don't want to sign, that's fine. In any case, here's your copy." He pushed the paper across the desk. Stanley picked it up. All in German.

"Now, Mr. Rosen," continued Weckerlin. "I think you must realize that this is serious. Very serious. The penalty for what you have done can go as high as ten years in prison. But it need not. The courts here are very fair. They always look most favorably upon men who cooperate with the prosecuting attorneys from the outset. It shows character. My suggestion to you is quite simple. Just tell me your story in your own words.

218

Why you stole this dossier? How you did it? Who has been working with you on this project? I'll have one of our secretaries take it all down, and then you can read it. I'm sure before the morning is out we will have a signed statement that ultimately will only help your cause." He spoke this in the voice of a kind man. At the end, he folded his hands.

By this time Rosen had returned to the almost paralyzed state he had entered into at the time of his arrest, which seemed now, in his confused mind, to have happened long ago in a murky haze.

"Now please, Dr. Whatever your name is, I must be able to consult with a lawyer. I know nothing of what you are talking about. I understand nothing of what's going on here. I need help. So please, let me talk to a lawyer."

"I've already told you that is not possible. Perhaps next week, or the week after that. A lawyer could be of no possible help to you. He would tell you exactly what I am telling you. Give us a statement. Give us the truth. Now shall I bring in a secretary?"

There was no response. Weckerlin just sat there for two full minutes, silent, watching Rosen. Rosen sat slumped in his chair; his eyes seemed out of focus as he stared almost straight ahead into nothing but the blank wall behind Weckerlin's desk.

"All right. Take him to his cell. Maximum precautions."

The man standing by the door took Rosen's arm and lifted him from his chair. With his other hand he reached toward to the suitcase which still lay open on the desk.

"No," said Weckerlin, "that stays here. And by the way, make sure Rosen and Bechot are in different cell blocks." Then he switched into German for a final sentence: *"Lasst den Kerl heute Abend ein bischen braten."*

Rosen disappeared through the doorway. Seconds later Bernoulli walked in.

"Could you hear everything all right on the intercom?" asked Weckerlin.

"Yes. It was all perfectly clear. Didn't get too far with him, did you?"

"That's normal. After twenty-four hours in solitary that will change."

"Maybe," replied Bernoulli. "The dossier, please."

Weckerlin handed it to him, and then asked: "What in God's name is in that dossier, Bernoulli? Sure, you told me that it would be there, and you told me about that gold Rosen bought. And you said there's a tie-in. But what is it?"

"I'm afraid that will have to wait. They want this dossier in Bern."

"Well, you can tell your friends in Bern that I've cooperated all the way, but they can hardly expect me to work in the dark for much longer."

"I would not say you're working that much in the dark. You know that this document was stolen from the home of the secretary-general of the BIS. And you know that Sammy Bechot did it and that Rolf Lutz put him up to it. And I think it is now equally clear that this man Rosen engineered the whole thing."

"But why the top-secret treatment of the dossier itself?"

"Weckerlin, I repeat, orders from Bern. So let's drop that subject for the moment. Lutz is much more urgent. You people tell me that they have just traced his movements to a small hotel in Zurich, the Hirschen. He stayed there last night and checked out around six-thirty this morning. Then nothing. His office in Geneva says they haven't heard from his today. What now?"

"I think we'd better first make a check of the airports—all three of them."

It was not until noon that they received the bad news. It was incredible but true. Lutz must have been on the same train as Rosen, coming from Zurich. Apparently he had gone directly to the Basel-Mulhouse airport from the station and just barely caught the flight to Frankfurt. The German police had been alerted. After lunch a Telex from the Kripo in Frankfurt told the rest of the story. Lutz had boarded a Lufthansa flight to

Lima, Peru. It had left two hours ago. Obviously there was no sense contacting the Peruvian authorities. They didn't even know the meaning of the word extradition in that country.

"Of all the bloody stupid carelessness." It was the third time Bernoulli had said that as he sat in Weckerlin's office.

"Don't blame yourself," said Weckerlin. "After all, we had to pick up Rosen first. He's the key man, from what you tell me."

"Yes, but we should have had Lutz under close surveillance the entire time. Ridiculous."

The phone rang. Weckerlin picked it up and then handed it across the desk to Bernoulli: "It's for you. Dr. Hofer himself."

They talked for about five minutes, with Bernoulli doing little more than grunting. When it was over, he just leaned back in his chair and lit a cigarette. He was already on his second pack for the day.

"What did he want?" asked Weckerlin.

"To keep us informed, he says."

"About what?"

"Well, he's protecting himself, and I suppose he is completely within his legal rights. He said he has cancelled all the transactions the bank did for Rosen during the process of the last few days. In fact, he claims that the bank has been selling part of that gold in the market today. He claims that it cooled off the speculators considerably when they heard that the General Bank of Switzerland had turned into a major seller of gold. Dr. Hofer's little contribution to international monetary understanding." The latter was said with more than a touch of sarcasm.

"That is all?"

"He asked if we wanted to temporarily block the cash funds Rosen has with them. Apparently it amounts to around $150 million."

Weckerlin softly whistled. "And?"

"I said we would let him know."

After that Bernoulli stood up.

"Well, off to Bern. I'll keep in touch. It seems highly prob-

able that we will have to meet early tomorrow morning. Here.
I know it will be Saturday. I hope you don't mind."

Weckerlin didn't mind in the least. His appointment as chief
prosecuting attorney had been a political one, and this obviously
involved politics.

Bernoulli picked up the afternoon papers after he left. They
confirmed what Hofer had told him on the phone. The word
had gotten out that the gnomes of Zurich, led by the General
Bank of Switzerland, had decided to take profits. The run into
gold had been met by massive selling of the metal in the Swiss
market. It had stabilized at $79.45. The foreign exchange mar-
kets had immediately reacted. The speculation against the
dollar had also suddenly subsided for the second time within
forty-eight hours. But it seemed nobody was taking any more
risks in face of the monumental gyrations in the markets during
the past couple of days. One after the other, European banks
had decided to stop trading early on this Friday. All pleaded
the need to catch up in their processing of the tremendous
amount of paper which had been generated by a week of unprecedented speculation. The headline in the *National Zeitung*
seemed to best sum up everybody's feeling: THE DOLLAR SAVED
AGAIN—UNTIL NEXT WEEK.

But this had been the week that counted. When Bernoulli
got to Bern a few hours later, the atmosphere of relief in the
office of the minister of finance was evident the moment he
stepped through the door. And when he handed the red
dossier over, it was truly a grateful handshake that was extended to him.

"Bernoulli, you've done a remarkable job. Truly remarkable."

"Without that anonymous phone call last night, we would
still be completely in the dark."

"True. No way of ever determining who that was, I guess."

"None."

At that point, the secretary-general of the Bank for International Settlements entered the room. His eyes went immediately to the red dossier still in the minister's hands.

Bollinger flushed. He immediately approached Bernoulli, took his hand, and shook it vigorously.

"You've actually done it," he said. "Unbelievable. But then this entire affair has been unbelievable from the very outset."

"But are the gold and foreign exchange markets under control?" asked the finance minister.

"They are. The banks have been closed for hours and those in the United States will soon be. Believe me, it cost the American government a packet—well over $7 billion to keep things under control during the past two days. But now we can certainly manage the last couple of hours."

"You are sure that the Americans are going to proceed exactly on schedule?"

"Yes, definitely. The American president will be making a special announcement on television in about six hours, once they are safely into the start of the weekend over there."

Then the man from the BIS turned to Bernoulli. "You are sure that none of this can leak to the U.S. government?"

"Well, certainly not tonight in any case. We have the red dossier here, and the man responsible for its theft is in prison in Basel, completely under wraps."

"But after this weekend? I think both of you must realize that if the true story of our involvement in this affair ever gets out it will have serious consequences for everyone in this room." Bollinger's eyes were on Jacob Gerber, the Swiss finance minister, as he made these last remarks.

"I don't get your point exactly, Bollinger," said Gerber.

"My point is this. Switzerland is the only country in the world which holds the vast majority of its reserves in gold. This American move will almost triple the value of these holdings. It would be extremely easy for lots of people to totally misinterpret our desire to keep this entire affair secret from the Americans."

"True," said Gerber. "What do you think Bernoulli?"

"I agree."

"But how can we possibly prevent such a development?"

"I think there may be a way," answered Bernoulli.

At this point Bollinger broke in. "But who has been behind all this, Bernoulli? And exactly whom do you have in prison in Basel?"

Minister Gerber glanced at his watch and then spoke. "That, my dear friend Bollinger, is truly a long story. Gentlemen, I suggest that Bernoulli tell it over dinner. Why don't we all head for the Schweizerhof. Tonight the drinks and dinner will be on me."

It was just after eleven when the three men parted. Gerber walked Bernoulli and Bollinger to the Bahnhof. Both took the last train back to Basel.

17

In maximum security cell 113 of the Basel prison a 500-watt bulb, protected by a heavy wire cage, relentlessly shone on the man huddled, head in hands, in the corner. There was no bed, no furniture; just a mattress and a blanket, both darkly stained. The cell had no heat.

The stench was overpowering, a mixture of defecation and putrefication. An open-pit toilet, at which two foot pedestals were mounted, was the source. Rosen's eyes, which swung regularly around the confines of the cell, always detoured this object, perhaps as the result of a reflex going back to childhood, when hope was still strong that things ignored may well not truly exist.

A bell tolled outside. Just one stroke. Quarter after eleven. Rosen knew, for since darkness had fallen outside and silence taken over the prison, it was this bell, and the passing of time it signalled, upon which his mind had seized. But had it been just one stroke? Perhaps it had been two, and he had somehow missed the first one. That would make it eleven-thirty, that much closer to dawn. No, it had only been one stroke. And it really didn't matter that much. For his light was still on. Please, God, he thought, keep it on all night.

And then a noise. Just a slight one. Coming from that corner. Rosen, not looking, tensed. Nothing. Probably something in the courtyard below. Then it came again. A rustling. A movement. Yet again, more pronounced—and close. Rosen forced himself to look.

"No!" he whispered.

But yes. Its beady eyes met Rosen's. They were unflinchingly aggressive. Then it moved again, and the glistening grey-brown skin slithered up into view between the two foot pedestals. It stopped, ears perked, both eyes still fixed upon Rosen as he sat, horrified, just six feet away.

"Go away," he said, and then shouted, "Get out of here! Please get out of here."

The rat just crouched there, eyes now moving, as if measuring the cell and assessing the chances of escape—not for himself, but for his prey. The thought communicated itself instantly, for it was then Rosen's eyes which began to wildly sweep the cell.

"Climb up onto something," his brain told him.

But his eyes told him this was impossible. The mattress upon which he squatted provided all of six inches elevation. That was the only object in the room. The walls, smooth and glistening with moisture, offered no shelves, no ledges, no footholds, no toeholds. The tiny barred window facing the courtyard was a full eight feet up.

Then the rat moved again. This time right to the edge of the pit, and right in the direction of Rosen. He began to shiver, first ever so slightly, but soon arms, legs, and then his entire body were shaking in uncontrollable convulsions, as his every fibre revolted against the utter horror of the situation.

"My shoes," he thought, in desperation.

But he had no shoes. They had been taken away. Nor did he have anything else with which to combat this enemy. The only items in maximum security cell 113 were one rat, one human, his shirt, his trousers, his socks, his underwear, one mattress, one dirty woollen blanket.

And then a second head appeared. Another grey-brown body oozed up from the drain, hesitating, perhaps adjusting its eyes to the unaccustomed glare of light in Rosen's cell. Suddenly Rosen remembered. The alarm bell! Just to the right of the cell door. Only to be used, it had been stressed, in cases of extreme emergency, of sickness which required immediate attention. The bell was twelve feet away. The rats, six.

Rosen moved ever so slightly, inching his way along the mattress in the direction of the door. Then he stopped. Neither rat had changed its position in the slightest. But they were watching. Rosen moved again. Still no challenge. Then he was on his feet. He moved his back against the cell wall and, gaining confidence, slid further toward the button which would bring deliverance. Still no movement in the open-pit toilet. He pressed the alarm bell hard, then again, and again. He forced his head against the steel separating him from the corridor, and within minutes he heard footsteps rapidly approaching. Then keys rattled in the door. It swung open, but no one entered.

"Stand back against the far wall!"

The man spoke English. Thank God.

"Back to the far wall," said the voice, this time harshly.

Stanley moved back, but only a few steps. The two guards, one with a drawn gun, just watched him from the corridor.

"Hands behind your head!"

Rosen obeyed.

Now one guard stepped in. The other remained just on the threshold of the cell, eyes wary. His revolver pointed at Rosen's feet.

"What's wrong?"

Rosen nodded his head backwards, toward the open toilet. The two men just stared at him.

"Rats," said Rosen, finally.

"What?"

"Rats," he repeated.

"Where?"

"In the corner. In the toilet pit."

The guard inside the cell stepped to the side and looked.

"I don't see any rat."

"Rats," repeated Stanley. "two of them."

Now the guard with the gun moved into the cell.

The two men in uniform glanced at each other, and then back at Rosen.

"We don't have rats here. This is Switzerland, a clean country. I think that you have rats in your head."

His index finger tapped the side of his head. His colleague

with the gun thought that was rather funny. Obviously he did not understand a word of English, but could hardly miss the meaning of the gesture.

"I tell you—"

"You," interrupted the guard, "do not tell me anything. We've been warned about you. That you're a troublemaker. Maybe. But although you might be able to make trouble in America, you're not going to make any trouble here."

"All right," said Rosen, "maybe I did imagine things. But could you somehow cover up the drain in that toilet? Please?"

"Do what?" was the incredulous response.

"Cover up the drain. That's where the rats came from."

"With what? A wooden plank? So next time you can hit us over the head? Don't be stupid. You know as well as I do that there are no rats here. Now what do you really want?"

Rosen just let one hand slip from behind his head, and across his eyes.

"Put those hands back where I told you."

No response. Then came a sudden jab, right into Rosen's gut. He doubled over. Both guards stepped carefully back.

"All right. That's enough of this. Your behaviour will be reported first thing in the morning. You, my little American friend, are heading for a lot of trouble in this place. One last thing. Don't press that alarm bell anymore. Because no one is going to respond. Get it? No more alarm bells!"

The two men backed out. The cell door slammed. The key turned. And immediately thereafter the light went out.

Rosen froze. Then he pounded on the door.

"Turn the light back on," he screamed. He pounded again.

"The light! Please turn on the light!"

But there was to be no light. Just the fading laughter of the two guards as they moved off. Then utter silence. Rosen slumped there against the door, now sobbing quietly. His stomach had recoiled into a hard painful ball after the blow. His heart began to flutter irregularly. Stanley was afraid. For his very life. Because he knew that he could not survive for long under these conditions, neither physically nor mentally. He was not a coward. But he was a Jew, and like so many of his race he lived his life with a memory, an abhorrence, of the unthinkable. Of Dachau, of Buchenwald, of the unspeakable silent extermination of six million of his race. In central Europe. In German Europe. The cynical accusations, the helpless confinement, and finally death—by suicide, slaughter, or simply the slow surrender of life through organic decomposition. In the dark recesses of so many Jewish minds this represented the ultimate horror, a horror which had to be kept deeply submerged lest the joy of life be lost forever.

'But now for Stanley Rosen it was a horror which had become reality, with stunning swiftness and brutal certainty. For no one could help him. Not tonight, or tomorrow night, or the night thereafter. They had him. Imprisoned. In central Europe.

As if in a dream, with mind paralyzed and spirit crushed, Rosen stumbled back into his corner, on top of the mattress. He pulled the blanket over his body, and then his head, curled into a ball, and entered a twilight stupor. All his senses simply turned off as, mercifully, his mind withdrew from a world which simply could not exist.

18

At just before ten the next morning, Saturday, November 8, the door to Stanley Rosen's cell opened again. He still lay, curled up, on his mattress.

"*Wach auf, du!*"

Rosen swung his feet to the floor, his eyes wildly moving toward the door.

"*Komm steh auf. Du wirst verlangt.*"

"Look, I don't understand German," said Rosen wearily.

"*Blöder Amerikaner. Immer dasselbe.*"

The prison guard did not waste any further words. He went to Rosen and pulled him to his feet. Then a second guard appeared, with Stanley's shoes, jacket, coat, even tie.

"*Anziehen,*" was the next order, this time accompanied by a few motions. Stanley got it. He put the clothes on.

"*Du sollst zum Staatsanwalt gehen. Verstanden?*"

For a crazy moment Stanley thought he had been freed. He pointed at himself and then at the door and said, "*Gehen?*"

"*Ja, ja.*"

Jubilantly Stanley lurched toward the open door.

"*Nein, nein. Bist Du verrückt?*"

Both guards grabbed Rosen, and it was firmly in their grip that Stanley Rosen left the cell. As the trio walked through the prison corridors, nobody took any notice of them. Within a few minutes, after the unlocking and locking of a series of doors, they entered the adjoining building. Soon Stanley was back into familiar territory, as he once again entered the office of the prosecuting attorney. This time he got the name, since it was printed in bold letters outside the door: Dr. Amadeus Weckerlin.

Weckerlin was on his feet as Rosen entered. He startled

Stanley as he extended his hand, but it was only to offer a handshake. Stanley ignored it.

"Mr. Rosen," said Weckerlin, completely unperturbed. "I would like to introduce a representative of our Federal Justice Department, Dr. Bernoulli."

The man who had been standing beside Weckerlin now also offered his hand. This time Rosen accepted it. He was offered a chair at what appeared to be a small conference table at the back of the room. The two Swiss took seats facing him. Immediately a girl appeared with three cups of coffee. On each saucer there was a small cookie.

"Do you take sugar?" she asked.

"Yes, please. That's very kind of you," replied Rosen.

"Do you mind if we get right down to business?" asked Weckerlin, as the girl disappeared.

"The sooner the better."

Now the new face, Dr. Bernoulli, took over.

"Mr. Rosen, as you know we have indisputable evidence that you have been involved in one of the most serious cases of economic espionage ever uncovered in this country. In that it was aimed at undermining the currency of our country, it was my duty to press charges against you."

"So that's—"

"Please let me continue, Mr. Rosen. And I will be quite blunt. As I said we have indisputable and irrefutable evidence. You will get five years at a minimum. We could argue back and forth all day, but believe me, I know our courts. Don't suffer from illusions that any forces on the outside would be able to help you. The entire affair involves matters of national security and matters which fall under the bank secrecy laws. The proceedings against you, from beginning to end, will be held in camera."

"Is your job to come here to intimidate me or what?" asked Rosen.

"That's a fair question," replied Bernoulli, "and it brings us directly to the purpose of our meeting this morning."

"And that is?"

"*I* am here to offer you a deal, as you Americans so nicely phrase it, Mr. Rosen."

"I read once that the Swiss authorities never make deals," replied Rosen.

"I'm sure you read correctly. This is an exception."

For the first time in many hours Stanley grinned.

"All right, let's hear it."

"I am prepared to withdraw my charges against you and Dr. Weckerlin is prepared to release you—immediately—subject to a few conditions."

"They are?"

"First, that you leave this country immediately. Second, that the fact of your short stay with us, and all circumstances surrounding it, are kept secret not only now but forever. That's all."

"Just as simple as that, is it? No hookers, no strings attached?"

"Not exactly."

"Well, perhaps you could be a bit more exact."

"Fine. All the cash margin you have paid into the General Bank of Switzerland during this past week will remain frozen for ninety days."

"And what about the gold I am supposed to have bought?"

"All those purchases have been cancelled. Also the foreign exchange contracts have been nullified."

"On whose authority?"

"Dr. Walter Hofer, the head of that bank, has been informed of most of the circumstances involving your person and he took this step yesterday. Our department agrees that he is fully within his legal rights, since the orders you gave his bank were a direct result of serious criminal activity, of espionage directed against Switzerland."

"And the cash margin?"

"As I said, under our order it will be blocked for ninety days. Thereafter, if you have shown good faith, the entire $150 million will be returned to you or transferred to any bank of your choice anywhere in the world."

"Fair enough. But what is to prevent me from telling this sordid story after I leave your wonderful country?"

"A number of things," replied Bernoulli.

"Like?"

"Like the fact that under U.S. federal law, any American citizen who buys gold bullion is subject to a fine equal to three times the amount of bullion contracted for. In your case, that would be around $600 million. There is also the possibility of prison for up to five years in hard cases. I would judge that they might regard this as rather hard, wouldn't you?"

Stanley said nothing.

"Then there's the entire record of your activities at the Basel branch of the General Bank of Switzerland during the past ten years. I am told that the use of numbered accounts in Switzerland to avoid American taxes is regarded as fraud in the United States. I also hear that the penalties in cases where the government has been swindled out of millions of dollars of taxes over a period of many years are rather severe."

"I see. And your famous bank secrecy laws?"

"Where criminal offences like economic espionage are concerned, these laws do not apply. In cases like yours, where obviously an international conspiracy is involved, there is nothing to preclude us from sharing information, pertinent to such a case, with foreign authorities. In your case, the U.S. Department of Justice."

"I hear that doesn't happen too often."

"As I said once before, Mr. Rosen, there are exceptions."

"I would call this blackmail."

"That is your privilege."

"How much time do I have to think this over?" asked Rosen.

Now Weckerlin interrupted. "As far as we are concerned, months—even years."

"Yeah," said Rosen, "I forgot. You fellows have never heard of habeas corpus."

"Well?" said Bernoulli a few seconds later.

"It's a deal."

"Fine," interjected Weckerlin. He picked up a piece of paper from his desk. "I have your release papers right here. I'd appreciate it if you would sign, right beside the pencilled X on the bottom."

Stanley signed.

"And now?"

"I will take you to the airport," said Bernoulli.

"What airport?"

"The Basel airport. We have booked you on an Air-Inter flight to Paris. It leaves just after noon." Bernoulli looked at his watch. "It's now quarter after ten. If we get moving, we should make it quite easily."

"You fellows were rather confident, weren't you?"

This time Rosen received no answer.

Rosen had already disappeared ahead of him through the door when Bernoulli turned and put a last question to Weckerlin. "What about Bechot?"

"Don't worry, even with this thing dropped, we have enough on him otherwise to guarantee that he stays inside for at least three years."

"Poor bastard."

Weckerlin just shrugged.

Rosen checked out of that Swiss prison in what must have been record time. He did not look back once after he had passed through the heavy doors. He just threw his suitcase into the open trunk of Bernoulli's waiting car and climbed into the front seat.

"How long to the airport?" he asked as they wheeled out of the courtyard into the narrow street, full of housewives with their baskets doing their Saturday shopping.

"Fifteen minutes," answered Bernoulli. He handed Rosen a newspaper. "Here's the morning *Herald Tribune*. I thought some of the stuff in there might interest you."

Rosen gave Bernoulli a peculiar glance. Then he unfolded the paper. The garish headline leaped out at him.

"My God!"

"What's wrong?"

"For Christ's sake, they've actually done it."

"What?"

"The U.S. has put the official gold price to $125 an ounce!"

"So what's new about that?"

"Well, I thought it had to come. I knew it had to be under-way. But just like that. Bingo. For Christ's sake!" he repeated.

"Come now, Rosen—"

Rosen put his paper down, and his face suddenly took on an almost enraptured look.

"Now I get it. *Now* I get it. Why, you dirty son of a bitch. You stupid son of a bitch. You dumb jerks have got the wrong guy. Somebody did the frameup job of the century, and you bastards fell for it like a ton of bricks. You stupid bastards. You pricks have just robbed me of a fucking fortune."

Bernoulli didn't say a word. They were now on the straight stretch of express highway that had them to the airport just a few minutes later.

It was a peculiar airport, probably unique, in that it was shared by both Switzerland and France. The border ran right through the middle of the terminal, and it was to this invisible line that Bernoulli led Rosen. Bernoulli carried the suitcase.

"Mr. Rosen," he said. "This is where we part. I don't expect we'll ever meet again." He offered his hand. Rosen ignored it and instead retrieved his suitcase.

"One minute," said Bernoulli. Rosen's heart missed a beat, and he suddenly had a terrible pain in his gut.

"What now?" he rasped.

"Your ticket," said Bernoulli, as he reached into the inside pocket of his jacket. "And your passport." After handing them over, he abruptly turned on his heel and strode out of sight.

Rosen passed through French immigration without a question being asked. Then he went to the men's room and vomited.

19

"Walter, these caviar canapés are delicious," said Sir Robert Winthrop.

"And the champagne superb." This came from David Mason.

Walter Hofer merely emptied his glass and then waved at the bartender for refills all around. The glasses were soon again brimming with Veuve Cliquot. Hofer glanced at his paper-thin watch.

"Gentlemen, why don't we take these drinks with us. It's well past noon, and I've arranged for lunch in a private room just here off of the bar."

The three bankers walked through the large glass-paned doors to the left, into a small but magnificently furnished suite. A table, set for three, glistened with its setting of crystal and silver. The centerpiece of delicately arranged flowers reflected the bright sunlight that was pouring through the large picture windows.

"Pleasant view, isn't it." As usual, Dr. Walter Hofer was right. The Grand Dolder Hotel lay high on the Sonnenberg overlooking the Lake of Zurich, surrounded by a golf course, which was in turn bordered by tall fir trees. Though only twenty minutes from the heart of Zurich, one had the perfect illusion of Alpine serenity. Even the prices were quite in line with the Palace, St. Moritz, or Gstaad. All that lacked were skilifts and idle royalty.

"I have given instructions to serve lunch at one. That will leave us sufficient time to cover the business at hand right now. Why don't we all sit around that coffee table over there."

Once they were settled, Hofer handed a set of neatly bound documents to his friends, retaining a third for himself.

236

"Well, there it is. All the necessary signatures of the South African government are attached. I and one of my deputies have executed it on our mutual behalf, thanks to your proxies. It was duly notarized here in Zurich on Thursday afternoon. Gentlemen, it represents an airtight document."

"Now let me summarize the details. Our joint corporation which is party to this contract was registered exactly five days ago, in the canton of Zug. We chose the name Intergold. The General Bank of Switzerland has subscribed to 40 percent of its capital, and both of your institutions have received 30 percent each. All the issued shares are in bearer form, and they can be assigned by you to whatever entity in your banking groups you desire. I'm sure taxation might play a role there. Both of your performance guarantees were received in good time. Thank you for your promptness, gentlemen. I know how difficult it sometimes is to expedite commitments involving such large amounts. As you know, David, your letter of credit in favour of Intergold has been deposited with us. And your sterling guarantee has been handled the same way, Sir Robert. My bank has given an unlimited, I repeat, unlimited performance guarantee to Intergold. I think we all agreed that this merited our receiving a slightly higher equity participation in the venture. By the way, since only bearer shares are involved, there is absolutely no way for the public to find out who stands behind Intergold. That may prove valuable. I'll cover that point later."

Both of Hofer's partners nodded.

"Now to the agreement itself. It runs for five years, starting January 1. The contracting parties are the government of the Republic of South Africa, Intergold as guaranteed by the General Bank of Switzerland in Zurich, Winthrop's of London, and the Republican Bank of New York. Under the terms of the agreement, dated just two days ago, Intergold has agreed to buy the total gold output of South Africa during the five year period following January 1st. The South African government has agreed to sell that country's total mine output during that period to Intergold on an exclusive basis. The only conditions which relate to this facet of the contract are that both parties agree that the amount to be delivered and paid for will not be less than 30 million ounces annually and will not exceed 35 million ounces in any twelve month period. The agreed fixed price in the first year is $80 an ounce. Each successive year thereafter, the fixed price will increase 5 percent. Key to the entire agreement is that these prices are irrevocably fixed and must remain so irrespective of the prevailing prices on the free markets in Zurich and London. These prices also remain fixed for the duration of the contract regardless of what happens to the official price of gold set by the United States government. I think you can appreciate, gentlemen, how very important this last condition has today become."

David Mason spoke up. "You are sure that after the president's speech last night there is no way the South Africans can break this contract?"

"None whatsoever. If they even try, they will be blackballed in every financial market in the free world. That they cannot afford. As I said at the beginning, this agreement is airtight from all standpoints. It has been drafted and approved by the best legal men in both Switzerland and South Africa. If it should ever have to go to arbitration, the Chamber of Commerce in Paris has been given jurisdiction. I think none of us would have to worry about which side they would favor."

"And if the government is brought down in Pretoria because of this?" asked Sir Robert.

"I hardly think that possible. You know as well as I do the nature of government in that country. It could only be overturned by revolution, and that would only arise out of domestic race problems. I don't rule that out ultimately, but I think it is highly improbable during the five years of our agreement. But then there's another factor to consider. The South African government entered into this agreement for very sound reasons. It allows their gold mines, the most important sector of that country's economy, to work with fixed prices for their output.

For years none of these mines could plan ahead, since the price of gold fluctuated much too much. A deposit of ore which can be mined quite profitably at $80 an ounce becomes a financial fiasco if the price dips back to $65 an ounce. By reaching agreement with us on a fixed price for their entire mine output, South Africa opened the way for an optimal exploitation of their gold resources."

"Yes," interjected Mason, "but as of last night they could be getting a fixed price once again from the American government: at $125 an ounce, not the $80 we have agreed to."

"That was totally unknown to both parties during the negotiations. In fact, for years the Americans have repeatedly expressed their desire to totally demonetize gold. They could just have well gone that route as the one they chose not so many hours ago. Then we, gentlemen, would have rather long faces this morning. That could have cost us billions. I repeat, this agreement was negotiated and signed in good faith by both parties, each fully cognizant of the risks inherent in such contracts. There can be no question of its validity.

"And you must not forget article xvi of the agreement. Both parties have pledged to maintain absolute secrecy concerning the existence and terms of this contract for at least ten years. If the South African government chooses, and I now suspect it might, it can easily conceal everything by merely making up the difference between what it will be getting from us and what the mines expect to get for their gold output after the American decision. They can take it from treasury funds. I'm sure they could bury the amounts involved in the defence budget. Such things have been done before, you know, especially in your country, David. No, gentlemen, all contingencies have been foreseen and covered."

Sir Robert Winthrop and David Mason were convinced. Then Winthrop asked the question, and he asked it softly.

"Walter, how much will our profit be?"

"Substantial, in fact quite substantial. I made a rough calculation last night after watching the president's speech on television. The Swiss TV carried it, you know. I must say, he made a very convincing presentation."

"I agree," said David Mason, "but what did your calculations show?"

"Let's take the first year," said Hofer. "Mine output next year is projected at 33 million ounces. Our gross cost, at $80 an ounce, will be $2.640 billion. Our receipts, upon resale to any central bank at $125 an ounce, will be $4.125 billion. That leaves a gross margin of $1.485 billion. Let's call it one and a half billion. Intergold expenses will be minimal, really nothing much more than the cost of compensating our banks for their performance guarantees. And transport and insurance, of course. In any case, I foresee a profit before taxes the first year of about $1.4 billion. The canton of Zug, where we have incorporated, has entered into a tax agreement with Intergold. The maximum tax rate will be 12 percent. That leaves an after-tax net profit of just a shade over $1.2 billion.

"My God!" exclaimed Mason.

"Yes," said Hofer, "it is quite amazing, isn't it. Of course, you must not forget that we have agreed to increase the price by 5 percent each year. It's a pity, but it couldn't be helped. That will mean that by the fifth year our gross margin will drop to under a billion. But for the five-year life of the contract, we should be able to clear $6 billion gross and well over $5 billion net after taxes."

"Absolutely astonishing," said Winthrop. "Walter, you have done a truly magnificent job."

"Sir Robert, the contribution you made during the past few days was invaluable, you know," replied Hofer. "Your intervention in the London gold pool proved totally successful. If we had not kept the price below $80 an ounce right up to the closing, I'm afraid the South Africans would never have signed. It was very touch and go at the last minute."

David Mason then spoke. "One thing I cannot understand, even now, is the behaviour of the Russians during the past week. From what we heard in New York, Walter, they started the entire speculation against the dollar and on gold, and then completely reversed field in midweek. Is that true?"

"It would seem so. Of course, their initial actions came within a hair of scuttling this entire project. Until something happened. I'm quite sure we will never know what."

"Is it possible they somehow got wind of what the Americans planned to do?"

"Hardly. David, I've been involved in countless numbers of devaluations here in Europe, and I cannot recall one which really went over perfectly. But not because of leaks. It's usually just because clever people, noticing this, hearing that, spotting something just slightly out of line with the usual pattern, start to get suspicious. All of a sudden the same conclusion is reached almost simultaneously by financial people in many different places, completely unrelated to each other. The German language has a word for this: *Fingerspitzengefühl*. The hunch. I suspect that this has played the key role in the events of the past few days. At least it did where I was concerned."

"Well, Walter," said Sir Robert, "here's to your *Fingerspitzengefühl*."

At that moment three waiters entered the room. Lunch had arrived. It lasted well over three hours. Dr. Hofer offered to take his two colleagues to the airport after a final scotch and soda in the bar of the Grand Dolder. Dusk was just closing in as they left.

Hofer took the wheel himself, explaining that he had given his chauffeur the weekend off. He proved to be a terrible driver, so for most of the journey his two passengers, quite sleepy anyway after the monumental meal, kept silent.

But as they approached the airport, Sir Robert said: "Walter, tell me, how much are you people ahead on your short position against the dollar?"

Suddenly Hofer, who could not have been more expansive during the preceeding hours, returned to character. "Robert, I'm afraid that is none of your business."

241

Winthrop just laughed. "I can tell you this. We made enough in just three days to put us well into the black for the year. And you, David?"

Mason just grunted. "We did all right."

By the time they exchanged farewells at Kloten airport the spirit of comradeship had totally disappeared. Theirs was, after all, just an ordinary business relationship.

20

Sunday morning, November 9, was one in which most financial people throughout the world slept late. The countless meetings and phone calls of the previous day, the hurried calculations and recalculations which had followed the American announcement of international monetary reform had left their mark everywhere. For some it was a day of triumph; for others, one of worry and despair.

Igor Josef Melekov was in the first category. With a still sleeping mistress at his side, he sat propped up in his vast bed in his apartment on the Moscow Hills, carefully studying a General Motors brochure. Yesterday had been the moment of supreme triumph: his appointment as chairman of the Foreign Trade Bank of the Soviet Union. Perhaps it had been sadistic to help Stepanov clean out his office. But still—the sight of him on that last trip down the stairs of the bank was a memory to be cherished. Today every one of those Georgians would be receiving their prizes: one-way tickets back to Tiflis. And now he would choose his own reward. In fact, the decision was already made. It was to be an Oldsmobile 98. He was positive that it would be the only one in the entire Soviet Union. The problem now was to get delivery. He shook the girl beside him.

"Natscha, wake up!"

"Not now, Igor."

"Natscha, how would you like to go with me to Helsinki?"

"Don't be ridiculous."

"What's so ridiculous about that?"

"I'll never get a travel visa."

"Ha! I will have that within three hours!"

"But why Helsinki?"

"Because I have urgent business there."

"What kind of business?"

"It concerns the automotive industry."

"Igor, why don't we get married instead?"

Melekov slumped back into his pillows. Now why did she have to go and spoil a perfect morning?

At the other side of the world, the president of the United States found himself in exactly the same position. Well, at least to the extent that he was in bed reading. The lady beside him was, of course, his wife. The bed was strewn with newspapers. It was the headline in the Baltimore *Sun* that summed it up best: "THE BEST-KEPT SECRET SINCE THE MANHATTAN PROJECT." The president chuckled. Yes, he had really caught the world by surprise.

Midway between Moscow and Washington, or close to it, Dr. George Bernoulli sat alone in the bedroom of his small apartment on the outskirts of Bern. He was not reading; just smoking and gazing at the ceiling. He had been doing that for hours. His stomach had been in a tight knot ever since leaving the Basel airport at noon the previous day. For since that time he had known. And there was nothing he could do about it. Not a single thing. The matter was closed, permanently, from the official standpoint. And thus it was closed, permanently, as far as he was concerned. For the first time in his life, Bernoulli's faith in the rule of law, in the inevitability of justice, had been shaken.

"Well," he said aloud, throwing off the blankets and stepping out onto the cold floor, "I guess father is right. This business is not for me."

He picked up the phone.

"Dad, this is George. I think I'll drop by for lunch. I've got something I'd like to talk to you about."

Not many kilometres away Dr. Walter Hofer was sitting in his living room, carefully writing in a loose-leaf notebook.

"Walter, would you like another cup of coffee?"

"Yes, Martha. And perhaps another piece of toast."

She soon returned. "Where would you like it, Walter?"

"Oh, right over there will be fine."

"How's the speech coming?"

"It will still take a few more hours."

"We should leave around four, you know. It will take us a good two hours to drive over to Altdorf. The Sunday traffic is always so terrible. I do wish you hadn't given Heinrich the weekend off."

The phone rang. Both appeared startled.

"I'll take it," said Hofer's wife. "It's probably Mary. Her young man from the bank picked her up very early this morning while you were still sleeping." She picked up the receiver.

"Walter, it's Lima, Peru. For you. I must say, at this hour on a Sunday morning!"

Hofer took the phone, listened very intently, said no more than two sentences, and then hung up.

"Who in the world was that, Walter?"

"Oh, just some unfinished business."

"Anything to do with those troubles at the bank?"

"No, Martha. Something quite unimportant that has now been completed—successfully. And about those troubles at the bank, they have also been dealt with, equally successfully."

"Oh, Walter, I'm so happy for you. Now you just go back to your speech. I've got a lot to do in the kitchen."

At four o'clock they left in the Mercedes. The trip took them around the Lake of Zurich, through Zug and Lucerne, and then down the east side of the Vierwaldstättersee. Soon they were on the famous, and dangerous, part of the Gotthardt route known as the Axenstrasse. In the 1930s kilometre after kilometre had been blasted out of the towering rock which bordered the lake at this point. Tunnel after tunnel, curve after curve. On the left hand side, the wall of rock; on the right, deep cold mountain water. Hofer, who knew fully well that his driving talents were limited, kept the car at very low speeds.

245

The traffic was sparse, since the heavy winter clouds had long ago closed in on central Switzerland, making an afternoon in front of a TV set much more attractive for the bourgeois Swiss than a Sunday drive around a lake almost totally invisible in the fog and often driving rain.

By the time the Hofers reached Altdorf it was dark. But they had no trouble finding their destination. The Oxen Hotel was right in the center of town, opposite the huge memorial to William Tell—the town's most famous, though legendary, son. The Oxen had been established in 1654. The old wooden timbers, small stained-glass windows, and the brightly polished bronze figure of an ox which hung on a massive chain above its entrance door made it a landmark known to travellers for many centuries. Its prize attraction for many generations had been the Goethestube. Even that great man had dined at the Oxen on his way to Italy to discover the culture which revolutionized his thinking.

Dr. and Mrs. Hofer were met by the Bürgermeister, flanked by both the Protestant pastor and Catholic priest of this ancient community.

The people of inner Switzerland are not known for ceremony. Soon after the Hofers had taken their place at the head table in the room which had already filled with the invited guests in their Sunday best, all sat down to dinner. The soup was followed by Holsteinschnitzel with Roesti. Dessert took the form of Zwetschgentorte and whipped cream. The wines were strictly Swiss: for those that preferred white, an Aigle; a dark heavy Dole for the rest. Coffee was served with a choice of either cognac or Kirschwasser. It was a solid Swiss dinner.

Silence was complete when the Bürgermeister rose to introduce the speaker to this audience of mixed religious affiliations whose mutual cause was that of promoting the ecumenical movement in a world which was rapidly coming closer together, even in Switzerland.

Hofer made a strong speech, pointing out that the time had come for the leaders of the community to raise their voices in spiritual matters. Demonstrated leadership, moral leadership, was the key to success whether in matters of church, government, yes, also banking. His was a plea for these leaders, many of whom he thought were gathered in Altdorf this evening, to take their fair share of the burden. To stand up, as good men, for the good of the community. He ended with an admonition, a citation from the ancient Greek New Testament, the Gospel according to Saint Luke, chapter 6, verse 45: πό ἀγαθὸς ἄνθρωπος ἐκ τοῦ ἀγαθοῦ θησαυροῦ τῆς καρδίας προφέρει τὸ ἀγαθόν, καὶ ὁ πονηρός ἐκ τοῦ πονηροῦ προφέρει τὸ πονηρόν.

The banker, having duly demonstrated his credentials as a scholar and humanist, then condescended to translate: "A good man out of the good treasure of his heart bringeth forth that which is good: and an evil man out of the evil treasure of his heart bringeth forth that which is evil."

Hofer's final words: "My friends, our record will speak for itself."

As the Hofers headed back toward Zurich, it was through an ugly night. The winds were high, whipping an icy spray off the white-caps and across the Axenstrasse. The road was totally deserted. Suddenly the headlights of the massive Mercedes struck a car, straddling the road in front of a tunnel entrance. Two men waved as he braked.

"Walter, don't stop for God's sake."

"Martha, now take it easy. I have no choice, and these people appear to need help."

The two men approached the car as Hofer wound down his window.

"Walter, be careful. They look like Arabs."

The warning came just a bit late. At precisely that moment an incredibly strong hand came through the open window and pinned Hofer's head to the back of the car seat. Another hand soon had the door open. Within seconds, a sharp blow, just one, had broken Walter Hofer's neck. Within minutes, both Walter and Martha Hofer were 110 metres below the surface of the Vierwaldstättersee inside their Mercedes 300.

Three months later a memorial was erected on the scene of

this tragic automobile accident. The citizens of Altdorf contributed the stone, the General Bank of Switzerland the gold plate firmly imbedded in the granite. The only inscription was a citation from the New Testament, the Gospel according to Saint Luke, chapter 6, verse 45, first half only: πό ἀγαθὸς ἄνθρωπος ἐκ τοῦ ἀγαθοῦ θησαυροῦ τῆς καρδίας προφέρει τὸ ἀγαθόν.